Some You Win

by

Fay Holt

Some You Win

ISBN 1 901442 0 3 9

First Published in 1997 by Pharaoh Press, Liverpool L3 5JY
0151 281 5131

Printed in England by Cromwell Press, Wiltshire.

1

She had travelled from London via Copenhagen, then taken the domestic flight to Karoup, a small military airport in Jutland, Denmark. As she came down the aircraft steps, she looked towards the main building, hoping to catch a glimpse of him, but the windows were of dark glass and appeared to be one-way.

She knew he would be looking for her. He would have an image of a twenty-year-old girl now going on forty-five, with flicked black hair, dressed in a Sixties-type gypsy skirt with extra layers of petticoat. The high stiletto heels were a must and he'd never expect her to be without those big looped earrings.

She'd been pleasingly plump in those days, always laughing, her face full of excitement and lighting up when she saw him - but that was a long time ago and she felt herself shiver at the thought of looking into those big watery blue eyes again. She knew the first words he would say to her, "Hello, *mine skat,* you are here, so everything be alright now."

On entering the building she noticed it was very small, so it was easy to mingle with people departing as well as arriving. At the end of the corridor a crowd of people were gathered to greet whoever they were meeting.

She noticed him immediately. He was still that big powerful man she had fallen hopelessly in love with. She waved to attract his attention, but he just glanced at her, deciding that she was waving to someone else.

Had she changed that much? She was aware of a slight feeling of annoyance. It was he who was to blame for changing her from the carefree girl she used to be into the cool-headed, slightly aloof woman she had recently heard herself called.

Well, she was a woman of the world now, she travelled extensively because her business interests were sometimes on an international level.

She paused to look in one of the many mirrors. She saw a slim, attractive woman with softly dyed blonde hair cut into a wedge, wearing a short-skirted suit, over which was a long, navy, cashmere coat. Her only jewellery was a diamond ring with a tasteful diamond bracelet to match.

It was at this moment she decided she couldn't meet him - not yet. She noticed a coffee lounge to her right, so instead of walking forward to where he was, she turned into the cafeteria. She felt in a state of panic. She shouldn't have come here. She bought a cup of that thick, black, Danish coffee and went and sat at the nearest available table. Even the coffee reminded her of him and there he was, standing yards away from her, waiting for her to arrive.

Oh, yes! He would wait. Hadn't he always waited for her the way she had waited for him? The intense love, then the rejection came flooding back. Oh, why have I come here? The minute I meet him, she thought, so many lives are going to be turned upside down forever and I don't relish the thought of his reaction, once he is aware of Paula's existence. There was no going back now, but she could delay the meeting for as long as possible.

She watched as he paced up and down. The crowd had departed and she realised they were alone, apart from a few people going about their duties. It wouldn't be long before he noticed her, so she moved to the far end of the cafeteria. Here, she was still within everyone's sight, but she didn't feel as exposed as she had been.

The realisation that her suitcase stood on its own waiting for collection suddenly hit her and she prayed silently that he wouldn't look at the label. However, he didn't appear to notice it and the airport staff soon removed it to a secure place.

What the hell was she going to say to him? Oh, she had known all along that it wasn't going to be easy, but the voices of everyone telling her to do the right thing had been too loud to ignore in the end and so here she was. Where were they now? she wondered. She should have paid for them all to come with her.

Funny, all those years ago, she hadn't needed anyone except him and now here she was, afraid to even say hello, but so much had happened.

She had been so lost in her thoughts that she hadn't noticed he had moved out of the foyer. Good, she thought and moved to get another coffee. As long as he was out of sight she felt more relaxed.

Did he really think that she could turn back the clock? There was no explanation for what he did to her. She had wondered constantly and now, perhaps when she looked straight into his eyes and asked him, he might find it too difficult to give her the answer she needed.

She stared into her coffee. Isn't it funny how

you blow things out of proportion when in a state of panic? She looked up and into the face of Evert Neilson. Yes, there he was on the other side of the cafeteria. She hadn't even noticed him come in.

She looked away from him, her mind drifting back to the events of the last two weeks. It had been a Wednesday morning when he had called her, out of the blue. She'd known she had a busy day ahead of her.

Her main concern had been to contact her customers to pay their invoices on time that month because the cash flow was giving cause for concern.

She wasn't too worried however, she had known most of her business contacts for over twenty years and as her company prided itself on giving an excellent service, they needed her as much as she needed them. They also knew that if they had similar difficulties she would not press them for payment.

In any event she had an excellent bank manager, but in these days of high interest rates that would of course be the last resort.

There had been no point in phoning at nine o'clock. These were the days of flexi-time, where it was better to get to work early and leave early or come in late and leave late, avoiding the rush hour traffic. Ten-thirty would be better.

Julia had come in with her coffee. It was the

one cup she allowed herself all day. After that, it was pure iced water with a touch of lemon. She had always enjoyed this time with Julia, who was always good for ten minutes' worth of gossip. She secretly wallowed in this, because some of the antics in that office were mind-boggling but as long as they didn't impede the work progress she didn't mind.

The telephone had disturbed them. It had to be fate because there had been hundreds of days when she had been miles away from the office at that time and yet here she was. She remembered Julia saying it was someone foreign for her and he said his name was Evert Neilson and then jumping up in alarm because she had gone deathly white.

She sent her out for some water and pressed her intercom. How stupid of me, she thought, to think it couldn't be him. Of all the countries she had ever worked in, Denmark was the one she had avoided. The memory of that place was too painful.

"Yes?" she had said, "Who is it?"

"Good morning," he had said, "my name is Evert Neilson, I call you long distance from Denmark. I want to speak to Kate Roberts, can you help me?"

"Evert," she had replied, "I am Kate Roberts."

"Kate, Kate," she had heard him whisper, "at

last I find you, everything will be alright now."

Yes, those were the words she remembered, because they were always his opening words.

"How did you find me?" she had asked him.

"Kate, I look for you for the past twenty years. You must know that."

No, she hadn't known that and as far as she was concerned, he could look for another twenty, because the time she had wanted him most he had rejected her and hadn't she ensured that no-one would get that close again?

She had missed most of what he had said because she had been in such a state of shock but she had quickly regained her composure when she had heard him say that he could be by her side within six hours.

"No! No! No! You must never ever do that!"

"Why? You are married?" he had asked.

"No," she had replied, "I just don't want to see you."

"Kate," she heard him say, "I will accept that you don't want to turn back the clock but I need to speak with you. I realise you are in shock, me too. I am overcome with emotion and need to get my head together. If I phone you back in one hour, will you make conversation with me? Please Kate, do this for me."

"Make it two hours," she had replied.

"You will be there then?" he had asked.

"Yes, I'll be here. Speak to me then," she had told him and replaced the receiver. She felt as if she'd done one month's work in one day. Julia had put her head around the door, asking whether it was alright to come in. "Kate, you're shaking," she had said, "who was that?"

"Paula's father," she had replied. "I'll ring my mum, she'll know what to do."

Her mother did know. For every problem of hers she had always given her sound advice. She had relaxed as she dialled the number. Her mother had come to the phone almost immediately. "Hello, Kate," she had said affectionately, "I was only saying the other day it's about time we were seeing you. It's been over six months since you were up here, you know."

"I might come at the weekend," she had replied, "I feel a bit raw at the moment."

"Why, lass, you're not ill?" her mother had asked, concerned.

"No, Mum, but I've just had a call from Evert Neilson."

She didn't know what she expected but it certainly wasn't complete silence.

"Mum? Are you still there?" she had asked.

"Yes, lass, I'm still here," she'd replied with a break in her voice.

"Mum, you sound upset. Are you crying?"

"Yes," her mum had replied, "I'm crying. I've been dreading this day, because you'll never forgive me."

"Forgive you? Forgive you for what?" she had asked but the phone had gone very quiet. "Mum?" she had said, "pull yourself together. I said that Evert Neilson had phoned me, why do I need to forgive you?"

"Oh, lass, I've wanted to tell you for years," came the tearful reply, "but something always stopped me. You were doing so well and I didn't want anything upsetting you."

She thought it must have been the only time she raised her voice to her mother. "What?" she had asked, "what do you need to tell me?"

"He came looking for you two weeks after you left and I told him I didn't know where you were. I thought it was for the best."

"Calm down," she had told her mother, "because it probably was. You couldn't do what he did and then two weeks later change your mind."

"No, lass," her mother had continued, "many's the time I've regretted not giving him your address so he could go to you."

She had put the phone down, promising to go to Liverpool that weekend. She had sat for a further half hour before deciding she would go there and then. She had needed her family around her. She would always think of Liverpool as her home. Oh yes, now she thought back to the state of her mind, everything was done in a rush.

Julia had cancelled her appointments and she had taken Evert's phone number so she could call him once she had reached home. She had walked into Oxford Street and into the private car park. It was expensive to park there but she needed the car at her disposal twenty-four hours a day. She couldn't envisage life without it.

She had decided not to go to the house, it was on the opposite side of London to where she wanted to be. Instead she had made her way to Brent Cross Shopping Centre. She had got all the clothes she needed there and justified it with the thought that it had been a long time since she had shopped for clothes.

Back in her car she had prepared herself for the journey: Staples Corner, up the M1 to the M6, turn off along the M6 and on to the M56, then along to the M53, through the Birkenhead Tunnel. She could have gone further on and through the new Wallasey Tunnel but Birkenhead had always been affectionately called 'the other side of the water' and that was what she needed at that time - familiar things.

She carved through the miles with ease in her

car. She loved her Audi automatic, as she had loved the two before that one. Maybe it was because it had been her first symbol of success all those years ago. She had never needed any other form of transport, as long as she had her beloved Audi.

She had been happy at her decision to go home. She usually passed through the 'shires which all had their own brand of humour and many different accents but that day she was anxious to get home so she had kept to the motorways.

She had thought of making a detour on the return journey to bathe in the feelings her designs had created. They could be seen in most high streets worldwide and her only disappointment was that England never felt it necessary to display the Union Jack. Reliance was put on the Great Britain label. Looking around her in the airport cafeteria, she was struck at the number of red and white flags everywhere.

She glanced across at Evert. Yes, his country might have a sense of pride but what had he to be proud of? At the first sign of trouble he had crumpled and let her get on with it. Her family had always been there for her and she regretted that she had even doubted them.

When she had arrived in her street a couple of weeks ago, what had it been like? You could guarantee that if there was to be a celebration the street would be first in line and what about when she had made that journey when she had first received his phone call? Those two boys in the street, "Mind yer car, missus?" She smiled as she knew the line by heart.

If she had said no, the answer would have been, "Well, it might get scratched," so she gave them one pound each and they had skipped along to the corner shop, the thought of minding her car furthest from their minds.

She had followed them to the end of the street. Yes, the two little shops were still there, Barlows and Salters. They sold everything, each trying to outdo the other and if one of them saw you in the other shop, you would feel obliged to say sorry.

She had noticed her mother coming down the street and had quickly made her way to meet her. She was always the same, whenever she met anyone she apologised first, "So sorry I missed you," or "Sorry I haven't got the kettle on." She was always sorry for something, even though most things weren't her fault.

"Oh, lass, yer got here. However did I miss yer? If yer hadn't come home today these eyes would not have closed all night. I'll be glad to get it all off my chest."

She had stopped her mother outside the front

door. "Mum, before you reproach yourself over me, I am very well aware that you would never do anything against me, even if you have made some wrong decisions, you would have thought it would be for my own good, so let the matter rest."

"I can't," her mother had replied. "Oh, lass, yer don't know how I've dreaded this day over the years. I just thought yer'd think differently of me if yer knew half of what I did."

She hadn't cared less what her mother had done, still didn't. As far as she was concerned, her mother could do no wrong. Never had, never would.

Although she was sitting hundreds of miles away, she could still recall the smell as she had entered that long dark hall and the baking trays had come out, ensuring that she had got the best possible welcome. It was the same story with her bedroom. It had always been named "Our Kate's" and everybody knew not to go in there even though she only used it for a weekend every six months.

She had felt guilty this time because it had been refurbished for her six months before. Each week they would have hoped she would visit them but they had never showed or even hinted at their disappointment when she merely called to ask about their welfare.

She had sat on the bed. It felt unusually warm and when she had pulled the covers back she had noticed a hot water bottle in there, airing it properly. Central heating hadn't reached most of these houses yet. She had never thought of having it installed, but now, she thought, that was a surprise they had coming to them in the near future.

The pine furniture her dad had done in the room was a work of art - no craftsman could have done it better. Her parents would have gone to St John's Market together to choose the gingham material for her curtains and bedspread and her mum would have got one of the neighbours to make them up, giving them a packet of cigarettes for their trouble.

As she had come downstairs, her mother had been sitting patiently waiting for her. "Come on, lass, let's have a nice cup of tea and yer can tell me what he said to yer, word for word and don't leave anything out, will yer?"

After she had put her mum at ease by telling her they had only spoken briefly, she'd then had the job of convincing her that there was no way he would be on his way to Liverpool. Her mum had still had her doubts, stating that he would know that if anything was bothering her, it would be home she would make for.

She had tried to stop her from going over the past but it was impossible. She had held her secret for so long she couldn't wait to get it out. "Ok, Mum," she had said, "you spill your guilty secret and I'll listen but whatever you've got to say won't make any difference to how I feel about you."

Her mum had played with her handkerchief. "As you know, your dad and brothers never knew why yer went away so suddenly. I kept it from them. It would have killed your dad, you know how he thought of yer. When that cablegram came for yer, if I could have taken all that pain away I would have but my own thought was to get yer away from 'ere before anybody found out. It's different now but in them days yer would have been an outcast. I thought it was for yer own good but it was the worst thing I ever did in my life.

"After yer got on that coach to London I was beside myself. I walked the streets and yer dad came looking for me. I explained away why I was crying by saying that yer'd gone on one of your trips and I'd had a dream that the plane would crash.

"Your dad told me not to be so soft and it became a laugh in the family for months after, but it was worth it, for them not to think badly of yer. About a fortnight after yer went Evert knocked at the door. I was frightened that one of them would come round the corner and the cat would have been out of the bag.

"He couldn't understand the change in me, so I told him I'd meet him in town at the old Reece's café. His first words were about the baby, so I told him yer'd lost it. To be fair, he seemed genuinely upset, but I wasn't really interested in what he had to say. I told him I didn't know where yer were because I knew yer didn't want to see him.

"I told him never to come to our house again and he just said, 'If that's what yer want.' Then I had an idea, I asked him to do me a favour and send me and your dad a card from the different places in the world he visited."

It was the first time her mum had smiled.

"He thought I'd gone soft. He asked me why I didn't want to see him but did want him to send me cards. When I told him I had my reasons he shrugged his shoulders and said he would. True to his word he did, for the first couple of years anyway."

She had got up then and reaching on top of the cupboard brought down all the cards he had sent - all written in his broken English with her name added at the bottom.

"Oh, Kate!" her mother had said, "I've told so many lies over the years. After a couple of years when the cards stopped, I told your dad and brothers that yer'd split up and you had gone to stay with your Aunt Cissy in London. Many a time I've slipped up and mentioned Paula and when anybody asked me who I was talking about I said she was just some kid up the street."

She still felt guilty that her mother had carried all the lies on for her, but she had told her fair share over the years as well. She'd denied Paula's existence and that was bad. When Paula had asked her had she any living relations she had told her they were all dead. How could she have said that? How could she have denied her family in Liverpool?

The rest of the weekend had dragged for her. She couldn't reveal her secret until she had seen Paula. She'd have to see if she would want to meet the family she never knew she had. Her mother had been relieved to get things off her chest and said she could rest easy in her grave once her dad had seen his only grandchild.

Oh, her mind had been in a turmoil that weekend, it was one of those times that you couldn't wait to get where you were going then once you arrived you couldn't wait to get away.

Paula had to be told, she also had to take Annie's feelings into consideration. She turned her thoughts to Annie. She knew now why she'd always had deep affection for that woman, she always made things seem so easy.

The journey back from Liverpool to London gave her plenty of time to reflect. Was it really twenty years since it all began?

2

It was a wild November day in 1962. She was nineteen years old. There had been a heavy snowstorm and she tucked her head down against it and made her way home.

She was at college studying design and she enjoyed it. After years of growing up with the dark browns and sombre greens of the war years, colours and music were at last beginning to light up everyone's life - and she was part of it.

Life was good. Her parents were working class and lived in a three-up, two-down in Liverpool, where the houses were back-to-back. She had been born in that house and knew everybody in the streets surrounding it. They would shout, "Hello, Kate!" as she made her way to and from college. Yes, despite the north-west weather it was a warm atmosphere to be in. Each time she arrived home her family were always glad to see her, because they knew she was home safe and sound.

It was Monday. She always looked forward to getting home quickly on Mondays because her favourite tea of Shepherd's Pie would be waiting for her, with lashings of that rich gravy only her mother could make.

Before she went to college, she had always helped by putting the meat from Sunday's joint through the heavy mincer which was screwed to the end of the table. The washing would be rolled into little bundles to be ironed on Tuesday, then put away for the rest of the week. That was another smell she always remembered. She liked that organised lifestyle and felt that being the only girl in a big family gave her a feeling of being well protected.

She was so engrossed in her thoughts that she didn't see the car skid on to the pavement, she only heard the noise. Then she was aware of being wrenched off her feet by a big body looming over her and thrown into a shop doorway. She looked up in a daze to see a big man lying motionless nearby. A crowd gathered and she could hear a siren in the distance. Then everything went black.

* * * * *

Kate opened her eyes in the hospital to the whole family looking at her anxiously. Once they realised her injuries were not that severe, they calmed down. They visited her in pairs over the next three days and were full of the usual Liverpool humour, but she noticed that when she asked what had happened, they became subdued and changed the subject.

She dreamed of a big man grabbing her, but the dream always ended before the final scene. One day, her dad had come into the ward with a strange woman, whom he seated next to the bed while he stood and turned his cap around in his hands.

"I'm the one to tell yer, our Kate," he said, "'cos I'm head of the family. Yer keep wanting to know what happened, well, yer were hit by a car."

"I know that!" she replied.

"Yes, well, what yer don't know is that yer would 'ave been killed except for this woman's son. He took the impact for yer."

Kate had felt the blood drain from her. "Is he dead?" she asked.

"No," replied her dad, "but we've 'ad a right time these last three days because it was touch and go. But they say he's goin' to be as right as rain."

Kate took hold of the woman's hand.

"No good talking to her, she doesn't understand a word yer say, but we've seen to her and she's staying with us. Seems a nice woman, but now he's on the mend we think she wants to go home to Denmark and we'll make sure she gets there."

Kate had pleaded with the doctors and nurses to let her go to him. She had to thank him. She had to say she was sorry because it was her fault he was in there. But she was to be discharged at the end of the week and was told she could make her own arrangements.

It was another four days before she could get to his bedside. He was still quite poorly but managed to say, "I'm so glad you are alright."

The days passed into weeks and Kate visited the big Dane every day to cheer him up and they were quickly on first name terms. Evert's face used to light up the minute she entered the ward with her basket of home-made cakes, dandelion and burdock lemonade and other titbits her mother had packed for her to take.

He spoke broken English and sometimes would say something in Danish that she didn't understand, but when she asked him to explain he would only say, "Whatever language I use it will only be to say good things about you."

The tone of his voice used to have an effect on her and she had never experienced thoughts like those before. It was a warm sensation deep in the pit of her stomach and one of the nicest feelings she had ever known. Was this the love she had read about between a man and a woman and was it right to wish that, when she kissed his forehead goodbye each night, he would enfold her in his arms and kiss her properly?

She was glad he was getting better, but sometimes she panicked when she thought he would soon be leaving to go back home to Denmark and she would never see him again. She never asked him about it because she didn't really want to know the answer, but it affected her family also - they shared so much laughter together and soon shared her innermost thoughts. They knew that the parting which would come eventually would have a lasting effect on her.

She was sitting by his bedside telling him how the tramcar had been held up along Edge Lane, when he said, "Kate, never mind about all that, they tell me I go home at the weekend."

She had felt the tears stinging her eyes and then they were rolling unchecked down her cheeks.

"Why are you so unhappy, Kate? Why you cry?

I think maybe it is because I go away?"

Kate nodded her head.

"But Kate, I could never leave you, anybody can break my bones, but only you can break my heart."

"Where are you going?" she had asked.

"I hope your mother and father let me stay with you for a while. You think they will?" he asked her then and waited anxiously for her answer.

"Of course they will. They wouldn't let you go anywhere else." She fell into his arms and was suddenly aware of the other patients and their visitors all laughing and cheering, but she didn't care. She was just happy he didn't want to leave her.

He had to sleep with her brother, Robbie, but he didn't seem to mind. He was welcomed as one of the family and it made him feel more at home. They all pooled their money together to buy a crate of Carlsberg lager every Friday night. The big home-made pies would come out of the oven, piping hot and as they raised their bottles they would all shout, "*Skol!*"

They became one happy family enjoying each other's company. The atmosphere was repeated over and over again. Then Evert announced out of the blue, "I must go back to my ship. I need to pay my turn. I cannot be a man if I do not provide for Kate and myself."

Her dad stood up and said, "Our Kate will miss yer and so will we. Yer can stay here as long as yer like."

They all nodded their heads in agreement.

"No, I think not," Evert told them. "You know, before I met you I would go to the sea for six months at a time. It didn't matter to me, one port was the same as another, but now, I think I try to get a ship that come to Liverpool every six weeks."

Then, turning to Kate he said, "Will you wait for me, *mine skat?*"

Kate's yell of "Yes!" was drowned by her family shouting for her.

Eventually, a letter arrived from the Mærsk Line. The trip was to be from Liverpool to Texas every six weeks. There was only three days leave in each port but he took over the watch in Texas, so he could get a full week's leave in Liverpool.

Kate saved to have a telephone installed, a rare commodity in the early sixties, but it was necessary to be aware of when his ship was coming into Liverpool. Once she got the message she would be on the dockside hours before, waiting for a glimpse of the one face that stood in the most prominent place, so that they could both wave to each other well before the ship docked in the harbour.

Yes, she always knew he would be the first down the gangplank, a sack over his shoulder containing little mementos from ports he had called at. Her family loved these little presents and laughed at some of the things he chose - like the four Davy Crockett hats with big fur tails hanging down the back, or the four Viking helmets he had sent over from Denmark - their faces were a picture.

He always brought a special present for Kate - and there was never any joke about them. Then came that magical moment. "Kate, I want you to be *mine gift.*"

"Mine gift?" she had asked.

"Yes, my wife. I love your family, but it is you I dream about every day. I realise my dreams must become real. We must find some way to be alone together."

She needed the same, but in the early sixties it was unheard of to go to bed together, especially in the family house - it would be too embarrassing. It just didn't happen.

"Next trip we call at Rotterdam for three days. My captain say you can come on board. Will you come to me?"

Kate told him she'd love to, but he would have to ask her dad.

The whole family had seen her leave. You would have thought she was going forever, not just three days, but they all shared the excitement as she got into the taxi that was to take her to Ringway

Airport in Manchester.

She had never flown before and felt sure the plane would crash and when it arrived at Schipol Airport in Amsterdam, she was more than grateful to get her feet on the ground - any ground, as long as she wasn't in that sky.

There was music playing over the system, *It Won't Be Long Now* by the Beatles, a group from Liverpool. Kate loved them. She laughed because she couldn't understand anyone. She went looking for a trolley to collect her luggage, then she heard him before she saw him.

"Kate! You are here!"

A big bunch of red roses was pressed into her arms and she was carried through the airport to the waiting taxi, where he paid the driver to sort out her luggage.

The drive to the ship was unnoticed because they couldn't take their eyes off one another. The words that came out of his mouth were of pure love and she basked in the romance of it all, knowing that she felt the same way and realising that the feelings she had suppressed for so long were about to be revealed during the magical night that lay ahead.

They lay in their single bunk in his cabin and she felt they were the only two people in the world. Nothing else mattered, only the two of them. She was sitting bolt upright when he asked why she wore clothes in bed with him.

All her modest thoughts disappeared as she let him slip off her nightie, whispering to her that she need not wear anything, that he needed every part of her and asking how could he explore her if she was covered in clothes.

She had no words to convey the intensity and longing that had been denied them, their being together then was enough, but he hesitated. "Kate, *mine skat*, you have never been with a man before. I am so afraid I will hurt you. I never want that I do that."

She felt a searing pain go through her body and she cried out for him to stop, but at the same time she could hear his comforting words telling her that this was the only time in her life she would get pain through him, that from now on, she was his, his alone and he would always be there to protect her.

They didn't move out of his cabin for three days. Food was left for them outside the door, with just a light tap to let them know it was there.

They showered together, each exploring the other's body under the soft, warm water and when she was tired he would sing her a soft Danish melody, *Oh, Maria, I will Come Home To You.*

Those three days she was to remember all her life.

All too soon the time had gone and she returned home, her heart downcast. She couldn't bear to be apart from him and she knew he felt the same way.

"Kate," he had told her, "you bring more meaning to my life. I ask my company can you sail with me, then I can show you all the places I have seen."

It was like a dream come true, an adventure and she was certain she would be with him for evermore. She went back to college but couldn't wait to get home to all those airmail letters. There were always dozens arriving because although he wrote every night before he went to sleep, he could only post the letters when his ship arrived at the next port.

One day there was no letter, just a cablegram with instructions to pick up a ticket to travel to him. Her mother assured her that all her clothes were neatly packed and she didn't hesitate. She got the first flight to be by his side.

The following three years were the most exciting of her life. She drank mint tea with him in Turkey, saw big fish in Bilbao and celebrated Independence Day in Texas. She watched as the barges made their way from one canal to another in Holland, listened enraptured as a little girl sang, *Buona Seva, Buona Seva* under the trees in Palermo.

One day he said, "I'll buy a wedding ring for your finger. We'll go to a jewellers and I will place a plain gold band on the third finger of your right hand so it can be exchanged to your left hand when we get married."

He knew she had no money but he saw to her every need. She didn't abuse his generosity because they planned to buy a house by the sea in Lemvej.

He knew she was ill on the three week sea crossing to Durban. She was constantly sick and a shadow of her former self by the time the ship docked.

Once the ship had discharged its' cargo, it would make its' way to Marseille and then on to Denmark where everybody would be paid off. Evert suggested that it might be better if she took a flight to England, then when she felt better they could meet up later and take a vacation together.

Kate welcomed the idea and felt better thinking of her own family taking care of her. Once home, he made her go to the doctor. After the doctor examined her, he beamed and gave her the news that she was two months' pregnant. She couldn't understand it. They had been careful to take all the normal precautions and that had worked well for the past three years.

She walked home with mixed feelings, but only because their dream home would have to be put on hold. She could stay in Liverpool and he could do plenty of extra hours so that they would be more or less in the same position with their savings.

She stopped by the main Post Office and sent a telegram to Marseille. She knew him, he wouldn't wait to reply, he would be on the first flight from France to Liverpool. She'd have to calm him because he'd be like a mother hen and make her believe she was the only woman in the world to give birth.

"Evert, darling," she wrote, "you are going to be a father. Cable me back as soon as you dock and I will come to Marseille."

She made her way home, deciding on the way to keep the news to herself. She didn't want anyone to know before he did, it wouldn't be right. They could tell them the news together.

His cablegram came by return and fell from her hands. It read simply, "Do not come to Marseille or Denmark, ever."

She was aware of her mother breaking her fall and her concern when she asked what the matter was. She replied, "Mum, I'm two months' pregnant and Evert doesn't want to know."

Her mother took over straight away, once she knew she was not going to faint again. "If any of them come in, just say yer've got the 'flu, that's why your eyes are red. Now leave everything to me, nobody need ever know except us."

* * * * *

Life was just a blur after that. She got the midnight coach to London, her mum telling her she would be a social outcast around there if anyone found out. She sat with her mother for hours in that bus station, her mother wanting to protect her from her dad finding out. She knew how much he thought of her, but yes, her mother was probably right, the shock would have killed him.

Her Aunt Cissy met her at Victoria coach Station the following morning. She was unmarried but liked it that way and didn't seem to mind the thought of living with Kate, pregnant or not. She was an older version of her mother again with only her welfare at heart.

The journey passed in a blur of emotion. She began to settle in and realised almost instantly that she didn't like London, it was too fast for her and nobody spoke to anybody else. It appeared a very lonely place. She needed to get back to her roots but how could she turn up with a baby in Liverpool? She had many conversations with Aunt Cissy and together they decided that the best thing to do was to have the baby adopted.

When her time came, Aunt Cissy went with her to the home run by nuns. The labour pains were the worst pains she had ever dreamed of. All she did was cry for her mum. If she was going to die, she wanted her mother to be with her.

Then all of a sudden the pain stopped and she heard her and Evert's baby make its' first sound. "What is it?" she asked the nurse who had been holding her hand.

"It's a beautiful baby girl," she replied.

Kate asked whether she could hold her.

"Well," the kindly nun replied, "I'm not supposed to let you, but just while I go and make you a nice cup of tea."

After that brief cuddle, the baby was taken from her. She asked at every opportunity to see her baby but this was always denied her. She was told in no uncertain terms to stop upsetting the rest of the girls, all of whom had seemed to accept their lot. She, however, refused to sign the final adoption papers until she met the person who was going to adopt her baby. No amount of bullying would make her change her mind, the fact that this wasn't allowed did not seem to matter. She wanted to see the couple who were to bring up her baby for herself. She was introduced to them in a side room and it was only when the woman with kindly eyes agreed to call the baby Paula, that she signed the papers that were pushed in front of her.

Finally, Aunt Cissy came to take her home. "Come on, Kate," she said, "it's all over now. You'll soon be back to normal. Will you go back to college when you get home?"

Kate broke down. Aunt Cissy took her hand. "Do you feel like staying here? Will it help to be near her?"

Kate flung her arms around her aunt's shoulders, breaking her heart until no more tears would come. She was not pressed into getting a job, but she couldn't put her sorrow on the woman who had been doing all the spare hours available these last few months to support her. But she had no work experience, she had only done her art designs and what could she do with those?

The answer hit her one day while she and Aunt Cissy were walking along the embankment. Her drawings and paintings. Colour excited her and some of her work sold for over a pound.

An exciting time followed. Within a month she had her stall set out and she enjoyed the antics of the other vendors trying to get potential customers to buy their wares. Sometimes she made as much as £10 a day, which must have been more than Aunt Cissy had made most weeks.

She bought Aunt Cissy the latest G-plan furniture and watched fondly as she polished it every day.

She got a letter from her mother every week, but did not reply because the postmark would reveal where she was to the rest of the family. She promised herself that once she had enough money to buy presents for the whole family she would make the journey home to Liverpool and they would believe she had been on her travels to various parts of the world.

She toyed with the idea of having a telephone installed, but in her times of depression it would have been too tempting to hear her mother's voice and any of them could have answered. This would have meant telling the truth or more lies, so she had left it.

She noticed the man each Sunday. He always looked at her work and sometimes he bought her designs and always paid more than the price she asked for. She looked out for him because his presence always meant she would have a good day and when she saw him approaching, she gave him a welcoming smile.

His name was Alex Montgomery. He told her he had many business interests, but had only become interested in design because decor was a major advantage in those days and he dreamed that in the coming five years England would beam with colour from John O'Groats to Land's End.

He asked her one day whether she would be interested in doing design work for him privately and handed her his card. She had thought about his offer all day and couldn't wait to tell Aunt

Cissy as soon as she got home.

Her aunt's reaction was just what she expected. "Kate, you're a beautiful girl. Are you sure it's your designs he's after? There are plenty of places he could go. Why you?"

They eventually reached an understanding that any work she did for him would be done from the spare room. She wouldn't go to his office until Aunt Cissy had got to know him as well. Kate didn't sleep the night she made her decision. She could taste success and knew she was doing the right thing. She contacted him at nine o'clock the following morning.

Alex was as good as his word. The only problem was, too good! The orders came from him thick and fast. There weren't enough hours in the day for her to complete them, but it was only when his associate started placing orders as well that she realised she had to get bigger premises and somebody to help her. And that was how her company began.

She found a little shop for rent near Aunt Cissy's, who insisted she still live with her. Her back and arms ached so much as she tried to do all the repairs herself. Had the shop been in Liverpool, her brothers would have had it finished for her within a week. As it was, any major jobs had to be done a month at a time as she could afford them.

The hard work was good therapy and she didn't have much time to brood over Paula. Throwing herself into her work was the only answer. However, Kate constantly thought about the baby she had given up and whatever spare money she had was used on private investigation, trying to find out where she was. Nothing worked and she eventually decided she was just throwing her money away.

Two years passed and she had been so busy that she hadn't really noticed how healthy her bank balance was. It was only when she got her first major order from a new market garden centre that she realised she could not continue as she was.

It was not in her make-up to admit that the job was too big for her, so she put it out to contract, insisting that every last detail was done to her specifications and that the order would be ready on the agreed date.

The garden centre was so pleased with her work that they ran an article about her on Gardener's World, saying that she was the designer of the future. This increased her workload further and she moved to a prestigious office in Stratford Place, off Oxford Street.

That was a good move. It always surprised her that if people thought you were struggling they didn't give you any leeway whatsoever, but if you gave the impression of extreme wealth, more work came in. It had happened on several occasions.

Her fame began to spread and she was approached about her subject at meetings and even on television chat shows. It never failed to amaze her that her commonsense answers to people's questions were considered to be so worldly wise.

The media coverage brought the work flooding in and her accountant suggested that she needed to get rid of some money. So, she moved out of Aunt Cissy's and into her own little house.

It took another three years to get it to her liking, because with working and travelling she just didn't have the time. But it was all hers and paid for, nobody could take it off her. House prices boomed in the Seventies, so her financial position seemed secure.

She made it home to Liverpool now every six months, going along with the story her mother had told them that she and Evert had fallen out and she had settled with her Aunt Cissy in London.

* * * * *

Julia, her secretary, had a new boyfriend who called in at regular intervals because his beat as a uniformed police officer was right outside the office. He was there that often that if she didn't know better she'd have thought he was on the pay-roll.

Julia knew all about Paula, and when she suggested that Rob might be able to help, Kate jumped at the chance. In less than a week he got the address she required. He was horrified when she offered him a considerable amount of money, telling her to be careful and to never disclose where she had got the address from.

She arrived at the semi-detached house and parked a short distance away, where she couldn't be seen. She heard them before she saw them, but as they came into view she saw a little blonde girl holding a woman's hand and chattering away.

They were oblivious to her presence, so she followed them and watched as the child was deposited safely at school. She then approached the woman. Anxiety and alarm registered all at once on Annie's face when she stopped her, for she recognised Kate immediately.

"What do you want?" Annie asked her.

"Please," she said, "I never want to do anything to upset you or her. I just needed to see her for myself."

"And now you have," Annie replied, "what is your next move?"

"I do not intend making any move, except I wouldn't mind, with your permission, giving her a present on her birthday and at Christmas, as if they'd come from you."

Annie relaxed and thought it over. She said, "Yes, I understand. I would want to do the same. She's a lovely little girl. I intended telling her about you, but knowing when is difficult. Maybe it's for the best now, because I didn't want her to find out when she was a teenager."

"Did you call her Paula?" she asked.

"Yes. I promised you that. I liked the name anyway."

Annie asked her whether she would like to see some photographs of Paula. She was on her own now, her husband had recently died and she made a point of stressing that Paula was all she had to live for.

They made their way to the house and Annie showed her pictures of Paula with a pride only a mother delighted with her child could have. They came to the arrangement that she could visit as long as she became Aunt Kate and Annie remained Paula's mother. She called after that at regular intervals during the next five years, ensuring from a distance that they didn't want for anything.

When she was ten years' old, Paula was told that she had two mums and once she knew the other was Aunt Kate she had no problem with it. In fact, she seemed to relish the thought that she was so special.

Kate fulfiled her life with her work and visits to Annie and Paula. Paula would sometimes slip up and call her 'mum' but she always remembered that her real mum was Annie, so there was no real problem. It was a pity that her family in Liverpool didn't know Paula, but that was a price that had to be paid. Too much deceit, it was best to leave well alone. Until Evert had phoned, then everything had to change.

So many emotions had been brought to the surface and once she had arrived at her house in London, she was well aware that Paula had to be told the truth and that it had to be now.

The panic she had felt came flooding back and she had made some feeble excuse that it was Annie she wished to speak to when Paula had answered the phone.

Kate had been relieved when she was told that Paula was on her way out and had jumped at the idea that she should spend the night with Annie.

They had seemed to sit for hours, waiting for her to come home and had both panicked when they heard her key in the door. Paula had been startled herself when she had seen them together, she must have wondered what bad news she was about to hear.

Annie had kept quiet while she had told Paula the truth. Paula had just kept looking from one to the other. Eventually, she got up, sat down again by Annie and linked her arm. Annie had put her free hand on Paula's head and stroked her hair.

"Kate," she said, "I have the greatest two mums in the world, but when I was at school, all the other kids had grandparents, dads, aunties, uncles and cousins. I never joined in because I didn't like them asking me questions. I know I could never have explained all those deaths. I have always intended to discover my roots, but at the same time I didn't want to upset either of you. Now, I hope you will make it easy for me, for I want to meet them. It's not too much to ask is it, for I am nearly twenty-one."

She had been relieved that Annie had intervened when she had told her not to think too bad of the situation because people thought differently now than how they used to when she was born.

Paula had realised the position when she had told her that today she would be known as a 'love child' but twenty years ago, she would have been Kate Robert's bastard.

"Sorry," she had said, "but the thought of having a really big family excites me. You two seem to have protected me, so I'll leave it to you when I can meet them, but please make it soon, won't you Kate?"

It had been left to her to make the arrangements

and the three women had parted on the same affectionate terms.

She had been glad to get to the office the following morning. Julia was already there, full of the news that Evert hadn't stopped phoning her. She could see all the messages all over her desk.

Julia had lifted the receiver and placed it in her hand. "Ring him now," she had said, "the business can wait for half an hour."

It had barely had time to ring when he answered it. "Hello," he had said, then she had heard the excitement in his voice as he said, "It is you! I am going crazy here in case you say no."

He appeared to panic when she had asked him what he thought she would say no to.

"No to speaking to me, no to seeing me, no to allowing me to come to you."

She looked over at him. He was now standing looking out of the window. Yes, that is why she had come here because if she hadn't he would have come to her and that was the last thing she wanted.

What was it he had said? "True love must never die. I am like Moses by the water, not knowing which way to go." Did he bother which way she had gone years before? Did he hell. However, she owed it to Paula to let her meet her father, then she was getting the first flight back. If Paula wanted to stay here for a holiday and get to know him she was old enough now to make her own mind up, but if he thought for one minute she was going to get involved again, he had no chance.

She felt like punching him hard. He'd upset her twenty years ago and now he'd done it again. As soon as Paula met him, she thought, she was going to tell him how she felt, then she was going home to lead a normal life.

She felt sorry for Paula. After that meeting at Annie's, she had appeared to be ringing her with the flimsiest excuses, but had never once mentioned Liverpool or Denmark. She must have realised how difficult it was for her to explain all the twenty year old lies.

Her mother had solved the problem for her. "I've told your dad," she said on the phone. She hadn't had a chance to ask what he said, because her mother had said that he was there and wanted to speak to her. She would remember his words for the rest of her life. She wasn't afraid of him, but to him black was black and white was white. He could never contemplate that there might be grey in the middle.

"Our Kate," he had said, "is this true what I have been hearing?"

"Yes," she had replied.

"Well, you've upset me, I can tell yer, yer kept me in the dark for twenty years and how come you didn't tell your daughter about us? It's all wrong, this, but you'll know that anyway. I've always been proud of yer, our Kate, but not today, not today. Were yer ashamed of us? Didn't we fit in with that lot yer mix with?"

She had never felt so low in her life. "Dad," she had said, "it wasn't like that."

"Well," he had replied, "yer'd better get yourselves up here and put everything right, or I'm coming down there."

"I will," she had said.

"I'll give yer until the weekend, to get yourself sorted out, otherwise I'll sort everything out for yer. I've had a grand daughter for twenty years that I didn't know about, what do you think you are all playing at?"

She remembered looking at the telephone receiver as she heard him slam down the phone. Her mother had answered when she had rung back. "He'll get over it," she had said, "but I've had a right time of it. It wasn't as though he was going to hit me or anything like that, he just seems down like I've never seen him in all the years we've been together."

She had spoken to Paula the minute she had got home. Paula had been excited when she told her about the conversation. "He sounds alright, just the type I like. I'm dying to see him. Are we going this weekend? Shall I ask my mum if it's alright?"

It only occurred to her then how like her dad Paula was.

She hadn't made any unusual arrangements around the office, she had had to re-schedule a couple of appointments but other than that they were used to her going away for weeks at a time, so nobody was aware of her personal dilemma except her loyal Julia, who wouldn't breathe a word.

Julia had blocked any calls, only telling her that he had called again. Julia was well aware that if Kate wanted to speak to him she had his number, but she had already agreed to meet him within the month at Karoup Airport and the month was up today.

She noticed he was now pacing up and down outside. He thinks he can grab hold of me and everything will be alright, she thought, but in the next hour, he's going to be so surprised, he won't know what's hit him and it's all his own fault.

He should have been there when she and Paula had gone to Liverpool the other Friday. The girl hadn't shut up all the way there. She was like a child who had been deprived of going to Disney World when all her friends had been, but now it was her turn.

"Fancy having a big family, after all!" she had

squealed with delight. "Do you think they will like me? Am I dressed alright?"

She had tried to answer all her questions and she had also warned her that her grandfather might not be his usual self because he was feeling very hurt at the moment. After all, it had taken him twenty years to hear about his grandchild.

"Don't worry, Kate," she had said, "I'll soon charm him round."

"You don't know him," Kate replied, to which Paula said, "No, I don't do I, yet!"

That was the only sign she'd had from Paula in the last few weeks that gave away the fact that she, too, was unhappy at being lied to for twenty years.

She had taken the scenic route, making the excuse that she wanted to show Paula her first designs, but knowing it was really because she didn't want to face her dad. It had always been important to her that he thought well of her, and although everything was straightened out now, she couldn't help remembering his words when he had said, "Got any more secrets like this you want to tell me about?"

They had come off the M53 at Ellesmere Port. "Why here?" Paula had asked. "Does it mean anything?"

"Not really," she had told her, but if the conversation had become strained they could always have related to the good times they spent as kids at the Rivacre baths. It had been as easy as keeping to the motorway. She had cut through Eastham Village, Rock Ferry and the Mersey Tunnel, which was just a stone's throw away.

She had been as stunned as Paula when they had turned the street corner and found yellow ribbons tied to every lamp post, every door and every bush. "What are they for?" asked Paula.

"I think they are for you," she replied, "to welcome you home."

3

On that day in Liverpool, she had never seen so many people come out of one house. There were aunts, uncles, cousins she had not seen for years - and in the midst of them, standing like the Rock of Gibraltar, was her dad. Nobody was going to welcome Paula until he did.

Paula didn't have the chance to get out of the car before he lifted her out. "Come on, me lass, let yer grandad see yer," and he carried her past the others into the house. The atmosphere had been overwhelming because it had been a northern welcome at its best. There had been enough food and drink to feed the whole of Liverpool for the following week and the presents for Paula appeared to fill the room.

Each person had been waiting expectantly for the presents to be opened, each one hoping that they had chosen the correct thing. Paula hadn't been able to cope with so much emotion and shed tears of happiness - tears were falling off the faces of most of the other people as well and her grandad had grabbed hold of her and took her into the front room saying, "Me and the lass are going in here for a bit of peace."

There was so much catching up to do. Not one of them had implied that they had had any knowledge of the words between her and her dad. Her mother had taken the big tablecloths off the food and everyone dived in.

"I'll just put these two little trays up and take them in to them. It might break the ice, Kate," her mother whispered, "put your head around the door and look at the two of them."

She had looked and could almost taste the feeling between them, the young and the old. There was no gap, they had their heads together. She had stood and watched them until her dad had noticed her presence.

"I'll tell you something, now, our Kate," he said, the tears choking him, "the day I first saw you I thought I had me birthday and Christmas cake all rolled into one, but it was nothing like today when I have got them iced as well."

"Come on, you two, everybody else wants to see you as well."

Her dad had got to his feet, given a big blow into his hankie and got hold of her and said, "You're still me lass," patting her shoulder.

Nobody had wanted to leave and so the gathering, which should have been for a few hours, went on all weekend.

It had been well past midnight when Paula had whispered to her, "Where are they all going to sleep?" She had looked shocked when she had told her in everybody's spare room. She had had to explain that northerners were a friendly lot and that's the way things were done in the north-west.

The excitement of the day had proved too much for her and she noticed that Paula was trying with all her might to keep her eyes open. "Tell me when you want to go to bed," she had whispered to her.

"Will they mind?" Paula wanted to know, whispering with her hand over her mouth so nobody would see her yawning. She had asked out loud, "Does anyone mind if we go to bed? It has been a long day."

"Of course not," they all chorused and her

mum added, "I've put you both up in your room, our Kate. Sleep tight, mind the bugs don't bite."

They had nearly been too tired to get up the stairs, but when they entered the bedroom, Rupert Bear was sat on one pillow and Paddington Bear on the other. They had smiled at each other and settled down in the freshly laundered sheets. There was a slight hint of lavender.

Funny, she thought, looking around the cafeteria, how certain smells remind you of home. Her mum had always believed it was the old fashioned formula for making you sleep. She laughed when she remembered the time her mum had got some new pills for making you sleep and insisted they all had one before they went to bed. The rush to the toilet the following morning made her hurry to get her specs on and she found she had given them all a dose of Beechams Pills instead.

She looked around to see if anyone had heard her laugh to herself, but everyone appeared to be deep in their own thoughts. She had been so lost in her thoughts of the past, she hadn't noticed the cafeteria filling up again. Another flight must have arrived. She was pleased, because once again she could take refuge in the crowd. She still had over an hour to wait for Paula.

Yes, she and Paula had indeed slept well that night and only awoke when the sound of someone creeping in and out of the room disturbed their dreams. They had dressed together and gone downstairs. There was only her mum, dad and one of her brothers at the table.

"Did I disturb you?" her mother had asked.

"Well," she had replied, "we heard something."

"Yes, well, it was me," her mother said, then pointing to her dad, continued, "he's had me going up there every ten minutes to see if you were alright."

"Well, we want our breakfast, that's why," her dad had retorted.

"Oh, no breakfast for me," Paula had said.

"Come on. Sit here with your grandad, me and you will have ours together. The rest of them can look after themselves."

Anyone could see the two had taken to each other the moment they had met.

"Oh, alright," Paula said, sitting down next to him, "you're the boss!"

"I don't think so, now you've arrived on the scene," he replied with his eyes sparkling at her.

"Bacon, egg, sausage, tomato and black pudding! I'll never eat all that!" exclaimed Paula.

"Course you will," the old man had said, "that black pudding will put a bit of meat on yer ribs."

It really had been lovely to see Paula and her dad. They were like two peas in a pod and they both loved each other's company, anybody could see that. She had planned to show Paula Liverpool and they could have gone to one of the better hotels for lunch, but there had been no chance of that.

The cars, when they did eventually leave the street, had been like a convoy. If Paula was going, they all were. She had been amazed at the Albert Dock - she hadn't known of its existence. The saw the Pier Head, St. George's Hall, St. John's Market, Cavern Walks, the two cathedrals, the Empire Theatre and of course, all the shops.

If Paula liked a jumper, she got half a dozen - one in every colour. In fact it got so bad she had had to remind them all she had a car not a lorry, to which someone had replied, "That girl's got twenty years of presents to catch up on from us."

It had been a waste of time really, talking to them. They had totally spoilt Paula and she had loved every minute of it. As soon as one person let go of Paula's hand, someone else took it. There had even been a small argument at one time, as they all wanted to be near her.

"Do you wanna see Liverpool's ground?" someone asked her, but before she had a chance to reply, one of her cousins had butted in, "If you do, you'll have to see Everton's as well."

They had turned the corner to the street where

the barrow boys were. "Apples a pound, pears . . " She had remembered as a child she had stood for hours listening to them and it was the same with the man who stood on the same corner every night shouting for you to buy the 'Echo'.

That had been a day to remember. Her dad had suggested they all go for a drink at the Adelphi - the fact that it had changed to the Britannia didn't seem to matter a jot because everybody still thought of it by its old name. It was opposite Lewis' with its statue of a naked man showing all his assets!

She smiled as she recalled the fuss that statue had caused when it arrived in the city centre. It had even been talked about on the six o'clock news and people would say, "Have you seen the man with the erection outside Lewis'?" and people would flock for miles to see it. The business world realised, of course, that it was a great advertisement for Lewis'.

Funny thing business, she thought, none of her family had been interested in going into business except her, but they all loved her stories when she came home - who she had met recently, what being on the TV was like, etc. Her sister's-in-law would not join in this conversation, they were too busy going through the bags she brought with her, eager to see the latest designs they knew would be the talk of the town before long.

She had loved that Liverpool crowd - still did. Sometimes their language was choice, but when Paula had met them for the first time, they had all behaved themselves. Even when they arrived back at the house after their day out and had started drinking, there still hadn't been one of them who had spoilt the atmosphere.

Trying to get them home had been difficult and it had been well past midnight again before the last one had left. With hindsight, it might have been better if they had stayed because her dad had taken off - but then again, she remembered, it had cleared the air.

She had made a pot of tea for the four of them before they went to bed and as she had come through from the kitchen she had heard Paula say, "Where did you work, Grandad, before you retired?"

"I used to tie up the ships," he had told her.

"Did you ever tie my dad's ship up?" Paula had asked him.

"Many a time," he had answered

She and her mum had got hold of each other, which her dad noticed straight away. "Didn't we say we would tell her everything she asked us? Didn't we make that agreement, you and me?" he had asked her mum, who had merely nodded her head. "Well, there you are then," the old man had said. Paula had looked alarmed and stated that she didn't want to cause any trouble.

The old man had ignored Kate and her mum and taking Paula's hand said, "You'll come to no trouble here, lass. Now's the time to ask all you want and I'll tell yer. I've lost twenty years of you, but what's gone is gone. But by the look of yer, you'll break someone's heart just like our Kate must have done to Evert Neilson."

He and Paula seemed to have forgotten Kate and her mum were still in the room, because Paula said, "Well, the way I heard it, it was Evert, my father," she corrected herself, "who dumped Kate."

"Well," her dad had replied, "there must have been two Evert Neilson's because the one I knew worshiped the ground our Kate walked on."

She had tried to stop the conversation, but the old man was having none of it. "Never mind, enough of this," he had said, "when I saw this girl yesterday, I saw her dad. She looks like that Ursula Andress and he has a right to see her like we all have, that's all I'm saying on the subject, except that she had been brought up by some woman in London that we don't know and she should have been here 'cos blood's thicker than water and that's that."

She thought back to the way Paula had tried to protect her. "Grandad," she had said, "I have a lovely mum in London. Kate has seen to my education and been there for me whenever I needed her. I've had a private tutor since I left school and next year I'll be going to university."

But, as always, her dad was having none of it. "Well, try to get into Liverpool," he had said, "so I can see you every day. I'll tell you both while you're here, me and her," he had continued, pointing to her mum, "came out of the mills in Lancashire to Liverpool because there was no work in the Depression and we settled here.

"I was lucky to get a job on the docks. You had to queue up every day and hoped you got picked to work, but as long as you were at the front of the line, you usually got a day's work. She brought the family up and I'll admit on a good week I'd spend a bit on drink, but not before I knew me family had a roof over their heads and food on the table.

"One more mouth to feed would have been no problem. What would it have been? An extra potato, a couple of pints of milk a week, but no, that decision was taken away from me. But in saying that, I'm proud of me family, always have been, always will be. But," he said, as he took Paula's hand, "there wasn't a prouder man in town today when I was walking around with you."

Paula had burst out crying and fell with her

head on the old man's knee. "Grandad," she had sobbed, "I love you."

"Well," he had said, "I have loved you from the day you were born and didn't know it, but they appear to have done a good job on yer without my help. So we're best leaving it at that. Now," he had said, "if you let me get up, I've still got to see to the other two women in my life," and he had come and put his arms around Kate and her mum's shoulders.

What a tearful time that had been. She had always valued her family unit and it had always carried her through any situation. Ok, she was successful now, but there had been times as she was building up her business, she had almost failed but she had always known in the back of her mind that if the worst came to the worst, she could always go home to Liverpool.

She and Paula had meant to leave on the Sunday, but had considered themselves lucky to have made an early start on the Monday. The Sunday dinner that had been served would have done credit to royalty. All offers of help had been refused, her mother insisting that it tasted better if you didn't have to cook it. The potatoes had been roasted to perfection in the meat fat, the carrots and swedes mashed with butter and pepper, the peas and a big piece of Yorkshire pudding with as much gravy as you wanted.

They all looked on that meal as the usual Sunday meal, but she knew that wherever she went in the world, the taste of food would never be as good as around that table.

Any thoughts of driving to London that day were completely out. They had already arranged that she and Paula go with them to the working men's club that night, telling them that there would be no trouble getting them both signed in.

There would never be another night like that again, there couldn't be. There were never any secrets around Liverpool and she would never forget the welcome they got in the club.

They had made an early start the following morning, this time keeping to the motorways and happy together in their own little world. They didn't make a lot of conversation on their way home. It was only when they had stopped for a drink at Keele Services that Paula had broached the subject of Evert. Thinking back now, she must have been trying to find a diplomatic way of asking her.

"Grandad liked Evert, didn't he?"

She had answered that everybody did.

"Well, when are we going to see him?" Paula had asked.

"Whenever you want," she had replied.

"Can I phone him tonight?" she had asked innocently.

"No!" she had heard herself shout, then she had to whisper that he didn't know anything about her. She remembered how upset Paula had looked when she had said quietly, "Well, I thought you had told me everything."

She had had to pacify her and explain that she had been told everything but her grandmother had told her father she had miscarried and so he didn't know she existed.

"Are you going to tell him about me, then?" she had asked.

"Of course," she had reassured her, only to be faced with the question of when.

"I thought when I go to Denmark," she had replied carefully, even though she'd no intention of going anywhere near Denmark before that weekend. But she had realised that Paula would want to meet her father and she had no intention of letting him come to London, he would expect her or Annie to put him up.

She knew she should have told him when she spoke to him after she'd been to Liverpool but, she thought looking at him, she hadn't wanted him to go to Liverpool either. And there was Annie to consider as well. What had Paula been like when they had finally arrived back there that day. She had jumped straight out of the car telling Annie how much she had missed her.

Annie had been concerned that she hadn't enjoyed herself, but she quickly put her mind at rest, telling her she had the most wonderful family back in Liverpool, especially her grandad. They had unloaded the car, Annie complaining good naturedly that they wouldn't have enough room for all the stuff.

She had left shortly afterwards because she wanted the privacy of her own home. She wanted to relax in the bath with those expensive oils she allowed herself and she remembered savouring the thoughts she had of that first meeting between her dad and Paula.

She wished she was in that bath right now. This meeting had been a fortnight away then and thinking back, a lot had happened in that short time as well. She had arrived for work the following morning with one day short in her week and her mother had phoned to ensure they had got home safely. She had thought nothing of it when her mother had asked for Paula's address so she could go on the family birthday and Christmas card list. It wasn't until the next Friday that she learned she had been tricked when she had got an urgent call from Annie that her dad had turned up on the doorstep and could she possibly go and sort everything out.

She had got to Annie's as quickly as she could. Annie had beckoned her to come to where the old man was sitting in the living room. "What are you doing here?" she had asked him.

"I wanted to see this woman for myself. She seems to have brought our Paula up right but I wanted to make sure. Nothing wrong in that, is there?" he had replied.

Annie had handed her a twenty-two carat gold watch chain which she recognised immediately as her dad's. "He wants me to have this," Annie had said, "but I can't accept it."

"Tell her to take it," her dad had pleaded, "I haven't got any money to speak of, but that is my most valued possession. It was my father's and his before that, but this woman's worth all the gold in the world for how she treated you and our Paula."

She saw a tear in Annie's eye. "Take it, please, Annie, it would mean so much to him if you would accept it, you can see that."

"Well," Annie had said, "He's kept telling me that, but I didn't want to do anything until you were here. Everything will be Paula's one day so perhaps it will end up where it should be at the end of the day. But what about your sons?"

"What about them?" her dad had asked, "make no mistake, I asked them all first did they mind, wouldn't have made any difference if they had, but I did give them a chance, but them lot take after me and the missus and were happy to have one less problem for them to worry about. Now, if you don't mind, our Kate," he had said, "I don't want to be a trouble to you any longer, so if you could just drop me at the station, I'll make my way home."

"Come on, you've always been an old softie underneath," she had said to him. What was he like? Only the best dad in the world.

Evert had been another matter. She had only had one brief conversation with him, she hadn't wanted to tell any more lies, she had merely confirmed the time of her arrival, telling him they could say what had to be said when they met up in Denmark. And there had been Paula. She had never been one ounce of trouble, but those last couple of weeks had certainly affected her. First she had said that when Kate met Evert she wanted to be there also and she'd had quite a job persuading her that it was going to be a terrible shock for him.

They had finally come to the arrangement that she and Paula would travel together from Heathrow to Copenhagen, where, after making sure she was safely installed in the VIP lounge provided by Scandinavian Airways, she would take the flight to Karoup, make him aware of Paula's existence, then

Paula would get the next flight two hours later and they would both be there to meet her.

Paula had been worried about how he would accept her. Well, she didn't relish the thought of even getting into conversation with him. She looked over at him and for the first time since she had arrived, they made eye contact. She gave him a weak smile then looked quickly away. She still had another hour to go before Paula's flight was due, so she could avoid talking to him for another forty-five minutes and spend five minutes waiting for the plane to arrive.

She was suddenly aware that someone was standing by her table and she looked up into the face of Evert Neilson.

4

Oh, my God, he had recognised her. "Yes?" she enquired of him.

"Oh, I am sorry, you are English."

"Yes," she said.

"Please excuse me, but I notice that you sit here the past hour. I think we both wait for the next flight from Copenhagen. Will you have coffee with me?"

"Yes," she replied weakly.

He called across the waitress, "Two coffees, please."

She had put her hands down on her lap so he

wouldn't see them shaking.

"Where do you come from in England?"

"London, I come from London."

"Yes, I have been there, but the best place I know is Liverpool. You know Liverpool?" he asked.

What a God-sent opportunity to tell him, but she just sat and stared at him. He was looking at her, waiting for an answer, but the words wouldn't get past her throat. No wonder he thought so well of Liverpool, he'd been treated like the prodigal son every time he returned there, but at the first sign of things not going his way, he had run.

"I know London better," she had finally managed.

"Yes," he said, "my wife is from London also. I think she miss her connection, but she be here within the hour, so I wait. I am so nervous, it is twenty years since I last saw her."

"You have not seen your wife for twenty years?" she asked, pretending to be shocked.

"Ah, she is not my wife but I call her that, because to me she always will be. There could never be any other but her."

She never answered him, but she was starting to see a side of him she had never known existed. Forget the bad past, gloss over things you would never forget and everything would go back to the way you wanted it to be. It didn't seem to matter how many people's lives you altered in the meantime.

She had spent twenty years living in London when she could have been with her family in Liverpool. If he thought that now he had found her he could get back what he rejected in the first place, he could go to hell.

"Why did you not go to see her?" she asked him.

"I didn't know where she was. I only just find her one month ago, after looking for her for the last twenty years."

"Well, if you thought so much of her, how did you lose touch in the first place?"

"I still don't know," he said sadly, "maybe in the next hour I will get the answer. I was on the sea and my wife came all around the world with me. For three years we have wonderful time together, until we make the trip from America to Durban in South Africa. She be very sick, so when we arrive in port, I tell her to take the aircraft to England. It will be better for her to be with her family in Liverpool, she would get better more quickly there than being tossed around by the water. So she go and I sailed with my ship to Marseille in France and on home to Denmark, where I get paid off and can take the flight to England, so I can be by her side."

"Well, what happened?" she asked.

"I don't know how it went so wrong, except that when I get to Marseille I get a cablegram from her that she is pregnant, she and me will have a baby together. I feel I am in heaven, but she say that she will come to me, but I never want that she travel anywhere, so I cable back I will go to her, but then I never see her again."

"Did you go to her?" she asked.

"Of course! Two weeks later, I take big parcel for the baby, but this puzzles me for twenty years now, her mother, who had always treated me like her son, was so cold to me. She not want to talk with me except to tell me that my Kate lose our baby. Sure I cry inside but that is never mind. I think that I still have her, but she is gone and I don't know where to look for her. That old mother knew, but she will never tell it to me, I know that. Are you alright?" he asked her suddenly, "you have not drunk your coffee. Is it too strong for you?"

"No," she replied, "it's fine," and took a big sip. She felt ill and a shudder passed through her, but he didn't seem to notice. She heard him continue.

"Two months ago, I looked at my television and I see her name, it stirred deep feelings within me. I never think it is her, but then it might be, because the programme is about decoration and my Kate always liked the colours. But it take me one month, twenty-four hours a day to trace her, because it was an English programme, but when she say 'Hello, Evert', I knew that my twenty year wait is over.

She should be in Copenhagen now, waiting to come to me. Years ago, when we were together, somebody cut the head off my little mermaid on the rocks in the harbour. My Kate didn't like that, she say she see it as a symbol from all the ships going in and out safely, so I took her to one side of the jewellers and I buy her a gold bangle. I wonder if she still have it."

She could see the sweat coming through the gold bangle on her wrist.

"We were engaged to be married and I buy her a gold ring when we were in Palermo."

Did he know? Had he recognised her? No, he was just rambling about all the things she knew to be true. She passed the pad of her thumb over the ring she was wearing.

"You meeting your man?" he asked her.

"No," she replied, "my daughter."

"I have no children," he said, "but my Kate and me we always dream we have four. This cannot be now, but," he added, giving a shrug of his shoulders, "so long as I have her by my side, everything will be alright."

"Will you please excuse me?" she said as she got

up, "I have to go to the ladies' room."

"Of course," he got up, "you will find it over there."

She made her way across the cafeteria, praying that her legs would carry her, otherwise history would be repeating itself and he would be protecting her from harm once again. She felt faint and was glad she had her make-up with her, she needed to splash her face with cold water and she needed to do it quickly or she would pass out.

She stayed there longer that she should. She was tempted to go straight outside and tell him. She had always been forthright in her business dealings and was well respected for it, so why not now? She'd never seen him really angry with her, of course, within the three years she had known him, they had had their differences, but when he was really angry he used to talk in Danish, as he had explained many times, he did not want her to know the words he would later regret.

She dreaded the next thirty minutes of her life. If only she had told him over the phone. Oh, yes, he would have come straight over, but she would have felt safer in her own home than here in the airport.

She went out onto the concourse, avoiding the cafeteria. She needed some fresh air, but damn, he too was there. He came over to her. "You're not well?" he asked her.

"Yes," she replied, "I'm fine."

"I like it if I speak with you, if you don't mind. I feel so nervous, I try to slim the last month, I lose eight kilograms."

"That's over a stone," she said.

"Yes, but it is important that I try to look the same weight. The grey hair I can do nothing about."

"I don't think it really matters," she told him, "it's what's inside that everyone looks for at the end of the day."

"Maybe," he said, "maybe."

They carried on the conversation until the tannoy announced the arrival of the flight. She saw Paula immediately, that honest, eager looking Nordic blonde, her hair done in two thick plaits. She looked at Evert, eagerly waiting, watching for a glimpse of the face he would not see. Paula saw them both and ran to embrace them, but Kate shook her head from side to side and Paula stopped and looked at her with a quizzical expression. Then she saw her eyes take on a hopeless look when she realised she hadn't told him.

Evert was looking really dejected. "Your wife not on the flight?" she asked him.

"No," he said, "and now I get very frightened because I know she leave London because I check with the woman in her office before I leave my house today. I get some change then I telephone her."

"She could be held up anywhere. Would you like that my daughter and I sit with you while you decide what to do?"

"I would be glad of that because I have nothing to do but wait. I know she will be here today."

Paula was standing by her side, not saying a word, just looking at him. She then moved forward and touched her father for the first time. "Come on," she said, "I'll let you buy me a coffee."

They seated themselves, all of them reaching for their money, but he interrupted them, "I will get the coffee," he said, "I am very grateful that you stay with me, for now, because I don't like that I be alone at this time."

As soon as he was out of earshot, Paula whispered, "You never told him, did you Kate?"

"No," she replied.

"Well, what are you planning to do? Let me sit here with him for the next half hour, so we've seen him and then go home?"

"Things have changed," she said, "you will have to give me time."

"Oh, Kate, I know this is difficult for you, but it is my father, for God's sake. I really want to know him and I hope he wants to know me and if you can lie to him that's fine, but I don't want to. I want him to know who I am. All the time I was in that airport in Copenhagen I could just imagine flinging my arms around his neck."

Evert came back, putting the coffee down in front of them. He then held out his hand. "My name is Evert Neilson," he said, introducing himself, "and you?"

She held out her hand and took his. "My name is Kathleen and this is my daughter, Paula."

"Oh, Paula," he said, "that brings back painful memories to me."

"Why is that?" Paula asked him.

"My wife and me, we always say that we get four children together. When we get a daughter we will call her Paula, it be after a song we sing together when we first met. Hey, Paula, maybe you are named after that song also."

She saw Paula look at her and decided that it had gone on long enough. She stood up. "Evert, I told you my name was Kathleen."

"Yes," he said.

"Well, in England, most Kathleens are called Kate. Allow me to introduce to you your daughter, Paula."

He looked at them, puzzled. "Sorry," he said, "I mistake what you say, could you speak to me more slowly please."

She sat down, "Evert, it's me, Kate."

* * * * *

"You? You are my Kate? But why you not say?" Then he added, "no, no I would know my Kate anywhere, sure you are a beautiful woman, but my Kate she have long black hair. I know her anywhere in the world."

"Are you crazy, Evert?" she said, "stop this, stop it now. Everything you have told me, I can fill in the rest in every detail. Evert, here is my passport, look at it. Look at my name, it is still Kate Roberts."

He took it from her, looked at her name and photograph. He never attempted to give it back, he just sat there looking absolutely stunned. It seemed like two hours, but it was only a few minutes before he said, "You say this girl Paula is your daughter?"

"Yes," she replied, "and yours, too."

He looked at Paula, "How old are you?"

"Nearly twenty-one," she replied. She went to put her hand on his, but he pushed it away.

"No! No! No!" he shouted, then to Kate and Paula's astonishment, the table was tipped up in front of them, the hot coffee spilling all over them. They didn't understand what he was shouting because it was in Danish. The Airport Security came running over and they seemed to calm him down.

They watched as he slumped in the chair

opposite them. There were no words between them until he broke the silence. "Ok, ok, I speak with you in the best English that I can. My wife, my Kate, she would never ever do that to me, she always would make sure that I see my own daughter and the same woman would never have been able this hour to sit and talk with me, of that I am sure. I don't know what trick you and the girl play. Sure you have correct documents and I don't know how you do it, but it is cruel, very cruel."

Kate got up, but he said harshly, "You sit down there," and looking at Paula he said, "you, too."

"Ok, I get the wrong Kate Roberts when I phone that office, but it seemed so real. Maybe all the English sound the same, but you make sure I never speak with you in detail these past weeks, only some woman, she would only know what you tell her. I never believe anybody in my whole life again. Maybe there is a law, maybe the police should speak with you, maybe I get them now."

"Evert," she said, but he interrupted her.

"Shut your mouth. I want no words off you."

"Then maybe you should get the police," she said, "I can tell them how my first meal on the *Mænsk* was twenty rashers of bacon and five eggs, or maybe I will tell them that I hate that dried fish you eat, or shall I tell them about all that black underwear you bought me in Texas, or that stupid leather camel from the Suez Canal?"

He sat and looked at her in disbelief. He got up. "Moment, moment," he said, "I need to translate from English to Danish in the computer in the back of my head. It is too much for any man to think of in one day - even one lifetime. You excuse me while I go to the bathroom? You wait here for me?" he asked.

"Yes, we will wait here," they both said together.

They watched as he made his way across the cafeteria. He looked as if he was drunk. "He's in a state of shock, Kate," said Paula.

"Yes, I know," she replied.

"What are we going to do?"

"I don't know," she replied, "I should be telling you, but I can't think straight at the moment. How did we get in this mess?"

"Maybe it started with all the lies twenty years ago?" suggested Paula, "perhaps you had better leave it to me. He doesn't know me and I don't know him, so we have no argument with each other. All sorts of things will be going through his head, but at the end of the day he knows it is his loss if he doesn't want to know me. Don't worry, Mum," she said.

"Mum? I've always been Aunt Kate to you," she said, surprised.

"Well, not today," Paula said positively, "it's not every day a twenty-year-old girl meets her mother and father together for the first time and that's how I'm looking at it anyway. If it doesn't work out I can always go home to my real mum and my Aunt Kate."

They watched the toilet door and eventually Evert came out. Paula got up and went over to his side. She didn't try to take his arm in case he pushed her away as he had before. Kate looked at them as they approached the table. She could see he had been crying, there was no mistaking the puffiness around his eyes. He looked at her, "You are my wife, is that right?"

"Well," she replied, "I was your girlfriend for three years."

He then looked at Paula, "And you say you are my daughter, is that right?"

"If what has been told to me is true, then yes, I am."

"Well, we will see in a moment," and turning to Kate he said, "you tell me now the words I use to you all those years ago, every time we meet."

She heard herself whisper, "You are here now, so everything will be alright."

"Say them again," he ordered.

"You are here now, so everything will be alright."

"Now say the words I use to you when we say

goodbye."

She tried to take his hand. He looked at her with his face like stone. "My wife," he said, "always know those words I use only for her, she never ever forget them. If you cannot tell me you had better fear that you will live because nobody can be allowed to break my heart so much. So, now you say those words, now!" he shouted.

She looked him straight in the eye, seeing Paula's white face to one side of him and said, "Don't forget, my Kate, no matter if we are apart, the same moon will always shine over us."

He looked from one to the other in disbelief, then he put his head in his hands, tears rolling through his fingers. Everybody was looking over at them, so they moved their chairs one each side to protect him. This time he didn't attempt to move away from them.

They heard him say through his tears, "You two be the reason that I make big fool of myself, but at the moment I need you both more than I ever need anybody in my whole life. In a moment I will take you both home. I will be the proudest man in Denmark because I now got the best feeling possible, but first I must take a double Schnapps, because I never be able to drive you without it."

"Shall I go and get you one?" Paula asked.

He got up, put his hand in his pocket and gave her a wad of notes, "Yes," he said, "why not. My daughter can serve the father with the Schnapps. Me a father, I cannot believe it. Sorry, I do believe it, it is just hard, if you understand me? My mind is crazy at the moment, so you will have to excuse what I am saying."

"Oh, shut up," said Paula, "I'll get you that drink."

"Not before I hold you," he said.

"Ow," she said, "you're hurting me, you'll break my bones."

"Only with the love I feel," he replied, as he let her go.

They both watched her as she walked to the bar. "She be lovely," he said, "and you Kate, now I not ask why, you can tell me later, but I'm so happy that you are here in Denmark. I always know that you would step on Danish soil again, I always knew me and you belong together.

"When we have our drinks, I take you to my house. It is the one we always dream of together, the one I build for you. That dream for me is always very real, it never die and maybe you know it now, because whatever went wrong between us is over. I make you believe in me again, you can be sure of that."

Paula interrupted them, putting three double

Schnapps on the table, "What's good for the gander is good for the goose," she said and she and Kate laughed.

"What does that mean?" he asked.

"Oh, nothing, it's just a saying, but I got it the wrong way round," Paula explained.

"*Skol!*" he said to them, "and you don't know the meaning of that, do you? It means I'm very happy that you are here with me and there is no other way I can say it. It never have a double meaning."

5

Walking away from the airport terminal towards his car, Kate was glad to breathe in the fresh air. She needed it. The past hour had been tense, to say the least.

He opened the door for her to sit beside him and guided Paula to the rear of the car. Instead of the excitement and conversation they had all anticipated, there was a reflective silence as each thought over the past and about the future.

Denmark was a beautiful country, there was no doubt about that, the flat green fields were similar to those in rural England, except there you didn't get those delightful little fjords. Evert was quick to point out the absence of any litter and that brought more memories back for Kate.

It had been the one bone of contention between them all those years ago that if she said something good about England you could be sure Denmark did it better - according to Evert anyway. She let it go this time.

She did, however, point out that there were fifty-eight million people in England, compared to only five million in Denmark, so she would expect Denmark to be cleaner. He smiled at her and remarked, "You still have that fiery spirit towards England?" She didn't answer, just nodded her head.

The roads were virtually traffic free and in all the little towns and villages they travelled through the red and white Danish flag was everywhere. They had travelled for nearly an hour and Kate was the first to notice the coastline. "You live near the sea?" she asked him.

"Yes, I always like that I live near the water," but that was all he said, he didn't elaborate.

Eventually they passed through two stone pillars that led along a drive and in the distance they saw a house standing tall and proud. Kate turned to Paula, she didn't say anything, just shrugged her shoulders. Evert was aware of the look that passed between them and turned to Kate. "This is your home, Kate, the one you and me always talk about. I built it myself because I always knew that one day you would be standing here by my side."

"It looks absolutely beautiful," she replied.

"Yes," he said, as he brought the car to a standstill, "I make sure of that. I build it for my beautiful woman, so everything I do must be correct for her."

He placed himself between Kate and Paula and took both their hands. "Come," he said, "I show you the interior."

Paula walked in silence, thinking that when she found love, she hoped she would encounter the same deep commitment as Evert had for Kate. They came to a halt inside a very large lounge, and still holding their hands Evert said, "Yes, you two are mine, I can see that now," his voice dropped to a whisper, the words becoming difficult to hear as he added, "you two must never leave me, otherwise I have to swim to you. I have to be by your sides forever, you know that don't you? Now," he continued, collecting himself, "I make the *Kaf* and then we can talk."

Paula gave a sigh of relief as he left the room and whispered to Kate, "Isn't he intense?"

"Yes," she replied, "but you will find that nearly all foreigners are emotional. To them the English are thought of as cold and conservative, but when you get to know him, you'll find he has a good sense of humour. I used to have some good laughs with him, in fact, we all did and you know what that lot in Liverpool are like for taking the mickey, but he used to give as good as he got and tell them that when they spoke correct English like him they may understand more. Do you like him, Paula?"

"Well, what I've seen of him, yes, I do, but that episode at the airport when he made you recite those words to him, I was saying to myself, 'Please God, let her remember'."

"Oh, that was no problem, I knew what he meant straight away, you never forget things like that, they stay with you forever."

"What do you think of him now?" asked Paula.

"Well, you have to remember that it is twenty years since I've seen him and basically people don't change. You do get older and your values in life change, you become more worldly wise. Life isn't love's young dream any more. I've altered since he knew me and I suppose he has as well, but we'll just have to wait and see."

"Yes, I suppose so," Paula replied, still whispering, then she added, "does he expect you to sleep with him?"

"Well," replied Kate, "I've been thinking about

that as well, but I'll cross that bridge when I come to it."

"I'd rather you than me," said Paula, laughing, "and I'd carry on thinking about it, if I were you, because it's gone seven o'clock now, so you haven't got that long before you have to decide. Good luck," she added.

Evert came back into the room, not walking, but in the form of a waltz. Behind him walked a woman aged about thirty, with long reddish hair, which she wore in a pony tail. She wore no make-up but she didn't need it - her skin was like pure silk with just a faint blush to it.

"This is Helga," Evert said, then he introduced Kate to her saying, "This is *mine gift*," and moving behind Paula, put both his hands on her shoulders and said, "and this is my daughter."

They were startled by the crockery clattering across the table and noticed that Helga blushed the same colour as her hair. "Come, pour the *Kaf*," said Evert, as he put the cups the right way up.

"No," replied Helga, "do it yourself, I have other things to see to," and she hurriedly left the room.

"Your girlfriend?" asked Paula.

"No, not my girlfriend," he replied, then turning to Kate he said easily, "there have been girlfriends, well," he corrected himself, "women. I tell you the truth, but you must understand that it is only because the man has his needs, but nobody come in this house ever, it was only for you and now my daughter, Paula.

"Helga," he continued, "is from the village. Her aunt ask me that I take her into my house to look after me. Her mother she die and the girl need a job, so I give her food, a room to sleep in and at the end of each month I give her the money that she can earn, but I pay every bill in here, every one. She know all about you, Kate, because when I take the Schnapps with the beer I talk too much, but now she see you for herself.

Ah, let me look at both of you. Yes, my life has been down many times, but never again. No," he repeated, "never again, because today, someone look down over me and say 'today it is your turn to feel good', yes, very good," he smiled.

"Now, do you want that I tell you what I do all these years, or do you want to talk and me listen? There are so many things I must say to you both and there are many things I must show you. I think maybe by the time we all finish, it will take us five years, you believe that."

"Well," said Paula, interrupting him, "we won't be seeing it all the time because Kate has to get back to work and my mum wouldn't like it one little bit if I was away from her for more than a week, let alone five years."

"You are with your mother," said Evert, looking at Paula and pointing at Kate.

"Well, yes," said Paula, as she held his gaze, "but I am lucky, you see, I have two."

"How?" he asked.

Paula took a deep breath. "I was adopted by a lovely lady when I was born."

Evert looked at Kate, pure bewilderment on his face. "Does that mean you sold her?" he asked.

"No!" said Kate, "I didn't sell her."

"Then what did you do?" he rounded on her.

Kate dropped her head, her voice so low it was difficult to catch what she said. Paula heard, but Evert said, "Kate, look at me. I want to know what you did when Paula was born."

She looked up at him and said, "I gave her away."

"You gave our daughter away?" they heard him shout. "You gave her away? Why did you do that?" he demanded.

"I got your cablegram that you sent me from the ship saying, 'Do not come to Marseille or Denmark' . . . "

They both nearly jumped out of their skin as he banged a great fist down onto the table. "I forgot to put four words," he said, holding up four fingers. "I forgot to add 'I come to you' on a bloody cablegram and you give our daughter away. You give away what you and me made together."

"Yes," replied Kate.

Paula and Kate didn't think they'd ever seen anyone so angry. His face was white with fury. They just sat waiting for him to speak. Eventually he said, "Why? You tell me now because I want to know."

"It was for the best," Kate said.

"The best for who?" he asked. "The best for you? The best for her? Because you can be sure it wasn't the best for me. Why you not wait to tell me, if you not want that little girl, you could have given her to me. I am her father, I would have taken her the day she was born. I would have loved that little girl, I would have looked after her, but you think it was for the best. Who gave you permission to make up your mind of what was best for me?"

He turned to Paula, "Do you know about Hans Christian Andersen?"

"Yes," replied Paula, a little puzzled.

"Yes," he said, "you only know the English way. When you were a little girl I could have sat by your bed before you go to sleep and tell you the Danish way. Who discovered America? Do you know that?"

"Columbus," she replied.

"No! It was a Danishman called Lief the Lucky. You see, I could have told you the truth. I could have learn you to speak Spanish, yes, even Russian. I could have teach you so many things if I was given the chance, but no, instead you were given away to some woman."

Then, turning to Kate he said, "You can be sure as hell that if I knew of this I never leave England, till I find you, never," he emphasised, then he added, "your mother, your brothers, your father who I take many beers with, they all agree I should be tricked? When you tell your father why did he not make contact with me, he knew which shipping line I belong to, why did he not get a message to me?"

"He didn't know," said Kate, "only my mother and me could have told you."

"Oh, only your mother. Yes, now it all make sense. I always think why she not let me in the house, why she was so cold to me, why I have to meet her in that café in the middle of Liverpool. Then she ask me to send her cards from all over the world. Why was that?" he asked.

"She had her reasons," said Kate.

"What reasons she have?" Evert asked and without waiting for an answer plunged on, "When did your father discover Paula?"

Kate didn't answer. "When?" he shouted at her.

"Two weeks ago."

"Now? You mean two weeks ago now?" he said incredulously.

"Yes," replied Kate.

"This is unreal," Evert said, "I think I go crazy." He turned to Paula, "Why did you not ask to see me? Did you not want to know who your father was?"

Paula did not answer.

"Did you know where I was?" he asked, then added, "more to the point, did you know? Were you ever told that your father was a Danish man?"

Paula shook her head.

"Excuse me," Evert said to Paula, "this is none of your doing. If you never knew then there was nothing you could do. I need to go for a long walk." He got up and walked towards the door, calling back over his shoulder, "the house is yours, do what you like with it. I need to go now before I go crazy."

"I'm so sorry, Paula," Kate said when he had gone. "I never expected it to be like this. I really shouldn't have come here."

Paula got up and put her arm around Kate. "Well, you can't blame him, can you? But I love my mum and if anything happened to her, part of me would be missing and if I hadn't been adopted

I wouldn't have known her, would I? Like I never knew I had relations in Liverpool, or a father in Denmark. My lifestyle certainly would have been different. Both you and Mum shared in making me how I am and I still think I am lucky to have had two mothers, despite what he says, but I do understand him as well. It is the same sort of shock for him as it was for me and I'll say this for him, he doesn't hold anything back, does he? He's honest with his feelings, isn't he?"

"Yes," said Kate, "he was always very honest."

"Well, why did you run to London without giving him a chance, if you knew that?" asked Paula.

Kate was about to answer, when Helga entered the room and cleared the table onto a tray. "She must have heard it all," said Paula, as Helga disappeared into the kitchen.

"Yes, but although she understood those words of English when Evert spoke to her, she might not have realised what was going on. When I was here in the sixties not many people could understand you unless you spoke extremely slowly."

"Good," replied Paula, "let's hope she doesn't, we don't want all our dirty washing done in public, do we? Did you see her blush when Evert introduced me as his daughter?"

"Well, I thought it was my imagination," said

Kate, "I'm glad you noticed as well."

"Most certainly did," smiled Paula, "but I'm not bothered about her. What do we do now, other than wait for him to come back?" and looking around she added, "you don't think he will be drunk, do you?"

"I don't know," said Kate, "but I'm not waiting to find out. We have to stay here tonight, so let's get our luggage upstairs and find a room somewhere."

The two women got up, the chairs clattering across the polished wooden floors. "Don't they have carpets?" asked Paula.

"No, as far as I remember, it's all wooden floors and rugs." Kate pointed to the wall. "See those pictures? He embroidered those for this house when he was on the *Mænsk*."

Kate walked over to them. "He's had them framed. Look at the dates, 1963, '64, '65. I remember putting some stitches in the '64 one, but you can't see them because they need cleaning. The colours, when they were first done, were lovely."

"Don't you have a lot of memories, Kate," observed Paula.

"You could say that, but it's what's to come that I'm worried about."

They found the bedrooms - all six of them - and were shocked into silence. One door had been named 'Evert + Kate', another 'Paul', then 'Paula', 'Evert Junior', 'Kate Junior' and 'Guest'.

Paula broke the silence, "Well!" she exclaimed, "I know which one is mine!" and opened the door. There was a double bed, which looked like two singles because there were two duvets and no pillows, just two little cushions, one on each duvet, in matching colours. The room had fitted wardrobes, a long unit and two little tables, one on each side of the bed. The only decoration was a picture of a little girl.

"You tired?" Paula asked, "let's get into these beds. He's not going to drag us out, is he?"

"I don't know what he's going to do," shuddered Kate, "Oh, Paula, what have I done?"

They seemed to talk for hours, Paula putting a brave face on everything and having to assure Kate that if the worst came to the worst they could always walk into the town and get a taxi.

"Did he ever attempt to hurt you?" Paula asked.

"Oh no! Never!" Kate replied.

"Well, then, leopards don't change their spots, they just get older," she reminded her, sounding more confident than she felt.

It was during the early hours of the morning when they heard the door slam. "Pretend to be asleep," whispered Paula.

They heard his footsteps on the stairs, they

heard him open what they thought to be his bedroom door then they heard him make his way across the landing. Their bedroom door opened and they felt his presence in the room. He just said, "Oh!" and closed the bedroom door. They heard him walking away.

"Thank God," said Kate in such a low voice it was barely audible to herself.

"Let's get some sleep," Paula suggested, patting her arm.

Neither knew who managed to get to sleep first, but when they awoke the sunlight was shining through. They found the shower room, got ready and decided to go and face whatever together.

The place was deserted. There were bread rolls and butter on the table, salami, ham, tomato and a tube of what looked like salad cream but turned out to be *Ramoslade.* A glass jug of black coffee was being kept warm on an earthenware dish which had a nite-lite inside it.

Helga appeared and put two cups, two knives, a serving fork and two bread boards on the table. "Oh! I remember!" said Kate, "they don't have plates to eat off, when they have a snack they use these boards." Turning to Helga she smiled and said, "Thank you," but the woman ignored her and left the room.

"She is one sullen, ignorant son of a bitch,

Kate!" exclaimed Paula, surprised.

"I've never heard you talk like that in your whole life before, Paula," said Kate, more than a little shocked at the girl's outburst.

"Look," said Paula, "my life has been turned upside down these last four weeks, all of our lives have been, but more so mine and my father's. Oh, don't worry, Kate, I will always be here for you, I just don't know where I'm coming from at the moment myself. There aren't any more surprises are there?"

"What do you mean?" asked Kate.

"There's no other relatives I don't know about, not more skeletons in the cupboards?"

"Don't be silly!" Kate replied.

"Well, if that's the case, I'm going to eat. The last time I tasted food was in that VIP lounge yesterday lunch time and I'm hungry."

Kate made do with some coffee, food being the furthest thing from her mind. She wished she'd never come here. She'd always been aware it was wrong to turn back the clock. Deep down, however, she knew the wrong had been done years ago, but admitting that would be accepting that her mother was not acting in her best interests and she would never believe that.

Helga appeared suddenly and began to clear the table. "I'll help you," Paula said, feeling sorry for her earlier words.

"No need!" she replied sharply and promptly left the room.

"Well, now we know she does understand English!"

"Yes," replied Kate, "and you can be sure she will be well aware of what went on last night, make no mistake about that."

"So what?" said Paula, "it all happened twenty years ago and it's got nothing to do with her. I need some fresh air and then I'm going to look for my father and make some sense of this mess. Come on, Kate, come with me. We have to face up to everything, don't we?"

"Yes, of course," Kate replied, "but I'll go and ask Helga whether she knows where he's gone."

She located Helga in the kitchen, busy preparing some vegetables. "Do you know where Evert is?" she asked her. Helga shrugged her shoulders and carried on, without even looking up. Kate tried again, "Excuse me, Helga, I know you can understand me, can you please give me some indication of where Evert is?" Helga ignored her completely this time and Kate, who had never used violence in her life, felt an overwhelming urge to slap her. Paula was right, she was sullen and ignorant.

Kate gave up and went into the lounge, where

Paula was waiting for her. Once outside, they surveyed everything around them. The views were breathtaking. The house was low-beamed with the roof coming down to meet the top of the windows. Across the windows were long brass rods with brightly coloured curtains going across the middle of the glass.

Kate had always loved the Scandinavian style homes and in fact, her London home was of similar decoration. The house was perfect, right down to the last detail.

Denmark is a flat country and the surrounding countryside could be seen for miles. An artist would have been in heaven here and could find enough material to last for years. Little houses dotted the landscape and the drive was a mass of colour. They both wondered what it would be like in the summer, if it was that beautiful now.

To the rear of the house was the water. Had they not known differently, they would have thought it was the ocean, it was so clear and flat as a piece of glass. Paula was the first to speak. "Kate, he did all this for you. Had you seen it before he altered it?"

"No," she replied, "I've never seen it before in my life, but had I come here looking for him I would have known which house was his because that's all he talked about. You get a picture in your head, you see, and you can really see it. He must be very proud of this house. We had better find him," she added, "but be prepared for the worst."

6

They started to walk along the drive towards the road they had travelled along the night before and saw a girl riding towards them on a bicycle. She drew level with them and stopped. "Hi," she said, "my name is Lis, Evert sent me to get you."

"Where is he?" Kate asked.

"Come," replied the girl, "I will show you. I have been waiting for you long times and if you do not come in the next hour then I would have to come to the house, but it is better that I meet you now, because some days Helga do not like it that I go there, so usually if I wish to talk with

Evert I go down to the riverside to do it."

She walked along with them, pushing her bike. "You speak good English," Paula said.

"Yes, I learn it from my school. Most people do now. You will find," she added, "that all young people speak good English, the older ones not so good. Do you speak Danish?"

"No," replied Paula, ruefully, "we only speak English."

"Oh, that is not so good! Everybodies should speak at least two languages. Evert seem very happy," she added.

"He does?" both women spoke together.

"Yes, he sing all morning. He have a nice surprise for you on the harbour. I think that you both like it, he describe every detail to me."

"What is it?" asked Paula.

"No!" replied Lis, "I think maybe he be crazy with me if I tell you."

"Leave it, Lis," said Kate hastily, "we don't want to upset him, do we?" she added, looking at Paula.

"You never upset Evert," the girl said, "nobody can upset Evert, he is so easy going, nothing can bother him. He did not know you were his daughter until last night."

Kate and Paula stopped dead in their tracks. "How did you know that?" managed Paula.

"He told me," said the girl, looking straight

ahead, "I think he tell me everything he know about the world. I know about his Kate everyday, because somewhere, your name is always mentioned by him, you can be sure of that. Everybody is knowing about you."

They had been walking for about thirty minutes, Lis leading them down the twisted pathways until they were in sight of the harbour. "Evert!" shouted Lis, "I get them for you!" They saw him by the side of a boat. He stopped what he was doing and made his way up to them.

"He has a boat?" Kate asked.

"Yes," replied Lis, "it is his pride and joy. I think maybe that you like it also."

As Evert came up to them, they could see he was smiling broadly. Kate and Paula felt a sense of relief between them but did not voice their thoughts as he was now within earshot.

"Ah!" he said, "you were sleeping when I get home last night and this morning I get up early because I have to put something straight as soon as possible. Come, I show you."

They followed him to the boat. "There," he said proudly. In old lettering was written *The Katie,* but in new neat stencilling next to it was written *Paula.* "See, my boat is now called *The Katie Paula.*"

Paula put her arms around him and they clung to each other, he being the first to break away. He rubbed his eyes and said, "I think the sea breeze makes my eyes water. Helga give you food?" he asked. "I tell her to make sure she give you what you want."

"Yes, we had food," Kate said.

"I don't think she understand much English," he said.

Oh, I think she does, thought Kate to herself and noticed Lis wrinkle her nose at the mention of Helga's name. She obviously wasn't keen on the woman herself. Lis broke the silence. "Paula, you like that we go to my house, get another bike, then we ride together where I show you many things. Then later we can all meet up. Is that alright?" she asked Evert.

"If Paula wants to, it's fine by me," he answered. He put his arms around Lis, "You get yourself a friend. I think that you and Paula be good for one another, she can be your eyes and you can be her mouth." Lis smiled happily.

Paula and Kate looked at each other, wondering what Evert was talking about. Evert noticed, "Lis not mind, I tell you. Lis is totally blind."

They both looked at her in astonishment and she turned towards them. "Tell me you did not know," she said. Kate and Paula moved at the same time, one to each side of her.

"No need for that," Evert said, "Lis know every

pebble."

Paula said, "But we had no idea. Your eyes move."

"Yes," said Lis, "because the nerve behind them make it so, but my eyes are totally false and you could not tell? Is that the truth?" she asked them.

Kate felt tears falling down her cheeks and Lis seemed to know she was crying. "Please do not feel sorry for me. I am not sorry for myself, it is only the last two years that I lose the eyesight, before that I see all things. At first, everybody treat me like I cannot walk, but now they accept that I can do everything. I ride my bike, I cook, I sew. I go to the disco, I dance, I drink at the bar, the only thing is that I do not see, but I can move in the dark, I am never frightened of that because for me it is always the same. If the fishing boats come in, Evert make sure I know how many because he explain everything to me all day, don't you?" she said, turning to him.

"Yes," he said, "she is the daughter I never had but when I tell her this morning she have a sister she cannot wait to meet you, she be up there for the last three hours."

Paula stepped forward, "Come on, sis," she said, "come and show me the sights of Denmark."

"Yes, I like that," replied Lis, "you want that I take you to our shops? We can take coffee together then I take you round the streets to see the clothes we sell in Denmark. I always like it when I go to these shops. Maybe I buy myself something to wear today."

The two girls departed, chatting like they had known each other for years. "What happened to her?" asked Kate.

"She have diabetes," he said, "she only have fifty per cent of her eyesight for the last five years but then they tell her they can improve that to seventy per cent, so she go to the hospital with much hope. When they do the operation, they take out one eye and put in a false one. That was bad time, I be mad as hell, but then two years ago they have to remove the other eye. Now she totally blind."

"But you really wouldn't know, would you?" said Kate.

"Yes, they do a good job, but she have to go there many times before they get it the way it looks today. Now, Kate," he said, "we must talk. Well, I must talk," he corrected himself. "The main thing being our daughter, Paula, but once we do it, I promise you I will never mention it again, because we start from today, that's the way it must be."

"You have a deal, Evert," said Kate.

"Come," he said, "we sit here and you can tell me all that happened since I see you in South Africa."

* * * * *

A long time later, when she had finished, he said, "Maybe I understand more than yesterday. I walk long time last night and I know that 1966 be different from 1987. The world has moved on. In Denmark, things like that always never matter, but in England, maybe you get plenty of trouble, so, yes, I understand. But I still feel sadness here," he said, touching his heart, "that you never trust me. You knew the dreams we made together, there was only ever you. You must be sure of that, even then.

"Twenty years without you, twenty years not knowing about her, is a long time in the life, but I think last night that twenty years might have been never, but although I am sad, I am also very happy."

Kate took hold of his hand, "I know this has all been a shock to you, but you are aware of everything now, so can't we use the next few days getting to know each other again and spending time with your daughter? We could just enjoy each other's company and think what might be to come in the future. I am different now to what I was - why, you didn't even recognise me, you must have changed, too," she added.

"No," he said, "I am still the same."

"No, we are not the same. We are adults now.

You worry me because you appear to be living with a dream of what I used to be, not the reality of what I am today," she said gently. "The only thing in our favour, is that neither of us is involved with anyone, so let's take it easy and live one day at a time."

"You don't want to sleep with me?" he asked.

"I didn't know what to expect," she told him, "but now I believe that if I fall in love with you again that would be wonderful, but at the moment, I look on you as a past lover who is also a very dear friend. My daughter has now found her father in you and she is our daughter, yours and mine. See the situation for what it is, Evert and let's relax."

"Yes," he said, "that is alright, but I'm still madly in love with you, but I know we must take it easy, but I never admit I do anything wrong all those years ago. We should never be apart, but you have your work in London so you will need to go to that and Paula, she have her second mother."

Kate broke in. "First mother, Evert. Annie is her first mother now."

"That I cannot understand," he said. "You are Paula's mother and I am her father, you'd better believe it."

"Evert," she said firmly, "you had better believe that for the last twenty years, Annie has allowed me to share Paula. She didn't have to do that, she loves her more than life itself and Paula loves her. Also, she would never want to think of anyone else as her mother. I have no objection, now that everything between us has been sorted out here, to you coming to London and meeting Annie. But before you do, it has to be on the strict understanding that you don't upset her. You have to accept her as Paula's mother."

"You think we can build our love again?" he asked.

"That is for the future," she replied, "so please, Evert, can we start as we mean to go on for now? Although," she added, "you have to answer my question first."

"I will try to accept things for how they be, you have my word on that. Maybe when I talk with Paula, she make me aware of her feelings towards her mother. The Danes are not stupid people. I will know it in her everyday words how she feel and that will be enough for me if she likes the life she get, but she have more feeling to get for me, of that you can be sure.

"Come," he said, "we go and eat, then if you like we go to visit my neighbour. The girl Lis, it is her mother and father. When I first find you again, they are the first people I tell. Well, besides Helga, but I never have to tell her anyway, but she think I go crazy because I shout all over the house, but I am so happy in the two hours that I wait for you to ring back I need some support so I go to my best friends, Pregan and Jenny. They calm me down. But Jenny, she make me promise for the last month that as soon as you step foot on Danish soil I take you there so she can meet you. Maybe she thinks we can be lovers again now."

He took her hand and led her away from the harbour, ensuring the way was clear for her so she did not fall. Kate felt a closeness to him. This was the way it had always been. She'd always believed he'd taken the place of her dad in being her protector. What a lot of wasted years, she thought. Maybe it could work out again. She smiled at him and he gripped her hand with added firmness.

"Kate," he said, "you are here. Everything is alright now. It has to be. My dream must become real."

7

Helga greeted them with a welcome fit for visiting royalty. Kate thought she was in the wrong house. "Would you like coffee first," she asked, "or do you like to take a shower, in which time I will have the meal served for you?" Then to Kate's amazement she added, "I'm so glad you found Evert."

They looked at each other, but Kate saw no trace of sarcasm or hostility in the girl's face. In fact, she looked perfectly genuine, so she replied, "Whatever suits you, Helga."

"No," replied Helga, "while you are here, you

get to do whatever you want to do. Just give me the times you and your daughter need to eat and I will make sure I have the food waiting for you."

Evert put his arms around her shoulders. "Helga, you make me proud. I make sure you get paid some extra money so you can treat yourself to something special."

"There is no need for that, it is the same for me to cook four meals as it is two," she replied.

There was no way a three-hour break could have changed her from the sullen individual she had been that morning to the nicely spoken girl she was now. Kate was just glad that they served food in dishes in Denmark and you helped yourself. Had it been the English way, all served on a plate, she would have been suspicious and remained hungry for the rest of her stay.

As it turned out, the meal was one of the best she had ever tasted. "Kate, you want more?" asked Helga, pointing to the food.

"Oh, yes please," Kate replied.

"Then help yourself," said Helga.

Evert was busy enjoying his food when Kate remarked that it was all cooked to perfection. He said, "It is always the same."

Helga didn't comment, she just squirmed with pleasure at the compliment. Kate got up to help her carry the dishes into the kitchen, but Helga stopped her. "Kate," she said, "you are on holiday here. Next week you have to go back to your work, so I do my work this week and look after you. There is no need for you to go near the kitchen."

"Yes," Evert agreed, "take it easy, Kate."

"Does anyone mind if I go for an hour's sleep? I didn't eat since the meal on the plane yesterday, didn't sleep very well last night and after that wonderful meal, I am very sleepy."

"I am so sorry, Kate, I didn't think. Of course, you must be very tired. I think I go to sleep also, then when we wake up we go to see my neighbour. Is that alright, Kate?"

"No," she said, "It isn't. You know we agreed that we take things a day at a time and that includes the bedroom. I have no intention of sleeping with you until the time is right."

"I never ask that you do," he replied, "we have six bedrooms in this house, not one."

Kate had never felt so stupid in her life. She looked at him but he was laughing. She laughed with him, "Ever felt like you've just had a smack in the mouth?" she asked him.

"It's alright, *mine skat*," he replied easily, then he put his hand to his lips, "sorry, I forget, *mine skat* is not allowed, is it?"

She went into the room marked 'Paula' and fell

into a deep sleep. She awoke to see Evert leaning over her. She had no idea how long he had been there. "You sleep the last four hours. Maybe we can get ready because my neighbours be on the telephone and I tell them to expect us in the next hour. Kate," he added, "you look beautiful while you sleep. You bring many memories back to me, but I never do anything you do not like so now I leave you to get ready. Is that alright?" he asked her.

She just nodded her head and watched him leave the room. Helga had the coffee ready when she came down the stairs, but as they were late Kate left half of it. "Oh, Kate," said Helga, sounding concerned, "you have not finished your *Kaf*. Evert, stop making her hurry, let her relax."

"Of course," he said, "five minutes more is not important."

Helga saw them to the door. "Enjoy your evening," she said.

"Thank you," replied Kate, taking her hand.

The neighbours, Jenny and Pregan, were waiting to greet them with Paula, Lis and their son, Christian. Jenny grabbed hold of Evert, "Paula has told us who she is and we are so happy for you. Pregan, give him a beer."

"Hello, Daddy!" Pregan said as he passed him a beer and Evert answered by raising his bottle, *"Skol!"* he said, "maybe you treat them with a little more respect now."

The atmosphere was extremely relaxed, a crate of beer was put at the side of the table, while every kind of spirit you could think of was also available and another bottle of wine was opened straight from the fridge once the previous one was empty. There was another table which looked as though it would collapse under the weight of all the food that had been prepared for them. There had been a great deal of effort put into the whole thing.

"That looks lovely," Kate remarked.

"You like it?" said Jenny, "Me, Lis and Paula we do it all day for you, we are very happy you are here."

Pregan got up and said, "I get all my tapes of Connie Francis out. You like her?" he asked. We play '*Who's Sorry Now*' first, then you can tell us how this bad situation come about. You may as well because when you go back to England he will tell us anyway! He never much good at keeping a secret!"

Evert put an arm around the back of his chair and said quite loudly, "You don't have to tell that nosy idiot anything, Kate."

Kate had never been put in this position before and looked at Paula for support. "Tell them if you want to, I don't mind," she said. Why not, thought Kate, looking around her at the friendly faces, why shouldn't she explain to them how difficult it was in the Sixties? She needed to convince herself now because these past four weeks had been horrendous and she was beginning to believe that everything was her fault. They were all waiting for her to speak, so she helped herself to a large brandy and related to them the events of the last twenty four years, leaving nothing out.

Paula was the first to break the silence after she had finished speaking. "What happened to Aunt Cissy?" she asked.

"She died," replied Kate.

"When?" asked Paula.

"Four years ago."

"I was sixteen then," said Paula.

"Yes," replied Kate and left it at that.

"You and Evert, you got the wedding rings on your fingers now?" asked Jenny.

"No, not yet," replied Evert, "but one day when my Kate ready we do it. Is that alright?" he asked Kate.

"Yes, one day," she replied.

"Then let the past be the past!" he said. "Now I think I get a little bit drunk."

Christian said, "Come, you two, I play you my tapes in the other room."

Lis turned to Paula. "You must have made a good impression on him, he never allow anybody near his music."

It must have been nearly two o'clock in the morning when Evert finally made the move to go home. Nobody wanted to break up the friendly gathering, but Evert said, "Ready to go home, Paula? Kate, she have her sleep, but you never got one so I think maybe you must be tired."

"Does she have to?" asked Christian, "another half hour and then I will walk with her home."

"If that is what you all want," said Evert, "but now me and Kate we get some air together."

They all embraced each other, arranging the same situation would be repeated in a couple of days, Evert and Kate playing host next time. He took hold of her hand and asked, "That will be alright, yes?"

"Oh, yes," she replied with enthusiasm, "that will be alright."

They arrived back at the house. It was strange how alcohol relaxed you and Kate was glad Evert didn't take advantage of her unexpected feeling of warmth towards him and was more than happy to accept his offer of a nightcap before they made their way to their separate bedrooms.

She drifted eventually into a contented sleep, only to be woken by Paula. "Kate, wake up!" she said, "wake up! I've got loads of news for you."

"What time is it?" she asked. "How did you get

home?"

"It's about three-thirty and Christian came with me. I've been outside for the last half hour talking to him. He's ever so nice," she added. "He's been telling me about Helga. You won't believe what he said."

"Try me," said Kate sitting up.

"Well, Christian doesn't think she is alright in the head. He says that she speaks to you one minute and ignores you the next."

"Oh, I know that already," broke in Kate.

"Yes, but here's the best bit," Paula went on. "Everybody around here says she is in love with my father, there's only him that doesn't know it. Pregan tried to tell him but he just laughed at him and said he was crazy. What do you think about that?" she finished.

"Well," replied Kate, "I think it's their problem, but if they haven't sorted it out in twelve years they are unlikely to now, are they?"

"That's the point! Christian says that everything was alright until you came along because he reckons that she thought in the next five to ten years he would give up any thoughts of you and turn to her."

"So that's why she was so distant yesterday," mused Kate, "but you didn't see her when we came back from seeing the boat. The meal she had ready for us had to be seen to be believed and you would have thought I was her long-lost sister. I think she has accepted the situation now."

"Well, I'd watch her. Christian says she can be very odd, he wouldn't trust her anyway. He was also telling me about Lis," she added.

Kate interrupted, "Oh, it's such a shame, she's so young. I feel very sorry for her."

"No, you mustn't," said Paula, "Christian says it's the last thing she wants. It makes her very upset. She just wants to be treated as if she has injured herself but will get better soon. He asked me to ask my father if we can all go on the boat tomorrow. Lis likes that and he told me that there he can make sure she is safe, without her being aware of his concern for her. He said that my father treats her like the daughter he never had and he hoped that I didn't mind if she still shared him."

"What did you say?" asked Kate.

"I just said that maybe Lis could become my sister, I always wanted one anyway. Do you think my father will take us out to sea? Will you ask him, Kate? He'll do anything for you."

"Ask him yourself," replied Kate. "In fact, why don't you three go together and I will go and look at the shops. That way, you and him will get to know each other without getting into serious conversation."

"Yes," said Paula, "I'll do that tomorrow morning."

* * * * *

"Mind if I don't come with you today?" said Paula at breakfast the following morning.

"Why, where you go?" asked Evert.

"Well, Christian wants to take me and Lis out on the boat and I said I would ask you if it was alright."

"What boat you get?" he asked.

"Yours!" Paula said.

"My boat!" he spluttered, "you three take my boat out to sea? You all crazy, I never let you take my boat unless I be there with you, be sure of it."

"Well, you can come if you like," she said, smiling at Kate.

"And you, Kate," he said, "you come as well?"

"No, not today. I want to look at the shops."

"The shops only open half day on Saturday," he said, "so if you like, you take the car. We will walk to the harbour and maybe you meet us this afternoon, say about two o'clock?"

"Yes," she said, "I'd like that."

"Hokey dokey, then we better move, otherwise none of us go anywhere. You call Christian and

Lis, maybe they're still sleeping. Tell them me and you be at the harbour in thirty minutes," he said. He turned to Kate, "tomorrow we all go to my club, if that is alright?"

"You have a club?" she asked.

"No, not me, but it is a club I go to every Sunday morning."

"Well," said Kate, "I don't really go to clubs and really I have no suitable clothes."

"What you talk about? It is not a nightclub, it is not a casino, it is Outland Club, but I explain tomorrow when we go. You will like it there," he added.

Driving on the wrong side of the road was fairly easy, she just followed the traffic. It was only when she came to town that she became nervous. Parking made her more so and she was just thankful that the car was automatic.

The continental shops were so different from those she was used to at home. They took so much pride in displaying their wares and made everything so inviting. Oh, yes, they could match them anytime in Harrods, Marks and Spencer and Sainsbury for example, but not in the little corner shops, not in the confectioners. There was only Thorntons or Carbonell Walker of Bond Street that was on a par with them.

She sought out the jewellers. Although she

didn't wear an excessive amount, the continental styles had always attracted her. In the clothes shops, she was more than a little surprised at the cheapness and the quality. There were a lot of Jaeger colours, together with the cloth cut in their Country Style range. She knew the Jaeger brand, it was a store she always made for and although they boasted of locations in London, Paris and New York, she wondered if it was here they actually got their ideas from.

The banks were closed but she had no trouble in using her credit card. She got back to the car with all her parcels and felt good. She decided the two thousand pounds she had spent in her three hour shopping spree had been worth every penny. Well, there was no-one to tell how much she'd spent and she didn't feel in the least bit guilty. It was her money and she had worked hard to earn it.

She made her way to the harbour and found a little snack bar. She parked the car and enjoyed a cup of coffee. She could have sat there by herself all day it was so peaceful. Did she really miss London? Not that much. But her business was a different matter, she wouldn't give that up even if somebody offered her ten million pounds that night. She enjoyed securing every new order so much.

The Katie Paula came gently into view and she made her way to the point, where she would have a perfect view of it at all times. Eventually they spotted her and waved for all they were worth. They must have been looking out for her and she was pleased they had bothered. It reminded her of when her dad used to take all of them to Blackpool in that borrowed Austin Ten and you went for miles hoping to be the first one to spot the tower.

They tied up, waited for each other to get off the boat and then all came running to meet her. Paula looked really healthy. "Kate," she said, "next time you must come with us! Can we go tomorrow instead of going to the club?" she asked Evert, hopefully.

"No, tomorrow you come and meet all my friends. There will be plenty of times in the future for you to be on the boat."

"Are Lis and Christian coming to the club with us?" she asked.

"If they like to," he replied.

"Great! We can all have another good day tomorrow."

"Come," said Lis, "I race you all to the car."

"No," said Paula, linking her arm, "I'm much too tired to do that."

* * * * *

There was no sign of Helga when they got back to the house, but the food was prepared - a cold and hot table, the latter in dishes in a heated trolley.

"Hadn't you better ask Helga if she wants to join us?" asked Kate.

"She will know that we are home. If she wants to join us, she will. Helga!" he shouted, "bring the *Kaf!*"

She shouted downstairs, "It is ready for you in the thermos. I will be there after to clear the table."

Pregan, Jenny, Lis and Christian came through the door. "We enjoy last night, so now we come to you!" Pregan got himself a plate and helped himself. "There is plenty for all of us," he said.

Evert went and got a crate of beer. "Did you all think that we were alcoholics, getting all that beer in?" Kate commented.

"We never get it for you," Evert said, coming back in, "every house in Denmark keep five cases of beer in stock because we drink in the house. We don't have pubs like you do, only hotels and little bars. It is too expensive to buy beer anywhere but the supermarket. Also, it is better that way because it keep the family together."

Dinner lengthened and it became another late

night, or rather early morning. They had to be at the club for ten o'clock the following morning, so it was a rush to get ready on time. Evert appeared rather the worse for wear after the night before, so it was left to Christian to drive.

"Where is the club?" asked Kate.

"Herring," Evert replied. "When I pay off my ship I finally get a job through my union in Herring as an electrician. I get the apartment off a private landlord and I work and save for my house by the sea. I never go drinking because that house is so important to me. Then I work with a guy who is a member of the Outland Club. It is a club where you can only be a member if you have worked outside Denmark for two years."

"Oh, so everybody has worked abroad," said Kate.

"No, not everybody," he replied, "you can take a guest, but they cannot become a member because the rules say two years away."

"Is it the only one?" Kate asked.

"No, there are thousands all over the world," he told her.

"I wonder if we have them in England?" she asked.

"I don't know," he answered, "we make good time," he said, looking at his watch. "You have no timepiece?"

"No," said Kate, "I don't have a watch."

"Why?" he asked.

"Because I don't like a lot of jewellery, I only have my ring, bangle, a couple of brooches and occasionally some earrings," she replied.

"What happened to that ring I buy for you in Palermo, the one you have when we got engaged? You gave that away also?" Then he added, "Sorry, I did not mean it to sound like that. Sorry, Kate."

"No, I did not give it away," she said stiffly, "I'm wearing it, but I had it covered with diamonds."

"That is it?" he said, looking at her hand.

"Yes, that's the one, that's the one," she repeated.

"Oh, Kate, maybe you do care."

"Yes," she said, "maybe I do."

"Your bracelet, I notice diamonds on that, too."

"Yes, you think right, it is the one you got me in Copenhagen," she said.

"And you always wear them?" he asked, "you wear them for the last twenty years?"

"Yes," she replied.

"I think I am stupid," he said.

"Why?" asked Kate.

"When I think that maybe you do not want everything for the best."

Paula laughed and said, "Well, that's debatable."

They both looked at her but she never elaborated, so they let it go.

All eyes were focused on them when they entered the club, the friendliness soon covered them, "Come, sit with us!" News travelled fast in Denmark. They all sat around one big table loaded with bottles of beer, Schnapps, brandy, coffee, rolls and butter. The walls of the club were like those found in an old country cottage, the ceilings had dark beams from which a hanging fixture displayed paper money from various parts of the world. Beakers, fans, vases and many other artifacts dotted the room and there were spears from Africa, rugs from Peru and hundreds of plates and farming implements.

The chairman stood up to speak. "Today we speak only English and for those who cannot understand, I will translate. Now you can tell us what you do in England and what you think of the Danish people," he said proudly.

Kate spent the next four hours talking about business in England. She hadn't meant to, but once she had answered one question it was followed by another. They were all interested in England's code of practice. However, she had already formed the opinion that they were well behind on the security side and told them so.

She could never imagine writing up a total night's bill on a beer mat, which she had watched them doing in the cafe by the harbour, but she had soon found that was the way business was done in the busy establishments.

She couldn't understand the lack of cash registers. Here, they had a bag strapped around their mid-drift where they collected the night's bills at the end of a day's drinking.

"Why not?" they asked.

"Well," she said, "you could be mugged and if not that then the customers would certainly leave without paying."

"Yes," they said, "that may happen in Copenhagen, but never here."

"You all come with Evert to my home," said one, "and mine," said another. There must have been at least a dozen invitations. "No, not this time," she said regretfully, "but when I come back, I'll make sure I do."

Evert put his arm around her shoulders, "Make sure you keep that promise," he whispered.

"I will make sure she does," said Paula.

"*Skol!*" they all chorused for the last time that evening. I could get used to this, thought Kate.

* * * * *

There were only three days left of the vacation and they had many things still to see. Kate realised what game Helga was playing - over the top when

Evert was there and complete silence when they were alone. She decided that Helga didn't like her and Paula, but as the feeling was mutual, it really didn't matter.

They never really went out in a threesome because it appeared taken for granted that Lis and Christian would come as well, but the laughter could be heard when they were in restaurants and bars along the beach and Kate felt more relaxed than she had done for many years.

Could old love be rekindled? she asked herself, then dismissed the thought. She had neglected her business these past few weeks and was looking forward to getting back into the office and catching up on things. Paula appeared to have taken over as Lis' guardian angel, but from a discreet distance. She'd even asked Kate if she could stay there for another month, but seemed to accept that she couldn't really once Kate had pointed out that Annie would be missing her dreadfully already.

These last few days had flown by, Kate thought on their way to the airport. Many promises had been made and Kate hoped they would not be broken.

The tannoy system was announcing their boarding time as Paula said her goodbyes to Lis and Christian and was rather tearful, Kate noticed.

Evert had grabbed hold of her, telling her to be

sure he'd never leave her again, then he turned to Kate, "I want to tell you," he began, but she stopped him.

"No, now I tell you," she handed him a package and added, "in the sixties, I could not afford to buy you anything, now I can. Open it."

"What is it?" he asked.

"Well, if you open it you will see," she replied.

Tears rolled unashamedly down his face when he looked at the plain gold band in which she had inscribed, 'Kate + Evert 1962-1987'. "Oh, *mine skat*," he said as he got hold of her like he would never let her go. They were only interrupted by Paula who said, "I have a present for you as well."

"What is it?" he asked again.

"He always wants to know what it is before he opens anything! Take a look!" she said.

He opened the package to see a plain gold men's bracelet with two gold bobbles on the end. He looked from Paula to Kate, "Does this represent Copenhagen?" he asked them.

"Got it in one," said Paula and with that he broke down completely. The tears were blinding him and there was no way he would have been able to see them board the aircraft.

8

"You know we have about three hour's wait at Copenhagen, before our connection to London," Kate reminded Paula.

"Good, it will give us time to have a talk about my future."

Kate looked at her, she was startled by the tone of Paula's voice, let alone what she said. "You know your future," she finally managed, "you're going to university."

"I'm going nowhere near there," said Paula.

"Paula! It's what you've always dreamed about, getting a place. What are you saying?"

"No, it's what *you've* always wanted and I went

along with it because I didn't know any different, but I don't want to discuss it here, I thought if we could get a table in that restaurant at Copenhagen airport, we could really be straight with each other for the first time in our lives. Don't let's fall out, Kate, that's the last thing in the world I want, but I have heard you discuss your feelings this last month but you haven't even asked about mine, so I intend to tell you. I couldn't have the same relationship with you if I had to pretend everything in the garden was rosy, because at the moment it is not."

Kate had never been as glad to see an air hostess as she was at that moment and she thought it must be an indication of the stress they were both under when they both ordered coffee, strong and black. They didn't speak to each other for the next half hour.

Paula was the first to break the strained silence when they were walking through the terminus. "If it's alright with you, I'll try to find a quiet table," she said. Kate had decided to listen to what Paula had to say and then tell her a few home truths, especially about Annie, who had made Paula her life's vocation. Yes, a talk would clear the air, so she willingly followed as Paula pointed out a remote table in the corner.

It was the kind of restaurant where you helped

yourself and got a fixed bill when you left, regardless of what you had eaten, so it was ideal because food was the furthest thing from their minds.

"Kate," began Paula, "I don't like this atmosphere between us, but I feel my whole life has been built on one lie and I've missed so much because of it. The biggest thing I cannot understand at the moment is how you could have told me they were all dead. How could you have said that?" she asked.

"I can understand you saying it about my father because you thought you would never see him again and also because you thought he had let you down badly, maybe you thought he would have hurt me in some way, but Grandad in Liverpool? What right had you to keep me from him, he'd done nothing to you, had he? You made sure you saw them every six months. Didn't you ever think that we had the right to know each other?"

Kate had gone deathly white, which Paula noticed immediately. She put her hand over Kate's cold one and said, "Don't be upset, Kate, I don't want to hurt you, I just need some answers, I think I'm entitled to them. All through my school years I heard my friends talk about their relatives, but not me, I didn't have any. Yet it turns out that I have more of them than anyone else had. Aunt Cissy, she knew about me, why did I never meet her?"

"You did," said Kate.

"When? How old was I? Did she like me?"

"Aunt Cissy was Miss Bainbridge."

It was Paula's turn to look stunned. "Not the Miss Bainbridge who once a year took me into Oxford when they lit it up for Christmas and told me that every star was an angel? Not the Miss Bainbridge who on the same day took me in a taxi to Harrods' children's department and told me to choose what I wanted, even though Mum had told me she didn't have much money, so to choose something cheap? Tell me Kate, it wasn't that lovely old lady I looked forward to seeing every year, was it?"

Kate just nodded her head. Paula looked at her, then she said, "I've just made up my mind. I'm nearly twenty-one years of age. What has been kept from me I'm going to get to know. You and Mum can come with me if you like, but I'm going to get to know my father and Lis and Christian, who I could have grown up with. I'm going to get to know everybody in Liverpool, especially Grandad.

"And how do you propose to keep yourself, while you do all this travelling about?" asked Kate.

"Well, you give me £500 per month, but if you want to stop it I'll get a job as a waitress or something and pay my passage that way. Oh, you can be sure my feelings for you and Mum are still the same. Nobody can take you away, only yourselves, but please try to understand, Kate, I need to know who I am."

"Paula, I *do* understand, but Annie would be lost without you, it is only you she lives for. Will you sleep on this when you get home and not say anything to her? Then I promise you, when I come over on my weekly visits you can bring the subject up and I will support you."

"Do you give me your word on that?" asked Paula.

"Yes, Paula, I give you my word."

"Then maybe we can all get over this together, maybe we can all be one big happy family. Do you think Grandad and my father would let Mum visit them?" she asked.

"Of course they will," replied Kate, "they will be only too pleased to see her," then she added, "Paula, you have a grandmother as well, you know."

"Yes, I know," she replied, "but Grandad shares his love around. The way I see it with Grandma, all her feelings are for her only daughter, you. Nothing must get in the way of your happiness. But you don't have to worry, I would never upset her because I like her, too."

"Can we consider the matter closed until next week?" asked Kate.

"Yes," said Paula, "but you're not going to like

this either."

"Like what?" asked Kate.

"Can I borrow next month's allowance so that I can get them all a present for when I see them next?"

"I suppose I owe you that, at least," Kate replied. She was glad to board the flight to London and was more than grateful when it touched down at Heathrow. Although taxis were expensive she couldn't wait to get one, the sooner she was back in her house the better.

The drive to Annie's was uneventful, she just dropped Paula off, leaving her to bring Annie up to date. She was relieved to be on her own once they had said their goodbyes and she instructed the driver to take her to the other side of London. She wanted to go home, get into her dressing gown, turn the heating on full and just relax. Tomorrow she would be back in the office with her life returning to some sense of normality.

9

She awoke early the next morning and left the house early to ensure she missed the traffic. There was only the night-watchman there at this hour, who commented that it was nice to see her back. She was pleased to get to her office and experienced the same thrill and exhilaration she had felt the first day when it had finally been completed.

Although she had thought about changing her lifestyle in Denmark, she knew that if she and Evert did get back together again, it would have to be over here, on her terms. Julia arrived, brought her some coffee and sat down. "Well, how did it go?" she asked.

"It was absolutely wonderful," said Kate.

"Not thinking of living there, are you?" asked Julia, sounding worried.

"Not that wonderful!" said Kate. "It was very nice, but you have to remember we were on holiday as well."

"Well, there's your letters. I've answered what I can, but those are your strictly private ones. Oh and by the way, John Kitchen said he needed to see you as soon as you returned."

"Anything urgent?" asked Kate.

"Didn't appear to be," said Julia, "but I've told you anyway," she added.

"I suppose you'd better tell him I'm home," Kate said. She gathered her mail together. The first one was from the bank asking her if she could make an early appointment with the manager. The next one was from her long time business associate, Alex. There was a tap on the door and John Kitchen walked in.

Kate smiled at him and his face lit up. He was ten years younger than Kate, but they had seemed to gel since they had first met when Alex had introduced him as a bright young accountant of the future.

"Would you like coffee, or something?" she asked.

"No, thanks, I've already had some." He came straight to the point, "We have a problem with our cash flow, we've pulled out all the stops but in the next couple of weeks we need to pay all the quarterly accounts that really should be paid by now."

"What are they?" asked Kate.

"Gas, electricity, telephone, rent, rates and on the 19th you've got the N H I," he replied.

"How much do we need?" she asked, her good mood evaporating.

"£40,000," he replied.

Kate exploded, "£40,000! No wonder the bank wants to see me! How on earth did we manage to get in a mess like that?"

"Well," he replied, "we've picked up some new accounts. Some of them are slow payers but there is a new national one that hasn't paid us for six months."

Kate got to her feet, "John, am I missing something here? Big national company or not, you're the one who's always telling the reps that profit margin and sales are no good, unless you get the cash in as well."

"I know that," he said miserably.

"Well, for God's sake get it in then," she said.

She got her appointment with the bank manager that afternoon. Actually, it would be a relief to get there. She could tell him anything, it was more like meeting an old friend. Her usual mineral water was waiting for her, together with the manager's pot of tea. He greeted her warmly and chatted about her holiday. Eventually Kate said, "You wanted to see me?"

"Yes," he replied, "nothing serious, but your business account doesn't appear to be running as well as it usually does and I wondered whether we should be talking over any problems?" he said pleasantly.

Kate had always been strictly up-front with him so she related the conversation she had had with John before she left the office and added, "So really, I needed to see you anyway, to ask for a temporary £40,000 overdraft."

The manager's face didn't change as he asked, "How temporary?"

"About four weeks," replied Kate.

"Let's make it six, to be on the safe side, that will bring us up to Christmas and we will be closed for three days."

So are all the companies' account's departments, thought Kate, but she kept quiet and listened to him say that he looked forward to her having a clean slate in the new year. "Just a bit of paperwork to complete," he said, getting some forms from the drawer, "shall we say three per cent over base just to keep head office happy?" he suggested, as he passed the forms over for her to sign. "Still in your own house, Kate?" he asked.

"Oh, yes," she replied, "I could never leave it, it's my sanctuary. I'm glad I bought it when I did, it's paid for now."

"How much is it worth?" he asked absently.

"About £200,000. House prices have gone crazy," she replied.

"Good, good. The money will be in your account today. Have a nice Christmas. If I don't see you beforehand." As usual, he walked her to the front doors of the bank. "You know," he said, "during the next six weeks we will have queues all taking money out, then there will be other queues of people all putting it back in. Funny old game, banking, isn't it?"

She made her way back to the office, telling John that they had a £40,000 facility and to get rid of it as quickly as possible, even if it meant spending all week on the phone. Once in her own office she asked Julia to get all her customer data and invoices outstanding. Then she rang Alex, she loved the man and she knew the feeling was mutual. Alex was her long time friend and confidante. "Yes," she agreed on the phone, "it is a long time since we have seen each other, I'd be delighted to meet you tomorrow, usual place, usual time?"

The Dorchester was Alex's domain and he had a special table reserved there between twelve-thirty and two-thirty every afternoon through the week. He was like one of the fixtures. Saturday and Sunday he kept strictly for his wife and children.

She decided to go home, she needed to soak in those special oils she used in her bath. She would use a face mask and completely strip her nail varnish. Alex was always immaculate in his dress and expected his dining companions to be the same. She would not disappoint him. She was glad to go home and once inside, made herself a sandwich from the hastily bought purchases she had gathered from the corner shop on the way home.

She had just settled down when the phone rang. It was Paula. Kate caught her breath, hoping she wasn't going to say she had revealed her plans to Annie, but she just wanted to tell her that Lis and Christian had called from Denmark, but she hadn't heard from her father and they hadn't seen him since they dropped him off. "Where would he go?" asked Paula.

"I don't know," Kate replied, "I'm not worried about him. Are you?"

"No," said Paula, hesitantly, "I was just wondering, that's all."

"Try ringing him," suggested Kate.

"What? And speak to that Helga? No thanks! Mum wants to speak to you."

Annie came on the phone, "Oh, Kate, she's full of it, she really enjoyed herself, didn't she? She hasn't stopped talking about her father or those new friends of hers over there, she really likes them. But I tell you, Kate, I really missed her and I'm so glad she's home again for good. I know it was only for a week, but we've never been apart for that long before."

"Well," said Kate, "you'll have to get used to it when she goes to university."

"I know," said Annie.

Kate felt like telling her the truth there and then, but over the phone would not be right, she needed to be there. "Don't worry," she said, "when she does go away, I'll make sure I spend more time with you."

"Oh, Kate, will you? That will make things a lot easier."

* * * * *

The next morning, Kate felt refreshed after going to bed early. She dressed, checking her appearance in the mirror on the inside of the outer door. She had got that idea from the staff room in one of the big stores. A big notice had said, 'All staff look, this is the way our customers will see you'. She felt satisfied with what she saw, so she made her way into London.

Once in her office, she took some phone calls, but her main objective was to contact her solicitor to instruct him to make the necessary searches at Company House on these new accounts Julia had lifted for her.

She arrive promptly for her meeting at the Dorchester with Alex and noticed he was already seated at his table. He saw her, got up and hurried across the room to meet her. He kissed her on both cheeks and escorted her to the table. "Kate," he said, "you always bring a smile to my face. You want the menu?" he said, offering one to her.

"No," she replied, "I'll leave it to you, as always. Your choice would be mine anyway."

"Shall we get a bottle of wine?" he suggested.

"Yes, of course, why not."

"Kate," he said, once the waiter had taken their order, "you know I have always looked out for you."

"I know that, Alex," she said.

"Well," he went on, "the business world is changing, these last few years the banks have been throwing money at virtually anybody who asked. As a result a lot of, shall we say, unscrupulous people or innocent amateurs, have come into our business and undercut us. My companies have suffered as a result like anyone else's and I will have to cut back in many areas, refurbishment being one of the first I must consider. Of course, your company will still get my requirements, but I do not intend to replace what can be left for another year to eighteen months.

"I am telling you now because I do not want you with a payroll you cannot afford. If it is left too late I realise that you are in serious trouble and I don't need to remind you that any unused labour is a commodity no company can afford. It is profit straight off your bottom line," he finished.

"I know Alex, I know," she said. They promised to meet on a more regular basis and although she never lost face in front of Alex, it was a very worried Kate who made her way back to the office.

She knew she was going to have to make cuts, but not before Christmas, she couldn't. She shuddered when she realised that so many people depended on the company to pay their mortgages, and she hoped the ones she had to let go found other employment quickly, so that their lifestyle didn't alter too much. In any event, the decision was hers and it was on a purely professional basis that she would make it.

Her mind was mulling over who would not be smiling next year and it depressed her. But she fully realised that for everyone's sake these unsavoury aspects of the business had to be dealt with.

Julia suddenly burst into the office, "Kate, you'd better speak to Paula, she sounds hysterical on the phone, I can't make out what she's saying."

Kate didn't wait for the call to be put through to her, she ran into Julia's office and could imagine Paula screaming before she picked up the phone. "Paula, it's Kate, whatever is the matter?" she asked.

"It's my father," said Paula in between sobs, "he's had an accident and they don't think he will live."

"Evert?" said Kate.

"Yes," replied Paula, "Lis and Christian have just told me. I want to go and I can't get there," she sobbed.

"Paula, stay where you are, I'm coming over now. Julia will make arrangements for us. Get a bag packed, we will get there somehow."

"Alright, I'll wait here, you're coming now, aren't you Kate?"

"Yes, Paula," she replied, "right now."

She gave Julia the necessary instructions and left the office.

10

Kate didn't really remember getting into the car, she just knew she had to get to Paula quickly, but that was easier said than done at that time of day. The traffic was often at a standstill and there was a protest march going on as well.

When she began her journey, she didn't know whether she'd even be able to drive, what with the problems the company was having, but she knew she had to stay calm for Paula's sake. She turned the car into a side street and found that plenty of other people had had the same idea. What the hell was happening? Kate thought. Since she'd met up with Evert again everything had gone wrong.

Paula was hysterical on the other side of London and Evert could be dead for all she knew and she had just about enough to cope with already.

Her mobile phone broke into her thoughts. Julia couldn't get a flight to Karoup until ten o'clock the next morning. Kate panicked. They would arrive too late, but there was nothing she could do about it, it would take at least six hours by car from Copenhagen, so she told Julia to arrange the flight for tomorrow.

Paula came running out of the house the minute she saw the car, with Annie following closely behind. "Where have you been?" Paula demanded, "he's dead isn't he?" she asked.

"I don't know," Kate told her truthfully, "I only know what you have told me. I got here as quickly as I could, Paula. We can't go today, there's no flight, so let's stop and think. Can we ring Christian?" she asked Annie, "and find out what the situation is?"

She didn't need to repeat the telephone conversation to Paula because she had obviously heard both sides. Although Evert was terribly ill, he was still alive.

"Let's go now," insisted Paula, "otherwise I just

know we'll be too late, I want him to know I'm there."

Annie took hold of her. "Paula, do as Kate tells you. She's doing the best she can. Do you want to stay here tonight?" she asked Kate.

"No, Annie, thank you, I'll have to go home and get some things together, we don't know how long we will be there, do we? We will just have to take things one day at a time."

Paula already had a case packed. "I'm coming with you," she said firmly.

Annie came with them to the car and watched as Paula threw her case in. Kate noticed the woman's lips trembling and she realised that Annie didn't know when she would see Paula again. Paula gave her a quick hug and told her she'd ring soon and jumped into the car.

Paula began sobbing uncontrollably on the way back and Kate tried to comfort her, without much success. Finally, Kate braked suddenly, with the effect that Paula stopped crying and looked at her with a shocked expression.

"Will you pull yourself together, you are only making things worse," said Kate, exasperated. "I cannot concentrate and I am doing the best I can. It would be better if you could help me," she finished.

"Sorry, Kate," sniffed Paula.

* * * * *

The next twelve hours or so were a blur. There were long periods of silence between mother and daughter and they arrived at Heathrow well before their flight.

"Kate? He will make it, won't he?" asked Paula.

Once again, Kate answered truthfully, "I really don't know."

The moment they arrived in Copenhagen, Paula was on the phone to Christian. Evert was still alive and Christian would be meeting them at Karoup.

They were both very apprehensive when the plane landed at the small airport in Karoup. "Is he still alive?" they asked, as soon as they saw Christian.

"Yes," came the welcome answer, as they hurried to the waiting car.

"What happened?" asked Kate.

"Well," said Christian, "I'm afraid he is totally to blame. When you left he took me and my sister home, but instead of going home himself, he went into the town and took a drink. He crashed the car down the bank on the way back, but he wasn't found until the following morning."

"Do you mean he was driving whilst drunk?" asked Kate.

"I'm afraid so," Christian answered.

"You mean he did it himself?" Paula asked, "Was anyone else hurt?"

"No," replied Christian, "there was only him involved."

At the hospital they couldn't believe what they saw, Evert was unrecognisable. He was unconscious and on a respirator. His legs and hips were in plaster and his skin was a mass of black and blue.

Kate couldn't understand how he had survived, if indeed he would still. She couldn't imagine how he could have driven the car after drinking, and her panic turned to anger. "How dare he put us through this for twenty four hours?" she managed, before breaking down for the first time and weeping uncontrollably.

Paula came and put her arms around Kate's shoulders, "Come on, Kate," she said, "you've kept up this far, please don't cry, Kate, for me, please."

"I'm just too angry to stop!" Kate spluttered. "Try and talk to him, I have to be on my own for a few minutes."

She watched as Paula knelt down beside Evert's bed and spoke gently. "Evert, this is your daughter, Paula. Kate is here as well. Open your eyes and look at us, please, we have just discovered each other, I'm not going to let you leave me. Give me a sign, Evert, anything will do. Do you understand?"

she almost shouted.

There was no response whatsoever, the only movement coming from Christian who took hold of Paula and guided her to a chair. Kate had never felt so hopeless in her life. Everybody expected her to do the right thing but the right thing spread itself in so many ways and she shook her head in despair.

* * * * *

She had been there for three weeks. There had been many phone calls from the office and many from Annie, asking when Paula would be home. Kate had to tell her she didn't know. Evert was still in a coma and Paula refused to leave him, so Kate was left in the house alone, facing Helga's open hostility and life was certainly very difficult.

It was almost Christmas. If she went home today - which she couldn't - she'd never have time to put everything in order before the New Year as she'd promised her bank she would do.

She stared at the open countryside from the kitchen window. There must come a time in your life when you ask yourself what's it all for? At the end of the day, who gives a damn? "You are here now, so everything be alright . . . " Evert's words came floating back. Why did she have to make everything right all the time?

Everybody was alright but her. Evert was going to get better, the hospital was sure of that, it would only be a matter of time and Paula was where she wanted to be, she was happy to be sitting there with Christian day after day.

Even her mum and dad had their own little world in Liverpool, unaware that anything was wrong. Everyone in her company would be planning their family Christmases and spending far too much, oblivious to the fact that she would spend the festive period huddled over the account's books - if she ever got back to London at all.

Annie would be lonely, but that would stop the moment she saw Paula and in the meantime, she was stuck here looking at Helga's sullen face. She made a decision, she was going home at the weekend even if she had to walk!

She went to the hospital to be greeted by a jubilant Paula, "Kate! Kate! Evert's regained consciousness!" she yelled, and gave her a piece of paper on which were scrawled 'Kate & Paula'.

"He did that?" asked Kate. Paula nodded her head and added, "The doctor has told him what happened and he's had steel pins put in his legs. His hip will need doing again and it will be about three months before he will be able to walk properly."

Kate grabbed the opportunity and said, "Paula, I have a business to run and Annie is missing you terribly, we should go home now."

"Annie's alright isn't she, Kate?" asked Paula anxiously, "she's not ill?"

"No," replied Kate, "she's not ill, but she is very lonely."

"Well, my father needs me more at the moment," decided Paula, "and I couldn't leave him now. You go, Kate and I'll stay here."

Kate felt selfish, but was relieved. She promised Paula she would be back between Christmas and the New Year and she would go and see Annie whenever she could, so she wouldn't feel too deserted. She almost ran out of the hospital in her hurry to get back to the house so she could book her flights for the following day. In the meantime, she spent as much time as she could with Evert and Paula and hoped she managed to conceal her delight at going home.

She returned to London the next day and was met by Julia at Heathrow. "Any major problems?" Kate wanted to know.

"Not that I know of, but there again, they wouldn't let me know anything unless I needed to contact you urgently."

The traffic was heavy as usual, more so in fact, given that there were just a few days to go before

Christmas. Everybody seemed to be shopping at once.

"Do you want to go home first to get your car?" Julia asked.

Kate shook her head. The sooner she saw John from Accounts the better she would feel. She put her head round his door as soon as they got to the office. "Shall we go to my office and see where we are up to?" she asked him. Was it her imagination, or did John look uneasy?

There were letters to be opened, but John rose and followed her immediately. "Did we get the cash flow under control?" she asked, when they reached her office.

"Well, initially we did, but now it appears to have slipped back again," he said miserably.

"We paid the forty thousand back to the bank, or at least part of it?" she demanded.

"Well, actually, we didn't pay any of it back. Everyone I have tried to contact seems to be at office parties or entertaining clients before Christmas." He added, "Kate, I've got some news for you that you won't like."

"What is it?" she asked, with a sinking feeling.

"You know that new account? Well, I got a cheque for half of what they owed, so I allowed another order to go through," he stopped.

"Yes?" said Kate, "go on."

"Well, the cheque was returned marked 'refer to drawer' and by the time it had gone through the system, the other work had already been completed."

"How much do they owe us to date?" asked Kate.

John mumbled something and Kate said, "John, I can't hear you properly. How much did you say?"

"£160,000."

If ever there was a day when Kate was going to have a heart attack, this was it. "How the hell does a company we have never traded with get to owe us £160,000?" she shouted. "How well do you know these people?" she asked accusingly. "What's in it for you to allow this to happen?"

John stood up. He looked in a state of total shock. "It's nothing like that, Kate, you should know that. I would never get involved in something like that against the company. It's true I do know all the directors because they have nearly all traded with us before in smaller amounts and have always paid on time, but twelve months ago they formed themselves into one company and opened up in every high street. I've been in a few of their shops, they are very cut price and appear to be very busy."

Kate interrupted, "Don't even begin to tell me,

John, it's the old sting; build up your credit until you're sure the different companies feel confident about you, then go for the kill and don't pay anybody."

"They are still in business," John said defensively.

"Mark my words," Kate said sombrely, "it will only be until after the Christmas trade."

"What can we do?" asked John, now looking quite ill.

"Nothing," she replied quietly, "absolutely nothing. It's already been done. Go back to your office and leave me on my own."

"I'm sorry, Kate," he said.

"It's too late for that, John, we need something a bit better than sorry now."

She began to open her mail, starting with the one from her solicitor which confirmed her worst suspicions. Being a limited company meant that the directors were only responsible for one hundred pounds' worth of the debts.

It just wasn't fair. The system failed to protect people like her. All her hard work over many years and the fact that she had ploughed everything she had back into the company meant nothing at the end of the day. There had to be something wrong here.

She pressed her intercom. "Tell John to come

to my office immediately."

He appeared in double-quick time. He must have been waiting for me to ring him, she thought. "Explain to me, John, the difference between thirty day's credit and one hundred and eighty day's. Where did the other one hundred and fifty days go?"

"In my own defence," he started, "nearly all our customers have changed their method of payment."

"Enlighten me," she said coldly.

"Well, our usual protection was to get half up front, but had we kept to that policy, we would have had no orders in this last twelve months. So it became the norm to allow everyone thirty days with the exception of Alex, who was sixty to ninety days."

"I know about Alex," she said, "go on, tell me about the others."

"The old way was to invoice on the 28th of every month so that we get paid at the end of the following month."

She interrupted him. "But that's thirty-three days at most."

He ignored her and said, "But companies, a couple of years ago, insisted that the invoices were dated the last day of any month, so that by the time they received them into their systems, they couldn't go out the following month after that, effectively making it sixty days. But," he added, "we contained that, because although we had some extra bank charges from time to time, the extra sales and profit took care of that."

"So why are we now on the verge of going broke?" she asked sarcastically, "if you're telling me that everything was contained?"

"It all happened this last year," he answered. "We got letters from nearly every accounts' department asking us to invoice by the 8th of any month. If they received the invoice by then, we would be paid by the end of the following month, which was seven weeks. We went along with it because now it wouldn't be sixty days it would only be fifty-three, which would be to our advantage."

"Go on," said Kate, "I'm still listening."

"The trouble this year is that a lot of people have used a delaying tactic of saying they never received our invoice, so we have had to do copy invoices which put payment back by eleven weeks."

"Did that apply to everyone?" she asked, "the seventy-seven days?"

"No, not all, but our better accounts have all cut back anyway."

"So how did the bastards get one hundred and fifty days? Tell me that, then."

"There really wasn't a problem at first," said John, "I realise now that we have been conned, Kate and I should have seen it coming, but keeping our staff employed was of the utmost importance. I never dreamed that they had no intention of paying us. At first, their requirements were modest and as I said, we never had any trouble with them individually before, so how could I even suspect that they would all be in it together?

"It was only when that cheque came back that I knew we were in serious trouble. I have seen everyone in the last three weeks and got a lot of money in. I even got the genuine customers to pay before they took delivery of their jobs, but it's still not enough, is it, Kate?"

"John, why didn't you tell me all this three weeks ago?" Kate asked.

"You seemed to have enough problems and I really thought I could solve this myself, without bothering you."

"Look, leave it be for the moment," said Kate, "I need to be by myself for a while."

John got up, "Kate," he said, "I'm really sorry about all this," and he left the room.

She banged her fist down hard on the desk. John was sorry, Paula was sorry, Evert was sorry. What good did it do?

11

Kate must have sat there for well over an hour after John left and other than making an urgent appointment with her bank manager, who she couldn't see until the following day, she didn't speak to anyone.

There had been many times over the years when she had felt concern over her cash flow. The last time had been in 1982, when the bank rates had affected everybody. But never had she been anywhere near the position she was in now.

'The buck stops here' said the sign on her desk.

Well, that was certainly true. What it didn't say, however, was that you were so dependant on other people making the right decisions for you and even if they admitted to fouling up, they could go home and leave you with a twenty-four-hour a day problem.

At times like this she thought of selling but always came to the conclusion that she had nothing really to sell, only contracts and anyway, any monies she raised would quickly evaporate in redundancy payments and holiday pay. She knew the business inside out and couldn't really imagine life without it. Apart from that, it did give her a good standard of living, one she wouldn't get working for someone else.

All she could really do was talk her way through it tomorrow and hope she could convince the bank manager to support her. She got up and started gathering her belongings together. She needed her bank's support, but tonight Annie needed her, and that's where she was going.

If she owed anyone anything, it was Annie. Oh, not in financial terms, but for the way she had allowed her unlimited access to Paula. Annie was not interested in business, so she said, but Kate had noticed over the years the *Financial Times* lying around. Once, when she had asked why she bought it, Annie had simply dismissed it by saying that she liked to see what the toffs were up to now and again.

Kate felt some of the weight lifting off her. She should have gone to Annie's an hour ago instead of brooding in her office. She hailed a taxi and directed it to drive to her house to pick up her car. Once inside, she dropped off her luggage, ignored the mail and the flashing light on the answerphone and, within ten minutes was driving across London.

She was surprised at Annie's appearance. At six o'clock at night, she was usually looking very smart and quite busy, but tonight she was in her dressing gown. "Are you ill?" asked Kate with some concern.

"No," replied Annie, "I just couldn't be bothered to get dressed today."

"What can't you be bothered with, Annie?" asked Kate.

"Oh, anything," she replied laconically, then added, "Paula's not coming back, is she?"

"Don't be silly!" Kate said, "I'm going over between Christmas and the New Year to fetch her."

"We'll see," said Annie.

Kate had never seen Annie like this in all the years she had known her. This couldn't be right. "Annie, put the kettle on and listen to me. Paula misses you and she sent me to ask whether you would like to go over with me. She made me promise that if you said no, I've got to kidnap you!"

"Oh, Kate," said Annie, "did she really say that? I'd love to go. Can you make the tea while I go and get dressed?" She stopped by the door. "It will be something to look forward to," she said, with a more cheerful note in her voice.

Kate stayed with her for a couple of hours. She knew that if Annie could have got her passport tonight she would have. It would be no surprise if she started packing the minute she left.

Paula must be warned before she had the chance to phone Annie, otherwise the woman would feel very let down by them both. So, as soon as she was out of sight, she put through a call on her mobile phone.

* * * * *

There were no welcome lights on in her house, but she didn't need that, just the peace she knew she would feel once inside was enough. This was safe ground. She owned every brick, every piece of furniture and she was proud of that fact. A doctor who had come to see her once had commented that it was very nice, very 'tasty' as he had put it.

Yes, if all else failed, she still had her house. She put a call through to Liverpool, telling them she would be coming home the week before Christmas, but didn't mention her problems. What would be the point of making them worry about her, Evert and Paula? She would fill them in when she got there.

She didn't bother with the television. What she needed was a good long soak in the bath, then an early night. The first two were easy, but getting to sleep was impossible, her mind was on all her problems and wouldn't rest. Was it Margaret Thatcher who had said you only needed three hours' sleep each night?

Well, thought Kate, maybe she was right, because after travelling from Karoup that morning, then facing all the problems at the office, going to see Annie and solving hers, she didn't even feel tired. So, at three-thirty in the morning, she was still walking around the house.

She didn't know what time it was when she finally dropped off to sleep, she only knew that when the alarm sounded the next morning she didn't have any enthusiasm for getting up. However, the day had to be faced, so she showered and dressed in her business suit and went out to face what was to come.

12

Her appointment was for nine-thirty, so Kate drove straight to the bank. She had always been completely straight with them, but today wondered whether it was the wisest course to take. She had to knock when she arrived, as the big doors were not yet open. When she entered, she was taken straight through to the manager's office.

"Hello, Kate," he said, as he got up from his chair, his hand outstretched to greet her, "sorry I was unavailable yesterday. Now, what can I do for you?"

"Well," replied Kate, "since I last saw you, I've had a look at our outstanding invoices and some of our customers appear to be taking longer than usual to pay."

"But not all of them?" he asked.

"No, not all of them."

"Well, sign of the times I'm afraid," the bank manager said, "but, providing you can generate cash flow through your long-standing business relationships, together with your profit from that source, you will clear your overdraft as agreed. In the meantime," he went on, "your outstanding creditors might settle, which will reduce your charges with us. You still look worried," he added, "but I'm sure if the worst comes to the worst, I can stretch your overdraft over a longer period."

Kate took a deep breath, "Could you increase it then, add £100,000?"

The bank manager looked startled, "Kate," he said, "we have always been totally up-front with each other. If someone asked me who was the customer I trusted most, I would not hesitate before I said you. Do you want to confide in me? The worst that can happen is that I send you away."

Kate took the opportunity and plunged in. When she had finished, he said, "Do you think you can trade out of it?"

"Yes," she replied truthfully, "I do."

"Well," he said, "I'm allowed to loan £100,000

without going through head office, so I will do this for you. I will cancel your overdraft facility of £40,000 and put it on loan, say, over two years, with another £60,000. Will that help?" he asked.

"Oh, yes," replied Kate, gratefully, "thank you. I won't forget what you have done for me today."

"Kate," he said, "wait a minute, there is a little tidying up still to do, before thanking me."

"What do you mean?" she asked.

"You cannot expect the bank to lend you £100,000 without some security. Now, you told me your house is worth double that."

"Yes," interrupted Kate, "but that is mine."

"I agree. But the company is yours also and it is in a very serious position right now. I would be failing in my duty as manager of this branch if I lent you such a sum without you being prepared to share my confidence that you can survive."

"What do you want me to do?" Kate asked.

"Well," he said, "it is not a question of me wanting you to do anything, but the only way you can survive the next few weeks without the bank helping you is to sell your house and very quickly," he added. "Therefore, I need you to sign a debenture for the amount loaned to you, plus, of course, any interest charges."

"Is this the only option open to me?" she asked miserably.

"Unless you have a large amount of money hidden somewhere, I'm afraid so," he replied, "although you could try one of the finance houses, but their interest charges are far in excess of ours. The decision is yours."

"I'd prefer to have all my eggs in the same basket," replied Kate.

"Good. I feel you have taken the right course. Now, as well as the debenture, we will need a current valuation, which, of course, we will pay for," he added hastily, "is that alright with you?"

"I think it has to be, doesn't it?" replied Kate.

"Don't worry," he said cheerfully, "you said yourself you can trade out of this. Could you let me have your final accounts, plus your projected figures for the next twelve months? Just as a precaution, of course."

"Of course," replied Kate and stood up.

"If I don't see you before," said the bank manager, shaking her hand, "have a lovely Christmas."

"You too," responded Kate and left the office. She realised, as she went out into the street that it was the first time he had not escorted her to the door.

Kate was really depressed now. A charge on her house. She hadn't thought of that. She'd watched it go up in value over the years and now, with charges over the next seven years, she owed

£100,000 on it, plus the eighteen per cent per year interest.

She could kick herself. She should have taken out one of the many pension plans she had been offered, but her house and business had been her pension. She had always been aware of the tax advantages had she taken a policy, but the premium had to be paid every month and she had preferred to keep the money within the company. Stupid! She could have used that policy now as security and not her house.

Driving to the office was a nightmare. Everybody seemed to be thinking about Christmas instead of driving. Well, she wasn't. In fact, the sooner it was all over, the better.

Walking into the office didn't seem the same these days. She had been away more over the last few months than she had since the company started and her problem had only been postponed, not solved. The staff missed her though and they were asking now what she would like for Christmas, as the customary bouquet of flowers wouldn't be a good idea as she was going away.

She made her way to John Kitchen's office. He looked as though he had won the pools, "I heard you were in and I was just on my way to see you. We have made considerable headway," he said, putting a list of promised payments in her hand.

She looked at it then gave it back, "Give me a guarantee that you can produce this list every month for the next two years and I might share your enthusiasm," she said.

She was aware of his astonished face, but she just turned on her heels and walked out. She didn't bother telling him about the extra £60,000 available, he would only feel better and relax his efforts and that would leave her in a more vulnerable position.

There was not a lot she could do at this time of year. It was always a bad period for orders. January and February were the months she looked forward to, as this was when her customers budgeted for the coming financial year in April.

She phoned Annie to tell her she was going to Liverpool and would be back on Boxing Day to collect her. Annie was in a happy world of her own. Paula had phoned and she was excited that her mother had decided to go. "Oh, Kate," she asked, "are you as excited as me?"

"Yes," said Kate, crossing her fingers, "I am." She ended the conversation and went to wish everyone in the office a 'Merry Christmas'. She deliberately missed out 'and a Happy New Year' because she didn't think it was going to be for most of them. They were surprised she wasn't staying in work for the last few days, but she really couldn't wait to get away.

As she drove up to her house, she felt sick. This was not her house any more, it was the bank's. How could she have let that happen? She went inside. She didn't need to pack, she hadn't unpacked yet since coming home from Denmark. She piled everything in the car and decided to do any washing in Liverpool. She drove off.

A new store which she had designed had just opened along the Rows in Chester. She needed to get some Christmas presents for the family and thought she could kill two birds with one stone. She loved Chester, with its Roman walls and old-fashioned street names and she remembered coming one Saturday a month to 'Brown's'. To her, as a twelve year old, it had signified pure wealth, with the plush, grey carpet with black lines that her shoes would sink into. She could almost smell the atmosphere of that shop and that's where she was headed.

She wondered if 'Hignett's' was still there. That had been the other side of the coin. Situated in Frodsham Street, it was the fish and chip shop that everyone made for. It even had sawdust on the floor - hygiene experts would have a fit now, but it served the best meals around. Fish, chips, mushy peas, tea and bread and butter, just one and threepence, which was seven pence in new money, but was probably more like two pounds today.

She could have kept to the motorways but decided to come off at junction nineteen for Knutsford. The countryside was so peaceful and she found herself humming *The Green, Green Grass Of Home.*

Sod the business, she thought, sod London, Denmark and everything else. She was going home to her mum and dad and there she would stay until Boxing Day. Then she'd go and pick up Annie. She decided to get everyone really nice Christmas presents and worry about what would come later.

Kate's mum screamed with delight when she opened the door to her. "Look who's here!" she yelled as they walked along the hall and not even pausing for breath added, "We weren't expecting you for a few days yet, love. Paula coming up on the train, is she? Get the kettle on," she yelled to her dad, "Kate's here!"

Kate was busy getting her cases and Christmas presents out of the car and by the time she went into the kitchen, the teapot was on the table waiting for her.

"Where's our Paula?" demanded her dad.

"Denmark," replied Kate.

"What's she doing there, then? I thought she'd been and come back?"

Kate sat down. "You won't believe all the things that have happened these last few weeks, right up to today, in fact and there's more to come with the New Year, too." She felt the tears starting to come.

"Come on, lass," said her father, "you know you can halve your troubles with us, that's what we're here for."

Kate told them everything, her parents listening to every word in silence, her father drawing long and hard on his pipe.

"Well," he said, when she had finished, "this all needs some thinking about. What if I go over there and make sure she's alright with that Helga, while you get on with what you have to do in London?"

"Oh," said Kate, "I'm not worried about Paula, it's my business and my house I'm concerned about."

The old man looked at her steadily and said, "Well, it looks to me as though you're worrying about the wrong thing. I'd be thinking about Paula stuck in a foreign country with a woman who doesn't like her. How can Evert protect her when he's in hospital?"

"Honestly, Dad," Kate said, exasperated, "Paula is quite safe, I wouldn't have left her there otherwise, would I?"

"Not if you say so, love, not if you say so."

Kate relaxed a little and her father went on. "This Kitchen chap, was he in with them?"

"No," Kate replied, "nothing like that."

"Well, how come he gave them so much rope they hanged you, then?"

"Look, Dad, once you start a job, you have to finish it. Also, once they owe you, if you refuse the next job, you have the added worry that they won't pay you for the work already done."

"Well," the old man said, "I work in more simple ways than those you talk about, but I do know that if you lend someone a pound and they can't pay you back, you don't go and lend them another one. It's common sense, lass, they can't pay one, so they're not going to pay two, are they?"

"Dad, it doesn't work like that," sighed Kate.

"Maybe you'd know where you were up to if it did," retorted her father, "and maybe you wouldn't be sitting here crying. I'm not going to pry, but you must be worth a few bob yourself, lass, where do you keep it?"

"In the bank," Kate answered, "but that's my private account."

"The same bank?" asked her dad.

Kate nodded.

"Well, maybe there's enough to cover what you owe them with the house, so if I were you, I'd get my money out of there and put it somewhere else, otherwise they'll have that as well."

"Dad, you're not listening. It doesn't work like that."

"Doesn't it?" he answered, "well, tomorrow morning I'll take you to plenty of people who it has happened to. People who have worked all their lives and who've been left with nothing. Me and her," he went on, pointing at her mum, "we've never been used to money, so we don't set much store by it, but you have, so you want to take a long and hard look at what you're doing. It's good advice I'm giving you, lass," he finished.

Kate went to bed early, her hot water bottle in place. Her dad worried her, he always explained everything in simple terms and more often than not, what he said was true.

She was worth approximately £37,000 at the moment and she decided she would move that money, just to be on the safe side, because, although she had signed for £100,000 today, with the interest charges it was considerably more and the repayments would really hit her hard.

She settled down further into the bed. She was going to stay there until her mum brought her a cup of tea in the morning and then she'd start enjoying her holiday.

13

The days passed quickly in the usual Christmas style, but despite all the protests she decided to go back to London in the evening on Christmas Day. For one thing, she needed to sort out some warmer clothing because it was bound to be cold in Denmark.

She laughed to herself as she picked up some old sheepskin-lined boots, she'd look attractive walking about in those, but if that's what it took to stay on her feet, so be it. Saying goodbye to her house and leaving her mail unopened, she made her way over to Annie's.

She really wished she hadn't asked Annie to go

with her now because then she could have made some excuse not to go herself. But it was too late and she couldn't let her down now, so it was with a false show of enthusiasm that she greeted Annie - who was so excited she had forgotten her fear of flying. Kate was convinced she'd fly the aircraft if she had to.

They arrived at Heathrow the following day and from the minute they took off, Annie's knuckles were white from holding onto the seat. "It's the safest form of travel," whispered Kate, "we are on radar the whole way."

"Does that stop you from crashing?" asked Annie, hopefully.

"No," Kate said, "but they would know immediately if something happened to us. Come on, enjoy your meal."

"I'm not hungry," said Annie, renewing her grip.

Paula was waiting for them at Karoup, "Mum!" she shouted, "Kate! We are here!" Kate watched as Annie grabbed hold of Paula and noticed that Paula was more than happy to hold on to her.

"We have been waiting for you for over two hours, haven't we, Christian?" she said.

"Yes," he said, getting hold of Annie's hand, "welcome to Denmark, Paula's mum, you will like it here because we make sure you have a good time."

"Oh," said Annie, delighted, "isn't he polite. Doesn't he make you feel welcome."

"He's alright, I suppose," answered Paula, as she guided them to the rear of the car. She herself hopped in next to Christian and Kate noticed immediately that there was a certain warmth between them. The conversation was punctuated with "didn't we, Christian?" and "you told me that, didn't you, Paula." Kate glanced at Annie to see whether she'd noticed but Annie was too busy hanging on to every word of Paula's.

They decided to drop the luggage off first and Annie was quite taken with the house, "Isn't it beautiful!" she exclaimed.

"Yes," said Paula, "Evert built it for Kate."

"No Helga?" asked Kate.

"Oh, she'll be around somewhere. Don't worry about her," she added, "all the time I've been here, she hasn't spoken a word to me, so I just ignore her. Anyway, I've spent more time at Christian's, haven't I," she said, looking at him.

"Yes," replied Christian, "and I make sure she is safe," and he put his arm around her shoulders.

Kate broke the silence, "You say your father is vastly improved?"

"Yes," answered Paula, "and he seemed better again once he knew you were on your way. Shall we go and see him now, because he knew what time you should have got to Karoup?"

"Yes, of course," said Kate, "we can't keep him waiting, can we?"

Helga came in with some coffee. "*Kaf?*" she asked.

"Oh, don't put yourself to any trouble for us. We will make it ourselves."

"Nobody go in that kitchen, but me," she replied and walked out.

"Mum," said Paula, "that was Helga and no, they are not all like that, are they Christian?" she asked him, taking hold of his hand.

Evert's face lit up the moment he saw them. "This is Annie, Paula's mum," said Kate.

"Oh, Annie," he said, "I believe we have a daughter between us!"

Annie blushed and answered, "Well, yes, I suppose we have."

"Let me say to you, Annie, when I first heard about you, I think I go crazy, because she not be with Kate or me, but now I got to know the girl, I think she is the best girl I meet in my whole life. Maybe you have some special quality to make her so?" he asked.

Annie blushed deeply again and didn't answer.

Evert continued. "Anything I have is yours. It has to be because you are willing to share your daughter with Kate and me. I think you are a good woman."

They stayed with him, Kate learning for the first time that he would be in the hospital for about four months. He'd have to have many operations on his face, but once they had taken place he would be virtually back to normal.

"Whatever made you drink and drive?" Kate asked him. "I didn't know you were so stupid to think you could get in a car when you couldn't even see straight, never mind drive."

"No, I would not do it also," Evert said, taking hold of her hand, "but when I saw you go into that aircraft I feel very sad, so I decide to have a beer with my friends, they buy me many beers because they know my mind is down. I mean to leave my car and take the last bus, but it is gone, so I think, because I am as drunk as hell, that I can drive home. It would be a long way for me to walk," he added.

"Don't they have taxis in Denmark?" asked Kate.

"Sure they do, but when you are drunk, you think that everything is under control. I'm so sorry that I put all the trouble on to you. I should be looking after you, I know that," Evert said miserably.

"Yes," replied Kate, "you should, but you're not and it is your own stupid fault, you only have yourself to blame."

He squeezed her hand, "I'm sorry you think so badly of me," he said, "your feelings, they go down towards me."

"When I thought I wouldn't see you again," answered Kate, "the twenty year gap shortened very quickly."

"You English are always so restrained, but not me, I would tell the world I love you!"

Kate was embarrassed and looked at Annie, only to notice a small tear coming down her cheek. Annie smiled back at her and said, "I think he's lovely, don't be too hard on him, Kate."

They promised to come back and visit him again later and made their way back to his house. Helga was sitting watching the television in the lounge. She didn't acknowledge them, so Kate asked, "Does anyone want a drink?" and then to Helga, "Do you want one?"

The girl jumped to her feet, "I tell you before, nobody goes in that kitchen but me!" she shouted, before walking away. Kate could feel herself bristling as she followed her.

"Helga? Can I talk to you?" The girl didn't reply, so Kate continued. "Look, let's get this straight, you don't have to like us and if you choose to ignore us, that is alright because we can manage quite well without conversation between us. Evert is in hospital and we intend to stay here, so shall we all make the best of it?"

Helga gave no indication she had even heard, so Kate added, as nicely as she could, "Helga, you don't have to cook our food, we will look after ourselves, why, you can even join us if you like." She held out her hand to the girl, but Helga met it with a look of pure hatred.

"You and your family will never ever come into my kitchen," she said.

"I think you are mistaken," said Kate quietly, withdrawing her hand. "My friends and family are more than welcome in any part of this house and you'd be well advised to make the best of it." She turned and walked away from the girl, back into the lounge.

The others had obviously heard the conversation and waited for her outburst. They could see her face was drained of colour in her anger. "So much has happened over the last few weeks," she managed, "my nerves are grating and nobody, but nobody gets to me more than her," she said, pointing to the kitchen, "I feel I could shake the living daylights out of her."

"Oh, Kate, she's not worth it," said Paula. "I've never seen you so uptight," she added.

Kate thought there was a reason for that, but didn't answer.

As it happened, they didn't get the chance to

prepare any food, Helga made sure of that. Whenever they went into the house, hot and cold food was always at their disposal. Everyone chose to ignore it, it was easier to eat at the Jensen's Steak House each day. If you went before six o'clock you could have a good variety of meals for almost three pounds.

Lis and Christian had decided to stay with them and were more than eager to drive them wherever they wanted to go. They were all allowed to spend many hours with Evert, which they took full advantage of, so they only really used the house to sleep and wash in - anything was better than having to look at Helga's sullen face.

They had only two days to go before they returned to England, which Kate would be more than pleased to see, for now that Evert was out of danger she needed to get back to the office.

Annie wanted to see the boat again, saying it was so peaceful there and Kate agreed. The harbour was always a welcome sight, the sea had always had a calming effect on her.

Paula, Christian and Lis were first out of the car, Kate waiting to help Annie. They heard Paula shout, "Who's done that?" and rushed over to them.

Paula was looking in horror at the boat and Kate could see that their names had been covered over in big blobs of black paint.

"I know who's responsible for this," said Kate, grimly and without waiting for the others, she turned and began to run back towards the house. She quickly found Helga, who looked frightened and Kate grabbed her by the shoulders and turned her round to face her. "Why did you do that?" she demanded.

"What?" asked Helga.

"Oh, you know what," said Kate, "why did you paint out our names on Evert's boat? Answer me!" she almost shouted, "because you're going nowhere until you do."

"Yes," said Helga, "I did it. You spoil everything. It is me that Evert loves, not you, not your daughter."

The others had caught up with Kate and were staring open-mouthed at the scene.

There was no stopping Helga now, her face was contorted with rage. "You, your daughter and all these people in my house. We were very happy until you come and trick him that your daughter belongs to him. Evert was a seaman, yes, and you go to bed with him all those years ago maybe, you be the prostitute, yes, maybe you still are the prostitute."

"Get out of this house, now," said Kate, totally controlled, with her voice as cold as ice.

"Never!" stated Helga, throwing her head back

defiantly, "this is my house, not yours."

"Then I will throw you out," said Kate, calmly.

Paula intervened, "Kate," she said, "where will she go?"

Kate turned on Paula and said sharply, "I suggest you all keep out of this. As for where she will go, that is her problem, not mine and not yours. This is between me and her, so please mind your own business."

Turning back to Helga, Kate asked, "Are you getting your belongings, or do I have to throw them out as well, because you have exactly fifteen minutes." She held Helga's furious gaze. "Now, I am going to make my family a drink in my own kitchen and I expect you to be out of this house by the time I have finished."

Helga didn't answer, she just turned and left the room. Kate was trembling with anger. Annie put her hand on the woman's arm, but Kate brushed it away, saying, "I won't be responsible for my actions until that girl is out of this house."

The coffee seemed to be ready in no time and Kate didn't even feel the boiling liquid coursing down her dry throat. She could hear Helga moving about upstairs and could barely control herself while she waited for the fifteen minutes to pass.

Eventually, Helga came downstairs with her bags and put some down in front of Kate saying,

"I will return for these later."

"No," said Kate, "you take them all, now," and she picked them up, opened the front door and threw them out, one by one, stating to Helga, "I never want to see your face again as long as I live."

"Oh, but you will," said Helga, on her way out, "I make sure you do!"

Paula and Annie were standing close together, and Paula breathed, "Wow! That was one mega row!" Almost at the same time Annie said, "Do you think she will come back?"

"Not if she knows what's good for her!" answered Kate. "Now, as far as I am concerned, Helga is history and I will not give her another thought. However, as I seem to have sacked Evert's housekeeper, I suppose I should go and tell him. Will you take me, Christian?"

"Of course," he replied, "but you must wait until I go and get my sister. When the trouble started she ran to tell my father, because we think Helga is crazy and he will take care of any problem with her."

Lis was laughing when Christian came back with her. "I wish I could have stayed here, sorry I missed that. My father gave her a lift with all her bags. Do not worry, Kate, her old auntie is still in the village, so she go there. She is crazy anyway. My father will come here soon, so you can be sure that Paula and Annie will be safe while Christian takes you to see Evert."

Christian appeared worried. "You know, Kate, you must be very careful of her, she is a danger to you now. Perhaps it is better if you go back to England soon. My father and me will take care of the house, you tell Evert that, we go everyday until he gets out of hospital."

"I know," said Kate, "it's a good job he has you and your family to support him."

Evert was surprised to see her. "You are alone and early," he said.

"Yes," she replied, "how are you?"

"The pains, they feel bad until I get injection, but I feel I get more well every day. The doctors tell me I have steel pins in my legs, but they have to be there, there is nothing I can do about it. You and Paula, it is too soon that you go back to England, but I know I cannot do anything about that also. It was my intention before the accident that I come to you, but that seems a long time away now," he said, sadly.

"Evert," she said, looking him straight in the eye, "I have some news for you which you may not like."

"You go and not come back? Is that what you tell me?" She saw the panic in his face.

She took his hand, "Don't be silly, I'll be back

before you realise I'm gone."

"Then there is no problem to what you have to say," he said, relaxing, "nothing else matters, only me, only you."

"I threw Helga out of your house," said Kate.

"You did? Why?"

"Well," said Kate, "we don't get on at all and if I'm going to come here regularly I couldn't bear to be in the same house as her. Paula feels the same way," she added, hoping it would add more weight to her reason.

"Do not blame yourself, Kate, the fault is mine, but you must be very careful of her, not relax, because I am not there to look after you. All my friends tell me she is in love with me, but I can never be in love with her, so I think it better that there is no words of it between us.

In the beginning, she was always smiling when I come home, she watch me comb my hair and tie my shoelaces. I was aware of everything she do, she even understand when I got drunk and talk of you. I think she know not to make a pass at me, because that would alter everything and then she could not stay in my house, but she never do that.

She seemed to accept things, she knew I got women in the town, but as long as I did not bring them to the house, she didn't seem to mind. She think I do it out of respect for her, but it was because I did not want another woman in that way in our house.

When I find you, I am so excited I tell her, in fact I shout it all over the house. She was distant from me for two days but then she seem happy that you come home, maybe it be a false happiness. You say she is gone for good?"

"Yes," replied Kate, "she knows not to come back while I'm there. Will you manage?"

"Of course!" he replied, "it is no problem for me. You not want to tell me why you have bitter words between you?"

"Not unless you insist," said Kate.

"No, I insist nothing from you, you know that. My main problem right now is you and me. We must talk Kate. You go back to England and I will not know when we see each other again. You have to give me some sign."

"That is not possible at the moment," said Kate, "I really shouldn't be here now and it has nothing to do with feelings or love or whatever, it's simply that I have a business to attend to and it is in trouble at the moment, so I need to get home quickly to put everything in order."

"Yes, I understand that, we have big recession also, many business they not be there anymore. My boat is my problem, I still owe 250,000 krona on it and if I not fish I will not be able to pay the monthly installments, but we each have a house that is paid for, so together we can live comfortably, either here or in London. You believe that also?" he asked.

"Well, I did have my house paid for, but last week I had to sign it over to the bank for the next seven years."

"Oh! Maybe that is the best news I get. I am sorry, but I think maybe I can be what a man should be and provide for you."

"I am too independent for that," Kate replied.

"Well, perhaps it is time for you to be less so," replied Evert.

Christian looked round the door, "Is it alright for me to come in?" he asked them.

"Yes," said Evert, "there is no problem."

Kate saw the relief in the boy's face. "Christian and Lis are taking me to the airport tomorrow," she said.

"Yes, I know that and I think that Christian be a bit more sad that you go back to England, especially Paula, eh Christian?"

Kate saw the boy's face change colour and he said, "Yes, it will be a black day for me."

Kate looked from one to the other. "Am I thinking what you are thinking?" she said.

They both nodded. "And what about Paula? What has she had to say?"

"I don't know," replied Christian, "because we

never discuss our feelings to each other. Maybe we both know that there will be too many complications," he added.

"You'd better believe it!" said Kate, "could I ask you both not to say anything to her?"

"Of course," said Christian, "but what if she makes her feelings known to me?"

"God forbid!" replied Kate in horror.

He looked startled, "Kate, I thought you liked me, in fact, I was sure of it."

She put her hand on his arm, "I am very fond of you and your family, but it is too big a change and everything must be taken much slower. Annie has seen Paula every day for the last twenty years and you don't know how you will feel one month from now, so I don't want you to cause her concern, when there may not even be a reason."

Evert said, "We say in Denmark that whatever will happen, it will happen, it never pass you by. Do not look so worried, Christian, you must let Kate and Paula do what they need to do. They will return to us, otherwise we go to them. Now you must go, you have plenty to do."

When they finally got back to the house, Christian didn't come in. "Where's Christian?" asked Paula immediately.

"I think he has gone to eat."

"Well, that's good of him," interrupted Lis, "he

could have given me a lift."

"Do you want to eat with us?" asked Paula, "then I will walk home with you later."

"You can't!" said Kate and added hurriedly, "we are going to the hospital."

"I know that, Kate," said Paula, "it's already arranged. Pregan was going to take us, but I persuaded him to let Christian go, because tomorrow is our last day, so I will walk down with Lis, then me and Christian will come and pick you and Mum up."

Kate was worried, the sooner she got Paula on that plane, the better. Oh, she would be sorry to leave Evert, but it was his own stupid fault. Anybody could get stoned out of their minds and end up nearly dead. He'd been really lucky, she realised and she hated to leave him just now, but she had to get Paula settled back in England as soon as possible.

She'd make sure that when she wanted to visit Evert, she'd be there with her. "I've been thinking," she said, "when your father comes out of hospital, maybe he could come to London to my house and we can all take turns nursing him back to health."

"I've got a better idea."

"What's that?" asked Kate, already knowing the answer.

"I'll stay here and look after him."

14

New Year's Eve. Kate had never really celebrated it. Once Christmas was over, she had usually spent the following week doing her budget for the year to come. This time her figures were in London.

She wandered through to the kitchen, "What on earth is going on?" she asked, surveying a mass of home-cooked food and a delighted Annie.

"Well," said Annie, "I thought that seeing how it was our last night, we could throw a party for New Year's Eve."

"Oh, what a lovely idea," enthused Kate, realising just how home-sick Annie was. She wanted to be in her own domain, making sure that Paula's every need was catered for, but if that wasn't possible, she would have fallen in with Paula's idea to throw a party.

"I won't bother to go and see Evert with you tonight, it's your last night and it's not my place really, is it?"

"Annie, you're Paula's mother aren't you? Evert will look forward to seeing you. He'll be disappointed if you don't go."

"Oh, Kate, aren't we lucky to have worked it out so well between us? I must admit I was worried a few weeks ago, when he first got in touch, but he's ever so nice. Everything will be back to normal after tomorrow," she added and came over to kiss her.

"Did you pluck up the courage to tell him about Helga?" she asked.

"Yes," replied Kate, "there is no problem." She didn't want to worry her and it was another reason that she wanted Annie to go to the hospital - she wouldn't have settled with Annie being alone in the house, Annie would be no match for Helga.

Lis and Paula joined them in the kitchen, "That smells lovely, Annie, you have to teach me how you do it the English way!"

Paula nudged Lis' arm, "How can you do that? You can't see."

"I cook all the time," replied Lis, "because I can hear the instructions someone tells me and I can feel the heat on the cooker."

"Oh, Lis, I'm so sorry, I never thought," exclaimed Paula, hugging her.

"There is no need to say sorry to me, because I know you feel sorry towards me. You keep forgetting that I am blind because you always say, 'look at that, Lis,' but today you remember, so that is good."

"Don't worry," said Paula, with tears in her eyes, "I'll show you everything."

"When?" asked Kate, hearing a sharpness in her voice.

"When I come back to see my father, of course."

Was it Kate's imagination or did she see Paula tap Lis on the foot.

"Tell us what he said about Helga," said Paula, changing the subject, "was he alright with you?" Then she laughed. "Well, I suppose that's a stupid question, because sacking her was nothing compared to finding out about me. Remember when he said about Lief the Lucky? I didn't have a clue who he was!"

"He was the Danishman who discovered America, of course," said Lis.

"Oh!" said Kate and Paula together, "don't you start!"

"What have I said?" asked Lis, "what have I said?"

"Did he ask you what started it?" continued Paula, "did you tell him about our names being painted out?"

"No," admitted Kate, "I didn't mention that, because as soon as I said we didn't get on, he said it was his fault."

"Why did he say that?" asked Paula, "did he tell her to do it or something?"

"No," replied Kate, "she was jealous of me and you and he knew that, but thought she would accept the situation. Whatever you do, don't mention to him what she did because what he doesn't know he doesn't have to worry about. Lis," she said, turning to the girl, "can Christian paint? I wondered if he could put it back the way it was?"

"Yes," answered Lis, "and I will help him."

"Suits us fine," laughed Paula, "we'll be on the plane being waited on and you two will be up to your necks in rags and paint stripper. Come on, Lis, we want to look our best for our last night, don't we?"

As they went out of the room, Annie remarked, "It's a pity Lis doesn't live near us back home."

Kate had her own thoughts about that and quickly changed the subject. "There is a pile of letters for Evert and I'll give the keys to Pregan tomorrow," she stopped, then said, "where are the keys?"

There was a clip board on the wall, with messages and old photos of Kate clipped on with bright coloured pins. Along the bottom edge hung an assortment of keys. Kate gathered them together, "Let's hope these are the right ones," she said and then stopped, "I wonder if Helga has a set. I'd hate her to be able to move back in tomorrow."

It was with some relief that Kate realised she could make the house secure, but she remarked, "If Evert tells us she has got keys, I'm going to have all the locks changed before I leave tomorrow and I'm going to take these pictures from the *Mænsk* to be cleaned. The colours are fantastic, it will be a nice surprise for him, won't it? But now we'd better get going, otherwise we'll be late and that would never do on our last night."

* * * * *

"Letters!" said Evert, "you think I want to read letters tonight? Are you crazy?"

"No, but I thought I could answer them all for you so you don't have anything to worry about," explained Kate.

Evert laughed, "And how are you going to do

that? You can't speak or read Danish! No, Kate, it is not your problem. Pregan will do what there is to do. You make sure he gets the keys to my house, they are all in the kitchen."

"We found them," said Kate, "but we wondered if Helga has a set."

"No," said Evert, "not unless she take them from there."

"Oh, that's alright then, she didn't have the chance."

"No," said Evert, "I remember when you get bad spirit nobody get a chance to do anything, of that I am always sure. I'm so sorry that you have had trouble while you are in Denmark, if I not be here," he said gesturing around the hospital, "the problem would never be, but maybe it's for the best. You all go home tomorrow and I will be here not knowing when you will return. I know it's my own doing but I feel very down when tomorrow comes."

"Well, think of twelve weeks, I make you a promise that no matter what, we will come back then," said Kate.

"You promise that?" he asked her. She nodded her head. "Well, that is alright, then, I can manage that."

"We are having a party at the house tonight. It's New Year's Eve, so we will drink your beer and wish you were there, but it is your own stupid fault that you're not."

Evert nodded, then said, "You come here early tomorrow morning. I want to spend as much time with you as I can before you leave. I fix it with the nurses."

"You make sure that's all you fix with the nurses," laughed Kate, "well, we'll be off now, back to your house to make merry."

"No," Evert said, "you go back to *our* house, yours and mine!"

* * * * *

Pregan and Jenny came over once they arrived home and it was an evening of toasting Evert's recovery on a regular basis once the alcohol took a hold. Annie went to bed soon after midnight, leaving everyone to continue the party.

The following day, Kate and Paula were astonished that it was twelve noon before Annie woke them. "Why didn't you get us up earlier?" asked Kate.

"Because it was seven o'clock before you went to bed! You were all very drunk!" Annie said, tartly.

"But we have to pack and get to the hospital. I promised we'd be there early. Evert will be on tenterhooks!"

"I have everything ready," said Annie, "there's black coffee downstairs and the only thing left to do is to wash your dirty cups. Once you've showered and dressed, you won't be that late. Anyway, I couldn't let you both stagger into the hospital in the state you would have been in, not after all your remarks about alcohol," Annie finished, pointedly.

"I never get drunk," said Kate.

"Well, you did last night, because your laughing woke me up. I didn't know you liked Connie Francis that much either. If I hear '*Who's Sorry Now*' once more, I'll go mad. You must have played it twenty times. I didn't know if you were singing it to Evert or Helga!"

"Oh, God," said Kate, "I feel fuzzy." She got out of bed. "Is this what they call the shakes? Can you ask Paula to phone Christian and Lis, they're supposed to be coming with us."

"No need," said Annie, brightly, "everybody's still here."

Kate wondered whether everyone had fallen out, because although they passed each other constantly that afternoon, nobody said 'hello' or anything.

Annie really had been busy. The cases were lined up by the front door. She'd even remembered the three pictures that were to be dropped off in the town. The house was immaculate, all signs of the party had gone.

In the end, Kate was the one who hurried everyone along, as they all seemed quite content to sit there all day. She gave the keys to Pregan and they said their goodbyes. Kate was worried. Evert would be really depressed by now, he would have expected them about three hours ago.

"Oh," he said sourly, as they wandered in, "I thought maybe you had gone back to England without coming to see me."

"Well, maybe I didn't think of anybody else except me last night and got drunk," said Kate sharply.

"Kate, Kate, let's not have strong words between us, but it is no good to be sat here, I tried to phone you many times, but the lines they be broke."

"Well, they must be, because the phones never rang at the house," said Kate, looking at the others. They shrugged their shoulders.

"My father will see it is repaired," said Christian.

Kate was surprised to see Pregan appear on the ward. "Get him a chair," said Evert, "this is my best friend!"

However, Pregan didn't sit down, instead he stayed where he was, moving from one foot to the other. Kate wished he would stop, she couldn't concentrate on what she was talking about. It was with some relief when he said eventually, "Me and my children will go to the car now, you can say your goodbyes alone."

"I'll come with you," said Annie, getting up. She wished Evert a speedy recovery. "Annie," said Evert, "you will always be welcome wherever I am."

"I know that, Evert," said Annie, kissing him goodbye.

Kate felt annoyed, but tried not to show it. It was too early to go to the airport but she had no choice but to tell Paula that they shouldn't delay too long because they were dependant on them for a lift. Paula said a tearful goodbye and waved until she had got to the door.

They were alone. "Please come back quickly, Kate, I need you here. I am very sad today," Evert said.

"Well, don't be," said Kate, "I have promised that I will be back here in twelve weeks, but I think now I may make a flying visit in a month's time. Does that make you feel better?"

Evert nodded his head vigorously. Paula came back to the bed. "Come on, Kate, we have to go, everyone is waiting for you."

"Don't cry so," said Evert, taking Paula's hand, "it won't be long before you and me are together again. You like the life in Denmark?"

Paula didn't answer, she just stood there with

the tears rolling down her cheeks. "Ahh, that is answer enough," said Evert, quietly.

Paula came round the bed and linked her arm through Kate's, but Kate released it, "No need for that, Paula," she said briskly, "we are fine about all our arrangements, aren't we?" she asked Evert.

"Yes," he replied, "there will be no problem."

Kate bent and kissed him goodbye, then turned and walked towards the door. When she got outside, she noticed everyone was staring at her. Pregan stepped forward, "Kate, there has been a big fire."

"A fire?" replied Kate, "where?"

"The house, Evert's house. There is nothing left and the police, they need to see you."

Kate felt herself being guided to the car but hardly noticed the drive back. A crowd of people were standing around and she heard a lot of hushed whispers.

She knew she would never forget the sight that greeted her as she stepped out of the car. Could this smoking mass of debris really be all that was left of Evert's beautiful house?

She saw the police approach and speak to Pregan, but it was all in Danish. Turning to her, one of them asked, "You were the last people in the house?"

"Yes," replied Kate.

"Then I need you all to come with me."

"But we were on our way to the airport," said Kate, "we fly back to England today."

"No," corrected the policeman, "not today. It is better that you give me your passports, please." He looked at the documents but didn't give them back. "You come with me, now," he said.

As soon as they arrived at the police station, they were ushered into a room. The policeman left them and they looked at each other in shock and disbelief. Paula was still crying and Annie and Christian were both trying to comfort her.

Annie kept saying, "But I know I switched everything off, I checked."

"How long will we be here?" Paula sobbed.

"I don't know," replied Kate. "Poor Evert," she went on, "how is this going to affect him? How on earth did this happen? There was absolutely nothing wrong when we left. Could it have been a cigarette butt?"

"No," said Annie, "I emptied everything outside while you all sat in the kitchen. I know I checked everything, I know I did."

15

It seemed they were in that room forever. They could see different people coming and going, but they had no contact with anyone. Nobody told them if they were officially arrested, but it was looking that way. They were certainly not free to leave.

Annie looked terrified, her main concern was that she didn't have her passport. Kate had to console her by saying that they weren't in some small dictatorship state in the middle of Africa, but in a country whose laws were similar to their own.

Two men eventually came in and sat down. One spoke perfect English, which relieved Kate.

"We look at the situation, you understand?" he said.

"Yes," replied Kate.

"We believe the cause of the fire to be deliberate."

Kate took Paula's hand. "Deliberate?" she said in disbelief.

"A great deal of gasoline had been used."

"Helga!" they all said at once.

"Helga?" the detective said, "who is Helga?"

Kate heard Paula break into incoherent babble, even she couldn't understand what she was saying. She intervened, putting a comforting hand on Paula's arm. "I will tell you about Helga," she said.

The two men meticulously took notes while Kate talked, then got up. "You excuse me, please, for now you will wait here. Perhaps you will not have to wait so long," he added, smiling for the first time, "as soon as I have news for you I will return. Perhaps if you go into the passageway to wait, you will get some refreshment."

"Are we under arrest?" asked Kate.

"No," he replied, "but you must understand something very serious happened today, there is a connection to you, so we need your presence here."

"Helga wouldn't go this far, would she?" asked Paula, when the men had gone.

"I'd believe anything of her," said Kate. She looked at the others for some kind of confirmation.

Christian nodded. "It is the only explanation," he said.

"My head feels as though it is coming off," said Kate, "we need to sort ourselves out. For the first time in my life, I feel helpless, I don't know the procedures in police stations, but I do need a drink and the toilet. Can you go and explain to them, Christian?"

If they were under arrest, then it wasn't so bad, because they were all treated with the utmost civility and everything was done correctly.

"They never gave us our passports back," said Annie.

Kate put her arm around her shoulders. "Don't worry, they will, we will soon be on our way home. That is the least of my worries I can assure you. What concerns me is Evert's reaction. What is this going to do to him?"

They looked up as the two men appeared with Helga, who smirked when she saw Kate.

"I told you that you not to be in my kitchen," she said.

The men hurried her forward and they watched in disbelief as she walked away from them. Christian was very angry, "I could kill her!" he said.

"Shut up!" whispered Lis, "don't say that here, they might hear you."

Eventually the detectives approached them. "Here are your passports, you are free to leave. The woman has made a full confession, but I say to you she is very sorry."

"Very sorry!" Kate interrupted, "give me a minute with her and she really will be very sorry."

The detective held up his hand, "I don't mean that she is very sorry that she start the fire, I mean she is very sorry that you were all not in the house when it was alight."

"You mean she wanted to kill us?" asked Paula, horrified.

"Yes," he replied, "so you see the charge she face is very serious."

"But why?" asked Kate, "why did she want to hurt us?"

"We have seen Evert Neilson, he is fully aware of what has occurred, maybe he can explain it to you."

"How is he?" asked Kate.

"He is very much in shock, but he is also very relieved that you are all safe." Then, turning to Kate, he said, "When do you intend to go home to England?"

Kate looked at the others, "Well, it is too late today, but tomorrow, if we can get a flight."

"Well," said the detective, "that will be a problem. Maybe we get the paperwork done quickly for the others, but we prefer that you do not leave Denmark until everything is in order."

"You mean we all have to stay here?" asked Kate.

"No, that will not be necessary," he replied, "only you, because it is only you and her that get the trouble together."

Kate felt ill. "I have to get to London as quickly as possible," she looked at the detective, "I have a business to organise."

"Yes, that may be and I extend to you my sympathy, but you must understand there may be a charge of attempted murder and we need to complete our investigations thoroughly. You are in no danger," he added, "because she will be staying with us. Where is the place we can contact you?" he asked, getting his notebook out.

Christian spoke, "At my father's house. You have the address."

"Yes," said the detective, "now you are free to leave, but please keep yourself available, we will be in touch later."

On the way back from the police station everybody was talking but nobody was really taking in what the others were saying. "Can we go to the house?" asked Kate, "I want to see what she did. I want to see what's left."

There were a few people still at the house, but Kate didn't notice anything except the smouldering remains. She thought of Evert's pride when he had shown her his dream, the home he had built for her and she wept. She knew that even if the police gave her permission to get a plane home immediately she couldn't leave him now.

The others were equally shocked and upset and came over to join her. She turned to Christian, "Where did your father go? Do you know?"

"He will be at the house with my mother. If there is trouble they are always together," replied Christian.

"Can we go there?" asked Kate.

"Of course," replied Christian, "that is why I wait for you." He put his arm around her shoulder and led her gently to the car.

Jenny came rushing out of the house the minute she heard the car, "You come," she said, "Pregan, he is in shock."

Pregan was sitting at the table staring into space. He made an effort to get up but slumped back, putting his hands up in a hopeless gesture.

"It was Helga," said Kate.

"Yes," he replied, "I know that. Everybody know now what happened. That woman she is crazy. She could have killed all of you. The police have been here. I go with them to see Evert."

"You did!" said Kate, "how is he?"

"Very relieved that you are safe."

"What did he say about the house?" asked Paula.

"It is never mind about that, there are many more houses in Denmark, he is just happy that you are safe. You were so lucky, if you take the plane tomorrow, you would all be dead now."

"What do you mean? You must tell me what you know. The police have only told us that she tried to kill us," said Kate, sliding into a chair.

"You better have the big brandy," Pregan said, pushing the Martell bottle towards her, "the way it was told to me and Evert, she never think that you travel on New Year's Day but wait 'til the following day, so this morning while you sleep she cut the telephone wire. She think that this morning you go to Jensens as usual, but in the afternoon you all go back to bed before you get ready to see Evert at the night. So you see, there would be no escape for you because she spray the gasoline completely around the house. It spread so quickly you would have known nothing about it."

Nobody said anything for a while - there was complete silence. It must have been about ten minutes before anyone spoke and then it was Annie, "We have been so lucky, why don't you go and see Evert, Kate, don't you think he will need to see that you really are safe and well?"

"Yes," Kate said, "let's all go, you and Jenny, as well," she added, looking at Pregan.

Pregan stood up and hugged her, "Of course we will come with you, my family support you in whatever you need to do."

They walked into the ward and saw a nurse by Evert's bedside. She acknowledged them and left.

"I am so happy you are alive, this is the happiest day of my life, you better be sure of that," announced Evert, delighted to see them.

"Your house is gone, Evert, do you realise that?" asked Kate.

"Yes," he replied, "I know everything, but the most important thing is that you are safe, nothing could replace that. The house, you see, what I build for you, it was my dream to do it, but what good would it be without you? That bloody woman, she came to see me two days ago."

"Helga?" asked Kate, "Helga came to see you? What did she want?"

"She want that I send you and Paula back to England for good, so me and her can go on as before, but I tell her she was crazy. She also tell me why you and her have trouble together, maybe it upset her that I laugh, because she do not know that you are hasty and have spirit - sometimes bad spirit and I think that day she say the wrong thing to you."

"Why didn't you tell me?" asked Kate.

"Why do you need to know?" said Evert, "it was between me and her. I tell her that I always make sure that she was provided for, but there was no place for her in the house because it is also yours and you would not like that she be there. She look upset but then she gave me a kiss on my head and I think that maybe she accept what was to be, but I never believe that the crazy woman would try to kill you and burn my house down!"

"Evert," said Kate, "would you mind if we go now and come back later? I need a bed otherwise I'm going to pass out. I feel positively ill."

Jenny said, "Kate, there is plenty of room at our house, we go there now."

"Yes," said Evert, "everything is alright here, you never make yourself ill, but you get rest and come back quickly, you promise that?"

Kate just nodded her head and allowed herself to be led away. Jenny spoke, "Pregan and I want you to know that you can stay with us as long as you need to, we have no problem." Annie apologised but said she just wanted to get home.

"Don't worry," Kate assured her, "I'll make sure you're both on your way tomorrow. I will probably cope much better once I know you are safely on your way."

Annie looked relieved but it was short-lived, because once they got inside the house Paula made her shock announcement. "If I don't get a return ticket to come back here, I'm not going!" she stated.

Kate drew herself up in front of her daughter, "There really is no need for you to be here. Your place is in England with your mother. I will return as soon as possible and keep you up-to-date in the meantime. You cannot stay here. You can visit during the holidays but you must go home."

"None of you can make me!" declared Paula.

Kate was astonished. She'd never seen Paula like this and she didn't think Annie had either. "I don't want to make you do anything, Paula," she said, "but how do you suppose you'd earn your living here? You have no training for anything and you don't even speak the language. Besides, what about Annie? Do you want to leave your mother on her own?"

"No," replied Paula, "I could keep going back to see you, couldn't I, Mum?"

Annie just looked at her and didn't answer.

"You need money to keep going between England and Denmark. Have you thought about that?" asked Kate.

"Well, I have my allowance from you, I'll use

that."

"Let me tell you something, Paula. Annie and I have had our own agreement for years, your education has been paid for, together with any of your needs, until you could earn your own money. We have already spoken about what you were going to earn as a waitress."

Kate realised immediately what she had said and clapped her hand to her mouth, but it was too late.

Annie was looking from her to Paula, "Would someone please tell me what's going on," she asked, in such a small voice, you could barely hear it.

"Annie, please believe me, for twenty years, well, fifteen anyway, I have never kept a secret from you. Paula has something to tell you. I promised her I would be there with her, but I say sorry to both of you, because it is just not possible today, I cannot take anymore. Whatever needs to be said it will have to be done without me, I need some air and I need it now."

"Kate, do you mind if I come with you?" She looked around and saw the concern in Lis' face. She went over to her and took her hand, "Lead the way, Lis," she said, "perhaps you can tell me where I'm going."

Kate had never known anyone who was blind before. She always felt sympathy towards them, but she wondered if not being able to notice everyday occurrences gave them the added power of more understanding of situations. The common sense attitude of this girl was far in excess of her years. "Where did you gain your experience of people?" asked Kate.

"I have to listen," replied Lis, "but I never learn anything listening to myself."

"You cope remarkably well, don't you," observed Kate.

"Yes," said Lis, "sometimes it is difficult, but I just have to do it."

Kate stopped in her tracks and looked at her. "Why do we stay still?" asked Lis.

"Because you are the inspiration I need!" replied Kate.

"I am?" said Lis, happily.

"Yes," said Kate, "you most certainly are. Come on, Lis, we'll go back and face the world."

As they approached the house, Kate noticed the police car. She was pleased, because she didn't really want to face an in-depth discussion concerning anybody's future plans. As they went into the house, she noticed that Paula and Annie were sitting together, holding each other's hands.

"Did you think I'd run away?" she asked the detective.

"Maybe if I was you I'd seriously consider it, but

I can assure you that you have nothing to worry about, only documentation. Your family, they tell me they go back to England tomorrow."

Kate looked at Paula and Annie. Paula smiled, "Yes, my mother and I will be in London tomorrow evening."

The detective continued, "It is therefore important that we complete these two statements tonight. You will be here for a few days more?" he enquired of Kate.

"Yes," replied Kate, "about a week, if that's alright?"

The detective nodded. Kate listened as Paula and Annie gave their versions of what had occurred. Never in her wildest dreams had she believed that their lives would be changed forever, although she was aware that they would never go back to the way they were and she didn't know for sure if they all blamed her, but at times she felt like the one who shot Bambi.

Evert could accuse her of misreading that cablegram all those years ago, now he could add that if she hadn't thrown Helga out, he would still have his house.

Annie would believe she had been lying to her and making secret deals with Paula, who in turn would always hold it against her that she hadn't been told the truth from day one and would think she was trying to keep her away from Christian.

At least the redundancies had been delayed for about a week, but recession didn't physically sit behind a desk, so when the time came for her to tell them their services were no longer required, it was she who was going to have to face the accusations and shoulder the responsibilities. She just wished her mum and dad were here.

"Can I interrupt a moment?" They all turned and looked at her. "If I'm not needed, I wondered if I might borrow your car, Christian, to go and see Evert?"

He got up and smiled at her, "Of course, Kate. Shall I come with you?" he asked.

"No. Thanks, but I need some time on my own," she replied. She felt a weight lift from her shoulders the moment the wheels began to turn. She could have driven for hours but running away would solve nothing. Now Evert had been on his own for a few hours he would be over the initial shock and she would soon be aware of his real reaction.

Evert did not see Kate approaching. He was oblivious to everything, but as soon as he realised she was there, he came to immediately. "You get good sleep, Kate?" he asked her.

"No," she replied.

"I did not sleep either," he said, "I think only

that I am glad you saw the house I build for you before it is gone forever."

"No," said Kate, "not forever. Is it insured?"

Evert nodded his head, "What is the insurance money? It is nothing to what I want you to have."

"Now look," Kate said, taking his hand, "we never agreed all those years ago that you would build it on your own, we were always going to build it together, remember? So now, we can!"

He looked at her hopelessly, "I am old now, Kate, I have many broken bones . . ."

"Which can mend," she interrupted, "you're fifty years of age, Evert, not seventy, for goodness sake." He laughed and Kate continued, "and this time I will be here with you to instruct the builders in what to do."

"You promise that?" Evert asked her.

"Of course, I will," replied Kate, hoping it was a promise she would be able to keep.

"Then maybe it can be done," said Evert.

"Don't worry," Kate said, "everything will be alright now."

"Oh, Kate! You always make me happy."

"I try," she said, getting up, "but now I have to get Paula and Annie back to England, that is the first priority."

"Yes," Evert said, "you need to do that. The Paula and Christian problem must be put on hold."

* * * * *

Paula was sitting on the bench outside the house talking to Christian when Kate finally arrived back and although she was well wrapped up, it was absolutely freezing. "What on earth are you doing out here?" Kate asked them.

"I'm waiting for you, Kate," Paula answered.

Kate felt that if she had to face one more problem today, her mind would snap for good. "Kate, I'm sorry for the way I've said things to you these last couple of weeks. You must think I'm a spoilt brat."

"Is Annie alright?" asked Kate.

"Yes," replied Paula, "don't worry about either of us, just come back to London as soon as you can."

Kate hugged Paula to her, "Oh, Paula, I needed that. You've had a lot to cope with, I know that, but you never know, things might work out at the end of the day."

She watched as Paula put her arm through Christian's and said, "I know it will, no doubt about that."

It was pure relief when Kate saw them off at Karoup Airport the following day. Paula had said a tearful farewell to Christian, they had both seen

Evert before they left, but Kate was past caring what had been said. Now she and Annie were on their way, it was one less problem. The police needed to see her, but they could wait until she'd spent the next two days sleeping, because after the past twenty four hours, it was all she could do to keep her eyes open.

16

Kate was aware of Jenny bending over her, "Kate," she said, gently, "the police are here to see you."

She looked at the clock, was it really ten o'clock? She jumped out of bed, "I should have been at the hospital four hours ago!" she said.

"What? At six in the morning?" laughed Jenny, "Kate, it's ten o'clock in the morning, you have slept for seventeen hours!"

Kate couldn't believe it and apologised

immediately. However, when she went downstairs, it seemed everyone was content to wait. Pregan had served them with the traditional morning beverage - a bottle of Carlsberg.

Although there wasn't much difference between England and Denmark, the main one was the way in which people from each country made you welcome in their home. In England, you put the kettle on and made a cup of tea, whilst here in Denmark, they gave you a bottle of beer and if you were really unlucky, a cup of coffee with a glass of old Danish.

Kate had only tasted it once and it had to be the most horrible stuff. It was a standing joke that if Denmark were ever invaded, the Danes would serve each aggressor with a bottle of Schnapps and the old Danish drink. The problem would be solved in twenty-four hours.

"Come, Kate, take some coffee and food and relax, we have plenty of time." Jenny looked towards the detective, who nodded in agreement, "There is no problem, it is only the formalities we have to clear up."

"Where is Helga?" Kate asked.

"She is sick in the head, there is big mental problems, which the doctors have to deal with but she is no danger to you, you have my word on that. Eventually there be time to be spend in court but I feel that will be a very long time away."

The statement took about two hours, the detective explaining that although he spoke perfect English, it was more difficult to write it. They had letters she didn't have and there were extra letters in the English alphabet anyway. "Your English language is difficult to understand when I first start to learn it, because you have so many meanings for the same word."

"Yes," Kate agreed, "but I hope that you understand I must get back to London because I have a business to run."

"After I go from here," the detective said, "you are free to leave. There will be no problem."

Kate smiled at him, his favourite phrase seemed to be 'no problem'. She turned to Pregan, "Can I use your phone, please? I need to ring my office. I will pay for the call," she added.

"Kate, you do whatever you like," Pregan said, "there is no need for you to ask, we are here for you."

Jenny took her into the room furthest away from the noise, because the detectives and Pregan appeared to be getting drunk already.

Kate rang Julia first. "Kate, where are you?" Julia asked her, "we have been expecting you all morning!"

Without going into detail, Kate told her that

she had been delayed but would be back in London within forty-eight hours.

"I'm glad," said Julia, "John Kitchen needs to speak to you urgently, I'll just transfer you. Oh, hang on, he's here now, anyway."

"Kate," said John, "we have had our overdraft facility withdrawn and replaced with a £100,000 loan."

"Yes," said Kate, calmly, "I arranged it."

"Is that because I fouled up with that new account?" John asked.

"Yes," she replied.

"Do you realise that the repayments are £2,166 per month?" he asked.

"Yes, I do, for the next seven years, but what you don't know is that my house has been used to secure it, so it is important that there is always funds available to cover it."

"I think we will be safe now," John said.

"What do you mean, 'you think'?" asked Kate, "we'd better be, or I lose my house."

"Kate, I need to talk to you urgently and not over the phone. I will meet you at Heathrow."

"Can it wait until then?" she asked him.

"Oh yes," he said, "but there are things happening at the moment that could be to our disadvantage."

"Not another scam?" she asked, alarmed.

"Oh, no, nothing like that, but we need to be on our toes, that's all."

Kate replaced the receiver and wondered how Evert would react when she told him she was going home. She still felt in shock herself and would be more than a little glad to get away from here.

When the police left, she told Pregan and Jenny what she intended to do.

"I understand," said Pregan, "but maybe you get hard time making Evert feel the same way. You must tell him the truth and not give him false hope. I think he believe you stay here for good now."

Kate was prepared for anything as she walked onto the ward. "Oh Kate, you are here. You know, *mine skat,* if I not see you everyday, I think my life would be finished."

"I'm going home," she stated, "I need to be there. My business is in trouble and I cannot afford to be away from it any longer. You must make an effort to get well again quickly, then once the insurance is settled you can look forward to rebuilding."

"It will not be as easy as that," said Evert.

"Why? What is there to stop you?" Kate asked.

"Well, first of all, I don't think the insurance will settle quickly because the fire was started deliberately. Also my boat, I get into trouble over that."

"Why?" Kate asked, "what's wrong with that?"

"I owe 250,000 krona on it and if I cannot fish I may not be able to pay and I think the company who lend me the money be glad to take the boat back because it is worth twice that. Then there is my stamps," he continued.

"What stamps?"

"The stamps that I collect since I was eleven years old."

"What about them, Evert?"

"They were worth about £50,000. My plan was to send them to Phillips in London. That was my pension, but now they are gone."

"Didn't you have them insured?" asked Kate.

"No, I never do it."

"So tell me what money you have got, then," Kate said.

"I have nothing, only the insurance claim."

"You have no savings?"

"I have about 20,000 krona, that is about £2,000 in English money, but my tax was due at the start of January, so that must be paid. There is nothing left for me, only you."

She didn't believe it, but when she looked at his face, the hopelessness was quite genuine, she realised. She drove away from the hospital damning

Helga. If she ever got her hands on that woman they'd go straight around her throat.

Pregan came out to meet her. He put his arms around her, "Come Kate, we think you get into trouble with Evert."

"No, I didn't," she said, "but without me, he doesn't appear to have a reason to help himself, he has a 'what's the point' attitude."

"Yes," said Pregan, "me and Jenny speak of this. You are very welcome here, any of your family. You stay as long as you like, but Evert is a proud man and I never believe that he want to live with other people. He will be away from the hospital in about twelve weeks, maybe."

"Well, what do you suggest I do?" Kate asked, "take him back to England with me? That would be impossible, I could never look after him - I have to go to work. I am needed there now," she added.

"Yes, we realise that Evert put pressure on you, maybe without really knowing it. You never intend to stay here for so long, did you Kate?"

"No," she agreed. Pregan's voice was so understanding that she felt tears prickle her eyes. He squeezed her shoulder. "Why do you not rent a private apartment, so that he has somewhere to live when he comes out of hospital? Not here, but in a place called Herring, his club is there and he has many friends in that place. Do you intend to come here regularly?" he asked Kate.

"Well, yes, but only for the odd weekend for now."

"Then that is ideal, because Herring is only ten minute's drive away from Karoup, fifteen at most."

"Shall I ask him? Do you think he will be well enough?"

"The sooner the better, Kate, because I believe that Evert think that now he has found you, everything will fall into place, but his idea is that it happen in Denmark. Maybe you like the English way of life better and do not want to change, so now you have to tell him the truth of your feelings."

Jenny smiled at Kate as she entered the house, then she came forward and took her hand, "My family like that you stay here. I would like it also but we know that you have to give yourself the chance to be a free spirit again."

"Oh, Jenny, the pressure just seems to have left me, all I need to do is convince Evert."

* * * * *

"You do that for me?" said Evert.

"Yes," said Kate, "Pregan will show me how, so there shouldn't be a problem."

"Yes, there is a problem," said Evert, sadly, "to

get an apartment and furnish it you need money, all I have is black smoke, nothing more, but it is my own stupid fault."

"Yes," said Kate, "you could have killed yourself, or even worse, someone else, you realise that, don't you?"

"Yes, Kate, I know that."

She could feel herself bristling, "It's easy for you to say you know that, but why take the car at all if you knew you were going to drink? I'm not sorry for you, in fact, I feel that every drunk driver should be thrown in jail."

"Well, maybe you get your wish because the law in Denmark be that every drunk driver does get put in jail and maybe when I get free from here that is where I have to go."

"Good!" said Kate, "they should take your driving licence away from you too so that you cannot drive a car again."

"Yes, I think that they do that as well," said Evert.

"Well, so be it, because the likes of you destroy families."

"Kate, do not be so angry with me," pleaded Evert.

"I'm not anything with you, I just believe that all drunk drivers have no thought for anybody but themselves, but I thank God that in your case it is only you who is paying the price. Although I am paying too, because I have to stay here and help you."

"I am not making you stay," Evert said, sullenly.

"No," agreed Kate, "but where will you be if I don't, so don't look at me as though I'm your worst enemy, because at the moment you need all the friends you can get. Every time I meet you, you seem to be in hospital. Oh, sorry," she added immediately, "I didn't mean that, you did save my life, after all."

He laughed, "I think about that, also, maybe it be a good omen. The first time I meet you and the last time I meet you was in the hospital bed."

Kate nodded, the tension between them over. "Now," she said, "perhaps Christian knows where I can go to find an apartment?"

"Yes," replied Evert, "I think he will, in fact, I'm sure he will. Did he hear from Paula since she went back to England?"

"Not that I know of," replied Kate.

"Well, I would prepare yourself that they will be in touch with each other, in fact, you can be sure of it."

Christian was more than happy to go to Herring. Kate had her own thoughts about how he knew so much about private housing. He knew where the offices were to register your name and the rules that when you reached the top of the list you were offered first refusal.

As it turned out, there was nothing available immediately, but they advised her to ring daily. Oh, well, another week away from the office wouldn't do that much harm. She was in a catch twenty-two situation and she didn't like it one bit.

John Kitchen assured her that what he had to discuss could wait, he now had everything under control, but perhaps they could think about reducing their overheads once she got back.

Reducing the overheads - that had to be the understatement of the year. Half the company would have been nearer the mark. She thought of the thirteen people in her office, how much time was spent a year walking round with pieces of paper. It was funny how you never noticed things until you had to.

It was exactly two weeks since starting her search that an apartment was offered to her - not in Herring itself, but in a large village called Sunds. It was ideal, it had a bus route into Herring and was even nearer to Karoup airport.

Her outburst with Evert appeared to have worked miracles because instead of looking depressed at the situation, he was more than happy to co-operate.

17

Kate and Christian toured the main street. Yes, there was everything here: supermarket, barbers, bank, library, post office, garage, florist, stationers and lots of other little shops dotted in between. The church was set back and all the roads seemed to lead to it.

They found the apartment. It was one of four. From the outside, it looked like a large white house. It was surrounded by green fields and new bungalows were scattered around the landscape in the distance. The view would be nice, thought Kate.

There was a large tiled entrance hall, with four separate post boxes on the wall. Stairs leading to the two apartments on the first floor were over to one side. One of the two ground floor flats had a shiny nameplate on the door, the other was empty.

Inside, the apartment was extremely tasteful with wooden floors throughout. There was a spacious bathroom on the left by the front door, while to the right was a small cloakroom. Walking forward brought you into the large lounge, which had French windows opening onto a patio.

The kitchen was small but would accommodate a table and chairs and was fully fitted. There were two bedrooms and all that was needed here were the beds, because they were also fully fitted with lovely units and wardrobes.

The rent for the apartment was £800 per month, which was expensive for what it was, but Kate thought she could live quite comfortably here. However, she was not so sure about Evert, because the whole apartment would have fitted in his old lounge.

Christian broke into her thoughts, "I would like this for myself and Paula," he said.

"Are you and Paula in touch?" she asked.

"Oh yes," he replied, with a broad smile, "most days. You see," he couldn't wait to tell her, "we love each other, Lis and I tell her not to be afraid that you find out, but you have to know that she is afraid that she make her mother very sad."

"Christian, I've known for a couple of weeks now, but you will have to wait until I get back to England, then I will talk to Paula and Annie. Will you wait until then?" she asked him.

"Yes, of course," he replied, "but Kate, you will not try to talk Paula out of anything, will you?"

"No, cross my heart, I already tried that once."

"Thank you. Kate, you are not angry that we love each other?"

Kate gave him a big smile, "No, I'm not, but Annie is different. Oh, she won't be angry, but she lives for Paula and I don't know how she'd cope without her."

"Yes," said Christian, "Paula is afraid of that also, but we belong together, I will get an apartment like this for us and I will go to work to pay for it and we will be very happy."

Kate laughed, "How else do you think you're going to get one without a job, but seriously, Christian, don't take into account the allowance that Paula gets from me, because things are not so good in England at the moment, in fact, they are not good at all."

"Kate, you do not have to worry, I can work many hours to provide for me and Paula. £800 per month is heavy but you can get a nice apartment for £350 per month, you know."

"That's the equivalent of three week's wages in England," Kate said.

"Ah, but here in Denmark it is only one week, that is the difference. Can we go and tell them we take this?" he asked.

"Yes," she said.

Christian came over and kissed her forehead, "Now I not be frightened to register my own name, then you can go home to England more quickly, because we look after Evert."

"You two have it all worked out, don't you!" said Kate, with a smile.

"Yes, but it is better now that you know."

It was better for Kate, she had to admit, but she wondered about Annie. She would be distraught when she heard the news.

They drove to Herring and accepted the apartment, only to discover that they needed a deposit of three month's rent - £2,400. Kate arranged with the woman that it could be paid within four days and was allowed to sign the agreement.

"You think it correct that you sign?" asked Christian, "maybe Evert not like it there, what if he want to go to Herring instead?"

"Well, let's go and find out, shall we? And if he doesn't want it he will have to go and look for himself."

"But what will you do with it?" Christian asked her, "because you sign that lease for the minimum of one year."

"Well, we'd better just hope he likes it," she said.

* * * * *

"I cannot get it," said Evert, "because I do not have the money to pay for it. Sunds is a nice place to live but I have to get something very cheap until my insurance is paid."

"What bank do you use?" Kate asked him.

"The Unibank, why?" Evert replied.

"I will transfer some money into it, then you can pay me back once you are paid out."

"No!" exploded Evert, "you never do that! I don't want your money?"

"I don't intend giving it to you," she replied, "but maybe it is better for me to get some money over here instead of where it is. Yes, give me your bank account number, maybe we can kill two birds with one stone."

"Do you know what you are doing?" he asked her.

"Yes," she replied, "I know exactly what I'm doing. Christian will take me back to Sunds, won't you?"

"Of course, Kate, whatever you want."

She didn't know how the system worked, but she would feel safer if £30,000 out of her own private account was over here. All she needed was to sign a transfer at the Unibank in Sunds.

That phone call from Evert had altered her life, and Paula's and Annie's too, she realised. If she could turn back the clock, she wouldn't have come in the first place, but maybe it was meant to be and her dad was right, she should have her personal money somewhere else.

It took two weeks to get everything organised. She got a lot of pleasure shopping for furnishings and ornaments to make the apartment look attractive. She was surprised at how quickly the telephone was connected, it took hours instead of days - which was a blessing, because she could conduct her business from there until she was ready to leave.

Christian didn't leave her side, he was her personal chauffeur and took her into Herring every day. He knew where the best prices could be found for the same items and saved her a lot of money. When the shops closed, he would drive her to the hospital to see Evert and then take her home.

Eventually, the apartment was finally habitable. Kate stood back and admired it. "We didn't do a bad job," she said to Christian.

"I think it's very tasteful," he agreed.

"Tell me about it, Kate?" asked Lis.

Kate put her arms around the girl, "But you know everything we bought," she said.

"I know, but I need to know where everything is."

Kate hugged her close, "I'll make some coffee and then if it takes me all day, you'll know every last detail."

She couldn't wait to tell Evert that it was all finished and that she was going home. But she didn't get the chance, because he had some news for her. Apparently, the doctors were delighted with his progress and were prepared to allow him home now he had someone to care for him.

Kate put on a pleased expression, but she felt sick. It seemed to be one thing after another and it appeared that every time she prepared to go home, something else stopped her.

She didn't believe in fate. She thought that what happened to you was your own doing. However, recent events meant that she was beginning to change her mind about that.

Kate decided to get Evert settled in and then go home, no matter what happened. The doctors said he would need prolonged treatment as an out-patient and also future operations, but the medical departments in Denmark would have to provide that.

John Kitchen had assured her that everything was now under control in London, but he had hinted that he would be very glad to see her back in the office.

Just let me get on that plane, thought Kate, but she hadn't bargained on Paula.

18

Kate decided to move into the apartment. Evert was coming out of hospital in about a week's time and she felt it would be more comfortable if the place appeared to be lived in.

There was the hundred mile round trip to the hospital to be faced every day, but it was worth the effort, because at least it was private.

Kate missed her nights alone. She missed the peace and quiet of her own house. She could be called selfish but after living on her own for nearly sixteen years, it was what she was used to.

She had to get to know the people in the shops

in Sunds. She enjoyed the walk there which took her through a small avenue of trees, past the church and out onto the main street.

The shopkeepers always acknowledged her with a smile and those who spoke English went out of their way to make her feel welcome in the village. She appreciated the woman next door who would knock every day with two fresh savoury buns and two sweet ones. Kate had invited her in for coffee, but as neither spoke a word of the other's language, it was hard work trying to be friendly.

Yes, thought Kate, in about ten year's time I could live in Denmark. Not in Sunds, though, because once Evert was on his feet and the insurance claim was paid, he would start rebuilding. She would visit regularly though and really enjoy it.

She was curled up with a cup of coffee, alone at last and content with her thoughts, when the phone rang. It was Annie. Kate started to say how lovely it was to hear from her, but was cut short.

"Kate, I'm sorry to bother you, I know you have enough problems, but Paula is involved with that boy in Denmark and I don't know what to do."

"Yes," said Kate, "I know all about it."

"Oh, you do," said Annie, quietly, "you never mentioned it to me, you never thought to let me know. I thought we had a better understanding than that."

"Annie, please don't be upset, because I only just found out myself and as soon as I come home, you were the first person I was going to see."

"Oh, Kate, I'm so confused. It's not your fault. I know you haven't encouraged her. She wants to forget about university and move over there. What can I do, Kate?"

"Don't worry, Annie, I'll try to make her see sense when I get back."

"You won't though, all her stuff is packed and ready to go."

"Go where?" asked Kate, already knowing the answer.

"To Denmark," replied Annie, "she's intent on coming over this weekend."

"What?" Kate almost shouted, "you have to stop her. Let me speak to her."

"It's no use, Kate, she's not here. She was very quiet all the way back and although she put on a brave face, I knew deep down there was something wrong. So I sat her down and she told me she didn't want to hurt me but she had to be with that boy. She says he wants to live with her. Kate, she never even mentioned marriage, where have I gone wrong? I'm so upset. I don't know what to do."

"Annie," said Kate, "you sound like my mother, both of you never did anything wrong and as far as her marrying Christian, perhaps it would be better if she lives with him first to find out what it's all about. She's not really experienced on that side of things, is she? You never know, she might want to come back with me. Look how my life's changed these last few weeks."

"I've lost her, Kate, I know I have," Annie said, miserably.

"Well, you were going to sometime, weren't you? Imagine if she met a boy from Newcastle, you wouldn't think it was a problem to go and visit her, would you?"

"No," said Annie, "but that's in England."

"Well, you can travel quicker by plane to Denmark than you can by train to Newcastle and make no mistake, Annie, you and Paula will never separate, you think too much of each other. Don't let her leave on bad terms."

She replaced the receiver, she knew Annie would have liked to continue the conversation, but there really wasn't much point. She looked at the ceiling and thought, if there is someone up there who likes me, please give me some sign as to what I should do. Surely nothing else could go wrong. More had happened in the last few weeks than had occurred during her entire life. She was sure of only one thing, that Annie shouldn't be the loser in all this mess.

The following night, Kate told Evert and waited for his reaction. Christian had, as usual, driven her to the hospital, but she hadn't mentioned her phone call with Annie, so he was completely taken by surprise.

If there was one person who could be relied on to be straight, it was Evert. Kate knew she would abide by what he said, as he would take every aspect of the situation into account before making a decision.

"Kate," he said, "look at me. I know about Christian and Paula. My eyes see it, but I not really say because I do not want your life to alter until you want it to and if Paula came to live here with Christian you will come and see her, but really I want it to be me you come to see. That is my problem with the situation. As for her and Christian, I do not think that it is our business to tell them what to do. We must help them."

"Thank you, Evert," Christian said, sounding very relieved. Evert ignored him.

"Now there is Annie, a good woman, but I know that the older she get, the harder it will be to let Paula go, but I see Paula and Annie together and I know the girl will never let her mother be unhappy for long time, you can be sure of that. Today she is in love, so let them be, you want that they be apart for twenty years like you and me?"

"No, of course not," said Kate, "but I feel so sorry for Annie."

"You go and visit Annie," said Evert, "I know you need to go back to England, everyday you come and visit me but I always think I tell you to go tomorrow because I need you too. Maybe I feel more secure when I get to Sunds. I know you will come back, I would trust you with my life, so there will be no problem. Anyway," he added, "I have your money and your daughter."

Kate laughed, "Yes, you didn't do so bad in a couple of months, did you? Where will she live?" she went on.

"With me, of course," said Evert. He looked at Christian, "I do not want that you live together until you are sure about each other. I want to see it for myself. I want that Paula know the Danish way of life, it is much different to the English way."

"Not that much," protested Kate.

"Yes," said Evert, "it will be important that she learn the language. Then, when she get a job she and Christian can make it together. She must get a work permit, too. There is a lot to be done, but I will take care of it."

"You can't even walk!" said Kate.

"No," agreed Evert, "but I can speak. Now, once Paula gets here, you go back to England, maybe it will be more easy for you and I will wait for you to return. It will be black not seeing you but I can wait - I have waited for the past twenty years."

Kate knew that one day soon she was going to have to make a decision. It could never be the love she had known with Evert before, but there was something, because she felt so comfortable with him. She couldn't even call him her best friend, she just slotted in with him.

There had been no other man in her life. Years ago she could have got involved with Alex but he always accused her of putting up a wall between them. They had always had deep feelings for each other but those had been buried a long time ago when he had married suddenly and ensured that no other woman would come between him and his wife.

She had, over the years, accepted the odd invitation to stay at his house and never failed to notice that he and his wife spoke as one. Pregan and Jenny had the same commitment to each other, but in a different way. Their's was the way she and Evert used to have. Could they return to that? She doubted it, but who could predict what lay ahead?

She enjoyed her business lunches and she enjoyed meeting the people she had known for years. They always made time for her. But what really excited her was the challenge of securing a new contract against all other competition. She still had that fighting spirit in her and she didn't want to lose it.

Of course, there had been times when she'd wondered what it was all for, all this business hassle, but deep down she knew the answer, she did it for herself, because it made her feel good.

Evert had been talking to Christian, but now he tapped her hand, "You are deep in thought, *mine skat.* What you think about, Kate?"

She smiled at him, "Oh, nothing really, I was just mulling things over in my mind."

"I know," he said, "but soon you have to answer yourself with the truth. Go to England Kate and get your mind in order. Some days I not feel so good, but every day I feel a little better than before. I never be so ill I cannot keep everything in order."

"It wasn't so bad for you, was it?" Kate remarked to Christian as they made their way home.

"Oh, I knew it wouldn't be," he replied, "because before he knew about Paula, Lis and me were the children he never had. It has been like that for years, but it was even better for us because there are things in your life you be afraid to tell your parents about, but we could always go to him and he would break the problem a different way to them. Lis and me were always feeling very comfortable when we were with him."

"So when you heard about Paula, did you think

of her as a sister?"

"No, never a sister. I see her before I know she is Evert's daughter. I was sat in my parents' house and Lis walked in with this girl. I feel the excitement I have never felt in my life before. I don't know where Lis found her, I think maybe she just walk out of the sea, but I know my life changed at that moment."

"What do you think about her living with Evert? Don't you want to get your own apartment together?" she asked him.

"Yes, of course," he replied, "I like that we get one today, but Paula need Annie as much as Annie need her, so they need to see each other every three months. Paula and me we already speak of that. It is expensive to travel to England, but Paula would be unhappy not to do it, so the apartment will have to wait. She stay with Evert and I with my family. That is alright because every day we can be together once she is in Denmark."

Kate felt a surge of relief flow through her. She was more than happy with the situation now that they had stopped to take Annie into consideration, because the last thing she wanted was for her to feel left out.

19

They watched as Paula came down the steps of the aircraft. Christian's face was flushed with excitement. Lis stood with Kate, "Today," she stated, "I feel happy because I get a sister. Paula and me we go to the bar and disco together."

Christian overheard her, "Well, it will never be without me!"

"Ok," Lis said happily, "we will let you come with us."

Paula arrived. She only had a few steps to walk around the barrier, but Christian lifted her over. She flung her arms around his neck and then came to Kate's side. "I'm so sorry, Kate, but you must understand that I'm in love with Christian and I don't want to be apart from him."

Kate hugged her hard, "I understand," she said.

"Then you're not angry with me?" Paula asked.

"No, you remind me of myself when I was your age," admitted Kate.

"Oh, Kate, Mum said you were annoyed and you were going to talk me out of it. She couldn't even bring herself to wish me luck when I left, she just cries all the time. I cried as well, but then I realised that whenever I decided to go it would still be the same, so I might as well be where I want to be now as in another three year's time."

"Well," said Kate, "you seem to have it all worked out, but as I told you on the phone, your father will insist you live with him, on your own," she added.

"Yes, we know that, don't we, Christian?" she said.

"What about your education?" asked Kate.

"What about it?" answered Paula, "once I learn the language, maybe I can go to school here, but maybe I want to be a housewife and look after Christian. It is here that I belong, Kate, maybe you do as well."

"Oh, no! Not me! I love London and Liverpool, that's where my roots are. Don't worry about

Annie, I'll make sure she's safe and secure."

Christian interrupted them, "Don't you think we'd be better speaking when we get home? We are in the middle of the airport."

Kate looked around her, they must look an odd bunch, just standing there. People would be wondering what they were waiting for. They moved out towards the exit.

Once at the apartment, Paula unpacked her cases and took over all the wardrobe space. She's definitely staying, thought Kate, she must have paid a fortune in excess luggage.

"Paula," she said, "this is going to be a problem because although your father hasn't got any clothes at the moment, once he starts buying again, half of your clothes are going to end up back in the suitcases."

"Stop worrying, Kate," Paula laughed, "I will look after things until you come back."

"Oh, Paula, what about Annie? She will want to come and see you and where could she stay in here?"

Paula said quietly, "I don't think Mum will come to Denmark again. She's withdrawn into herself. Maybe when she's had time to think about it, she'll be alright. I promised her I'd phone tonight and then every Sunday. I hope she has accepted my going," she finished, sadly.

"Hey, don't forget I'm going to miss you as well," said Kate.

"Yes, but you have other things to occupy yourself with, she only has me. I have always known that. I've never joined in school holidays or sports' days away, but no, no matter what, I could not be away from Christian."

Christian moved to her side and said, "Kate, I look after her for the rest of my life. You never have to worry about that."

"I know, Christian," said Kate, "I know you will, but we have to make Annie feel the same as me, don't we? Anyway, let's go and see your father, Paula, then I'm going to get myself a plane ticket, pack my cases and go home to England."

Evert was delighted to see his daughter, the pride shone out of him as he looked at her. Kate tried to stop her selfish thoughts, but was glad he'd be occupied getting to know this wonderful girl, because her departure wouldn't be so traumatic. Oh, she knew she had some unpleasant tasks awaiting her back at the office, but at the moment, she was counting the hours until she boarded the plane home. Little did anyone know it would be months before she could even think about going anywhere.

"Well," she heard herself say, "I need to go and book myself a ticket. If I can get a flight today, I will be taking it."

"So soon?" asked Evert, in dismay.

"Yes, the sooner I get there, the sooner I will get back." She kissed him and noticed there were tears in his eyes, but he didn't offer any excuse for them. She knew how he felt and if things had been different she could have been persuaded to stay at that moment.

They called in at a travel agent in Lemvej and she used her credit card to ensure she had a seat on the flight that would leave in three hours. It would be nine o'clock in the evening before she got to Heathrow. Julia was more than willing to come and meet her but phoned to say that John Kitchen would be meeting her instead.

They waited in the same café at Karoup where it all began. Kate was half expecting to see Pregan arriving with some news that would delay her departure once again, but nothing happened and it was with great relief that she settled back into her seat on the plane.

Kate slept most of the way home and the announcement that passengers should fasten their seatbelts as they were just ten minutes out of Heathrow sounded like music to her ears. She liked Denmark but she loved England. She couldn't wait to get her feet on the tarmac.

She was one of the first through Customs and

saw John's anxious face looking for her. He helped her with her luggage and she settled in the car, surrounded by suitcases. John mentioned how tired she looked.

"Well," she responded, "there was certainly plenty to do. It wasn't my idea of a holiday."

"Don't think you've come back to one here," John warned her, "everybody is talking of us going into recession and a deep one at that. Just look at all the houses for sale," he said, pointing to the many bill boards they passed. "The parties I went to over Christmas were alright to start with, but I always seemed to end up in a corner with about half a dozen business people who all had the same story. The thing that depressed me, which I didn't want to mention over the phone, was that Alex is thinking of selling up and going to live in Jersey."

Kate felt a cold shudder pass through her, "Has the story been confirmed?" she asked.

"No. I can't find out any more. The person who told me that had had far too much to drink anyway. He said it was top secret and he'd deny telling me if the news got out."

"How much business do we do with Alex exactly?"

"A little under a third," he replied.

"You know I should have made cutbacks before Christmas," Kate told him, "but I didn't want to do it then, because the timing wouldn't have been very good, would it? But it's the first thing I have to do tomorrow."

"Well," said John, "if what I have told you turns out to be true, those cuts will be very deep, because you will have lost one third of your sales and in this economic climate you won't replace them overnight."

"Coming in?" she asked, as they drew up outside her house. John appeared a little taken aback by the offer, because in all the years she had employed him, this was the first time he'd even seen the house.

"I like my privacy," she explained, "but in the next few months I'm going to need a lot of help with an assortment of things, so I think it's about time I confided in someone."

He looked surprised, "And you trust me after I let that credit run wild?"

"Yes," she said, "I do. You were up against a load of crooks and unless you are one yourself, you don't think the way they do. I could say you were very naive, but that's all."

"Kate," John said, "I was so frightened that if I stopped their order they wouldn't pay us at all. I knew we were in trouble with them and I did delay, but we were up to just over £100,000 then, but because of the delay I had no contract at all, so

I renewed it by sending them a small consignment. They sent back a cheque to clear the outstanding invoices and on the day I received it I let all the other work go ahead. Five days later I got the cheque back marked 'refer to drawer' and by then it was too late."

"Why didn't you tell me, John?"

"I thought I could put it right but it was three further days before I found even one of them. They were always unavailable. When I saw him he convinced me it was an oversight on a transfer of funds from one account to another."

"Have they gone now?" she asked.

"Yes, it was just like you predicted, except you said Christmas and they actually did the January sales as well before the shops were cleared. You see a lot of those labels on the market stalls, some items that were twenty pounds you can now get for one pound, ninety-nine pence.

"Not bad, is it? They have had top mark-up in the shops, half price sale, probably had thousands of items left that they would have sold off in job-lots for merchandise they would not have paid for in the first place."

"Can't the police do something, Kate?"

"Maybe," she replied, "but they will have to find them first. It will have been well thought out, you don't honestly believe they would not have sold their own properties well before, do you? They'd rent a house, a top of the range car, bank just enough to keep everybody happy then skin the rest off to some numbered account. Alex might meet them in Jersey," she laughed.

"How can you laugh about it, Kate? I feel like going to find them and killing them."

"If I didn't laugh I'd just sit and cry my eyes out. Look, we've got to try and save the company because if we don't, now the bank has a charge against my house, I will lose everything."

"Do you want me to work through the night, Kate and have everything ready for you in the morning?"

"No," she replied, "tomorrow we'll do it together. Do you want a coffee or a glass of wine?" she asked, feeling sorry for him, "come on, cheer up, you won't be the first - or the last - to be taken in by these people."

She saw him relax a little, "Thanks, Kate," he said, "I've not really slept properly for the last few months and I'll make sure you soon have your house paid for again."

"Don't make promises until you are one hundred per cent sure," she warned him.

"Sorry," he said, miserably.

"There are scams which are legal, you know. One of my brothers told me about one that happened in Liverpool."

"What was it?" John asked, "if it's legal, I'm tempted."

"You won't be," she laughed.

"Just try me," he answered with a rueful smile.

"Well, a man set up a business called 'Ultra Sensuous Sex Aids' and opened a bank account in that name. He then went to Amsterdam and bought ten of these aids for twenty pounds each. He came back and placed advertisements in all the papers saying 'straight from the continent, should be twenty pounds, once only offer cut price of ten pounds'. He got thousands of replies, banked all the cheques he received in the business account and posted off the ten sex aids to the first ten who bought one."

"Didn't the ones who didn't get the goods ask for their money back?" asked John, puzzled.

"They didn't need to, because he sent them all a letter saying 'due to popular demand, we have run out of stock', and enclosed one of his own cheques for ten pounds. However, because the name on the cheque was 'Ultra Sensuous Sex Aids', about seventy-five per cent of the customers were too embarrassed to pay them in. Even if they had, he would still have had the interest on the money for thirty days."

"Isn't that deception?" asked John.

"Well, yes, I suppose it was, but with any crime, you have to prove the intent and what police station would be bothered to investigate a ten pound problem?"

"Do you think we should go into that business?" John joked, "sounds alright to me. How much did he make?"

"About £150,000," she replied, "but I think we'll pass on that one."

John raised his glass, "No," he said, "you don't seem the type to deal in sex toys."

"Do you feel like going home?" she asked him, "I don't mean to be rude, but it's past midnight and we have a heavy day tomorrow."

He got up immediately, "Sorry, Kate. I know the months ahead will be hard but I feel so much better for this talk."

"Goodnight, John," she said, as she closed the door, "try to get some sleep."

"You too," he replied, with a wave.

Kate needed her bed. She showered quickly and slid under the duvet. Any problems could wait for eight hours.

20

If she felt at home last night, it was no comparison to how she felt when she arrived at the office. She had known on the drive through London there was no way she could leave for anybody. The traffic was always a problem, but apart from that, she was happy here.

Julia came in with the coffee, "I enjoyed making you this today," she said, "it's not the same when you're away. Are we ready to start work, then?"

"Yes, I can't wait. Give me ten minutes to sort the mail and I'll be with you."

Three letters from the bank! The first told her

she had a new manager, the next one said he wanted to see her urgently and the third wished her all the best from the old manager, who informed her he was leaving the banking business altogether.

She didn't bother opening the other letters but pressed her intercom to get John to her office immediately. He came in, looking flustered. "What's going on with the bank?" she asked.

"Nothing as far as I know, why?" he asked.

"Oh," said Kate, relieved, "you've heard nothing from them?"

"No, not a word. Let's phone and see what they want."

She couldn't even make an appointment until the following Monday, let alone speak to the manager over the phone. Kate couldn't understand it. She told the woman on the other end of the line that it was the first time in twenty years she hadn't been able to make an appointment for the following day.

"I'm sorry," said the woman, "but things are changing for us here. See you Monday."

"I wonder what she means," mused Kate, "oh, well, it gives us a chance to show ourselves in the best light possible. I have to see the new manager on Monday, so you've got until Thursday at the latest to show us how we survive. Meanwhile," she continued, "I'll go and see Alex, then we'll know the real story. I'll press him if I can to give us an extra bit each month, that should help."

"Good luck!" John said, leaving the office.

Alex answered the phone immediately, the warmth of his voice coming down the wire like silk. "I've been away," she said, "it's time we got together."

"Any time today," he answered, "come to my office."

"What about your table at the Dorchester? Shall I come before you go, or after?"

"I no longer have a table at the Dorchester," Alex said, "it was an expensive commodity I no longer have any use for."

Kate felt as though a hand had just flipped her stomach over. Perhaps the rumour was true, after all.

"Can I come over now?" she asked.

"I look forward to it, Kate. Walk right in when you get here, I'll be waiting for you."

Now she was sure there was something different. She had never been told to walk right in before, his secretary always introduced her. Well, in the next hour she'd find out.

Julia looked at her as she went past, "Are you coming back?" she asked.

"Yes, of course. Why?"

"I just wanted to talk to you for about half an hour, that's all."

* * * * *

Alex greeted her with open arms. "You look tired," he commented.

"I've had a busy couple of months," she told him.

"Haven't we all!" he replied.

"Alex, can I come straight to the point?" she asked, "I've heard a little rumour that you may be selling up."

"Not selling, sold," he replied.

"Could I ask to whom?"

"No, not yet, give me another week and then I'll tell you."

"But why, Alex? I thought you were doing so well. Your shares have gone through the roof, when most are going down."

"Kate, there is a time to be born and a time to die. It is the same with a company. There is a time to buy, but you have to be aware of the time to sell, also. The base rate is ten per cent, mark my words, in another year it could be thirteen, fourteen or even fifteen per cent. Many businesses will not be able to afford that and I don't need it.

"So now I'm going to spend time with my family. This company has had over twenty years of my life, so now I think it's my wife's turn. So, as soon as the final details are in order, we will settle in Jersey. The house has already been sold."

Kate's mouth felt dry. "Will we keep the business?" she asked, "are you free to tell me that?"

"I doubt it," said Alex, "but when we last met you said you were going to reduce your costs. Did you do that?"

"No," admitted Kate, "not yet."

Alex looked startled, "Maybe you've left it too late. Why did you delay? I'm surprised, Kate, I always thought of you as astute."

"Alex, you wouldn't believe me if I told you, but things are not that bad out there, are they?"

"I'm afraid so, Kate," Alex said.

"You couldn't put in a good word for me, could you? With your purchasers?"

"They already have their own department for the commodity you supply," he said.

She got up and took the hand he was offering. "I'll let you know where we are in Jersey, you'll be very welcome to spend some time with us, Kate, when you need to escape the rat race."

How could she have been so stupid? He'd almost told her his plans at that lunch in the Dorchester. A third of their sales had gone, just like that. She'd try to bluff it out with the new bank manager but how long would that last?

She returned to her office. Her head was spinning. Julia stood up, "Kate, are you alright? You look terrible."

"I feel terrible!" she replied, "the things that are happening to me lately. I feel as though I must have run over ten black cats."

"Annie has been on the phone. She sounds upset you haven't phoned her. She's rung three times in the past couple of hours."

"If she phones again tell her I'm not here."

"That's not like you, Kate. Look, shall I get us both a drink? I don't want to pry, but a problem shared is a problem halved, you know."

"Julia, get me some black coffee and come in, I need you to be a psychiatrist for a while."

It must have taken about two hours to tell Julia all the details. "Right," she said, when she had finished, "you be my shrink."

"Phew! I don't know how you've coped, but there are other things more important than this company or money. You could make yourself ill with all this worry, stress is a killer, it's heart attack stuff - and, by what you say about Annie, she sounds as if she's suffering as well.

"Look," she continued, "do what you can to save the company by all means, but at the end of the day, if the worst comes to the worst, we are all experienced enough to find other employment, aren't we? I don't want to leave here, but if it helps I'll go of my own accord."

"Let's just wait and see, shall we?" said Kate.

"Why don't you go over and see Annie?" suggested Julia, "she must be very upset. I think you owe it to her to at least put her mind at ease and it will take all the worry away from you for a few hours. You can't do anything here until you get those figures and I'll make sure you have them for tomorrow morning."

"Yes, you may be right, Julia. If Annie phones, tell her I'm on my way."

Kate arrived at Annie's at seven-thirty. She was surprised there was no light on, but all the curtains were drawn. She felt a feeling of panic begin and knocked louder than she would normally have done.

She was relieved when she saw the bedroom light come on and Annie eventually opened the door. "Oh, Kate, it's you!" she said, opening the door wider.

"Are you ill?" asked Kate.

"No, I just thought I'd go to bed early."

"Annie, it's only seven-thirty!"

"Yes, but who have I got to wait up for now Paula's gone? I assume you couldn't talk her into coming back, then?"

"No, I never tried," answered Kate, truthfully.

"What about her education? What about her home here? Do you agree with her throwing all that away?" asked Annie, sharply.

"No, not really," replied Kate, calmly, "but I don't want her to feel she has to stay here, it would serve no purpose and only make your relationship bitter. Look, she might even decide to come home herself."

"Oh, I hope so," said Annie, fervently, "I really hope so. I can't stop crying at the moment, I feel so lost. Everything revolved around her."

"Well," said Kate, "do you really think that's a good idea? After all, she was going to go away sometime. You did, I did, everybody leaves the nest at some stage. Why don't you join a social club, write her some cheerful letters, go and visit her every three months? You know the red carpet would be put out for you and the travelling would do you good."

"No, I don't think so," said Annie, "oh, don't worry, Kate, when she phones I'll put on a bright voice. I just miss her so much."

"It's not Paula I'm worried about, it's you, Annie. Are you eating properly? You sound very depressed."

"Yes, I'm eating," said Annie, "and I suppose time heals, they say it does, anyway."

Trying to sound as bright as she could, Kate said, "Well, you've still got me and I'll make sure I come over more often. Why don't you come and stay with me sometimes? We could go out for a meal, have a good old chat and possibly even go to the theatre."

"Yes," said Annie, "that would probably fill the void."

Kate left Annie in what she thought was a better frame of mind. She waved goodbye and watched as Annie went back inside. Kate drove off, but stopped up the road. She decided to go back for another hour, but when she reached the front of the house, it was already in total blackness once again.

Kate wished Evert had never found her. Everything seemed to have gone wrong since that first phone call and appeared to be getting worse day by day.

Oh, she was glad her mum and dad had met Paula, especially her dad. He acted like a twenty year old when she was about. She was also glad that Paula and Evert knew of each other's existence. Was she being paid back for lying all those years? But Annie had done nothing wrong and what was her life like now?

Kate could have done with speaking to Evert, he would have told her to get on a plane to Denmark and everything would be under control, but that would not have solved anything and she couldn't speak to him anyway, because he was still in hospital. Just thinking about him had a soothing effect on her and that's what she needed right now, she had pins and needles at the top of her head.

When she went into her house, she was determined not to dwell on what was in store for her over the next few days, but that was easier said than done. No matter how hard she tried to think about something else, she couldn't shake the feeling that the worst was yet to come.

There was a big pile of mail to read, but that was the last thing she wanted to do. She'd take them all to the office with her in the morning and deal with them there.

She should really have gone to bed, but she knew she wouldn't sleep, so she opened herself a bottle of wine and settled back with it. She wished she had a newspaper then she could have done the crossword, not that she ever finished them. Well, she had a few times in the last twenty years. It was strange how she couldn't finish one herself, but if someone needed an answer, she could usually find the right one.

She sat up, that was it! If someone asked a question, someone else would answer it. She'd call in the accountants, Kitson and Sykes. She disliked accountants, but the law said you couldn't sign accounts yourself, so their yearly audit was usually her only contact with them.

She'd call them immediately she got to the

office in the morning. Perhaps they would spare her some time that day. She admitted her timing wasn't that good because they were always busy this time of year, but they had received about £150,000 from her over the last twenty years, for doing virtually nothing. The accounts John Kitchen and his department prepared for them normally needed very little work.

If she had that £150,000 now, all her problems would be solved. She could see the need for company accountants but not these outsiders, not when you had VAT inspections. The Inland Revenue audits should be enough to satisfy everybody.

The Customs and Excise visits were the worst, you felt like a criminal the minute they entered the building! She remembered when one of their thorough checks had been to the company's advantage and they had enjoyed a twenty-six thousand pound refund. The Inland Revenue had only been once, at five o'clock one afternoon. They had taken all the paperwork with them, but it had been returned by eight forty-five the following morning. They obviously didn't find anything wrong and hadn't bothered her since.

She got up, the bottle of wine was starting to have an effect on her and now she'd thought about her problems and put the world to rights, she felt more relaxed.

She felt warm inside when she thought that Evert would be asleep now after saying goodnight to her. He had told her once that every time he went to bed he would say, "Goodnight, Kate and I hope you do the same." She had said she would, but she always forgot.

Evert just didn't realise the problems she had. If she tried to explain and got uptight in the process he would tell her to take it easy, it wasn't the end of the world if things didn't work out the way she wanted them to.

She had noticed all the fatty food there was over there, every course had something to do with the dairy and although she had tried to avoid it, it was quite impossible, because the way the food was presented was so tempting.

She decided not to have a shower, it would only wake her up and anyway, after a bottle of wine, she thought she might sleep after all.

21

The minute she arrived at her office the following morning, she called Kitson and Sykes. A visit was a little difficult at the moment, but if it was a matter of urgency, in view of their long-standing relationship, the time could be found. They arranged to be in her office by two o'clock that afternoon. "By the way," Kitson added, "do you think you could raise our cheque and I'll collect it while I'm there?"

"What cheque?" asked Kate.

"Last year's," he said, "for six thousand."

"Yes, of course, I wasn't aware that you hadn't been paid."

"I was a little surprised myself," he said, "because we have altered our policy and now, before we even touch a set of accounts, we need payment up front."

"So, what are you saying?" asked Kate.

"Well, to keep your business in line with our method of trading, it would be to your advantage to pay the two year's together, which reduces your costs, because you do not have to be charged for monthly reminders and, perhaps we'd better leave any other debate until we meet, because we do now have a timed phone call charge, which can be quite considerable on long drawn-out conversations."

Kate couldn't wait to put the phone down. She was definitely in the wrong business! The hidden charges made now by professional companies just had to be seen to be believed.

She had heard John's voice while she had been on the phone, so she got up, opened the door to her office and invited him in.

"It's not looking too healthy," he said, without preamble. "Oh, the cash flow is fine, but without the loan we would be in considerable difficulty."

"Did you take an assumption of the sales we could look forward to from Alex in your projections?"

"Yes, of course, because even if the rumour is

true, his purchaser is going to need to carry on short term, but you were hoping to squeeze some information from him. Did you?"

"You'd better start your projections again, John," Kate said wearily, "because any figures you allocated on behalf of his company are not viable any more."

"If that's so, then I'm afraid we'll find it very difficult to survive, Kate, our overheads are far too high once his requirements need not be met."

"If we cut right back to the core, is there a chance?" she asked.

"Well, yes, I suppose so, but you have redundancy payments to think about, which affect the cash flow immediately."

"The accountants are coming at two o'clock and they need a cheque for twelve thousand pounds."

"What for?" John asked.

"Six thousand for last year and six thousand up front for this year."

"They can have one six thousand," he said, "but the other invoice they can wait for. We'd never have another order if we did that," he added.

"New bank manager, Alex selling up, redundancy payments," Kate leant back in her chair. The first people to go were the salesmen. Thank God she had them on commission payments only, so redundancy didn't affect them. She had initially done all the selling herself, but it had become too time consuming to keep returning in the hope of an order, then having secured a sale, keeping the account active.

She had decided to employ reps one Friday when she had been called to a meeting in Bristol at five o'clock. The problem was that she was in Newcastle at the time and the traffic was horrendous. When she did finally make it - on time - she was met by a twenty-two year old newly appointed executive, who simply wanted to see what she looked like.

Actually, he had placed many orders with the company, but he always insisted it was Kate who dealt with him and although they were now quite good friends, she had never told him she could have murdered him the first time they met.

Those reps had been a thorn in her side over the years. She gave them a good salary, a company car and it was not unknown for them to spend their afternoons on the golf course. When she went the other way and provided a low salary with commission, they would sell the most lucrative contracts to the highest bidder among her competitors, leaving you with just enough to keep them in employment. Well it worked better that way, as she was always the highest bidder.

Did those people whose sole intention was to

con their way through life ever stop to think how many families they destroyed? She didn't think so, but if they did, would it make a scrap of difference anyway? They had just taken away from her the last four year's profits and she was very near to throwing in the towel, but she was made of stronger stuff and would battle on. It would only take one more mistake though to bury her for good.

She had always worked on the principle that you could be conned on every deal, but never by the same one twice and any time she had been deceived in the past she had quickly stood the loss and ensured the company never had any contact in that area again.

What worried her now though, was with the loss of Alex's business, could she afford to be that choosy in the future? If the worst came to the worst she could go to Evert in Denmark, he would welcome her with open arms. But would that work, she reminded herself, it had been twenty years and they were both now set in their ways.

She opened her personal phone book and picked up the telephone, she had three and a half hours to secure what future orders she could and half an hour to consolidate the figures before the accountants arrived. She was determined to show the company in the best light possible.

She afforded herself a smile when she remembered her first big order from a national company. They had insisted on seeing her offices. When they arrived, there was only herself and two other employees, but when they asked how many she employed, she told a white lie and said thirty. It would be easy to contract the work out. She had made the office look well staffed, even down to a false holiday planner, which looked very impressive with all the names of her relatives on and some bright stickers.

She had even hired a typewriter and adding machine for the day, and once the room looked spick and span decided it looked too orderly and spent another hour carefully disorganising it again.

Well, she didn't have to do that now, she had all the office equipment she needed and more people than she could currently afford to pay.

She put the phone down, the buzz from it disturbed her and she needed to think things through. She had to take into account that if she had heard the rumours about Alex, then the accountants would certainly be aware of what was going on and when they cast doubts on her losing a third of her sales input, she wanted the ammunition to assure them their fears were groundless.

Picking the phone up again, she dialled the first number. She felt a certain amount of satisfaction that her main contract was available and was delighted to hear they had decided to increase their orders in the current new year's budget.

When she replaced the receiver over an hour later however, she wondered if this was the wisest method, because the main theme of the conversation had been about their respective holiday periods, where they were going for their holidays that year and the forthcoming recession. It was little wonder the phone companies made massive profits, there must be hundreds in her position chasing every potential order in the quickest way possible.

She looked at the clock, she had only been able to make eight calls in three and a half hours, but what she had achieved had been worthwhile.

The accountants arrived and Julia escorted them into her office, both immaculately dressed as usual, their voices oozing charm. She responded in the same tone, telling them how delightful it was to see them again.

The first thing they presented her with was copy invoices, saying that in case she had mislaid the original ones and to save her accounts people time, they had brought them so the problem could be resolved while they were there.

Kate looked at them and said, "There is no problem paying you for the accounts you have produced and we know that in two months we will have to pay you for the first ones for this year, but you have given me invoices here for almost twenty thousand pounds."

"Yes," replied the senior accountant, "my colleague apologises for the error. When he spoke with you on the phone he only took into account the payment in arrears and the forward method of payment, forgetting the current year we are now preparing for."

He turned to his colleague, "We did discuss this at length on our way here, and we came to the agreement that should you suggest that due to losing one of your main sources of income you would benefit from placing your business with another firm of accountants who still implement the old method of payment, we feel obliged to warn you that they would not have the experience of your particular needs as we do. So we have an alternative option. You can clear the outstanding invoices today and place the remaining ones on direct debit on a monthly basis."

Kate looked at them, so they did know that Alex's order would disappear this current year. They would pick up in the accounts that £160,000 worth of sales had gone into liquidation and the minute they looked at the bank statements they would see the £100,000 bank loan.

She had no option now but to tell them everything. When she had finished, the senior man said, "My goodness, you really do need help and of course, that is what you pay us for, but I have known you a long time and I have every confidence that you will trade out of it with the contacts you have in the trade. May I suggest that our internal department help you on a month to month basis."

"What would that entail?" Kate asked.

"We will virtually run the account and at the first sign of difficulty we will be on hand to advise you on the steps to take."

"Will you be doing it yourself?" she asked.

"Oh, good gracious, no! It would cost you far too much, but of course, I will oversee it."

"So it would be one of your junior accountants who will actually do the work?" she ventured.

"Yes, but of course, the charge to you will be greatly reduced."

"Oh," said Kate, "how much will it be?"

"Say, two hundred and fifty pounds per week," he replied, "excluding, of course, any major expense."

Kate had never looked a viper in the eye before. She got up, "I'll just go and get your cheques. We will take your option for the current year."

Walking to John Kitchen's office, she felt like turning back and throwing them both out, but at this stage of the game, she needed as many friends as she could get. Once she was over this, however, she would deal with them in the nicest way possible.

John Kitchen was very reluctant to pay both invoices. He suggested they pay one and post-date the other, but she insisted they be paid the full amount and instructed him to arrange a monthly direct debit with the bank for the coming year.

On the way back to her office she thought of the fees she had paid the accountants over the last twenty years and realised it all amounted to nothing in the end. Loyalty didn't count.

Kate gave the two men a big smile as she entered the room, "There you are," she said, handing over the cheques, "oh, I forgot to mention that after our conversation this morning about your requirements to be paid up front, you gave me the idea that perhaps we should adopt the same policy. Before you arrived I had an hour long discussion with a long-standing client and told them that we would require half payment up front ourselves, so you see, it isn't all black."

She continued brightly, "I have just had a word with John, my company accountant and he will give me a day to day analysis, so should we require your assistance we will call you. Of course, there will be a one-off payment. Good day, gentlemen."

Both men took her outstretched hand and left the room. She closed the door behind them.

22

The minute they left, she reached for the calculator. She had had it for years and many hundreds of thousands of pounds had gone through it. She usually added or multiplied her figures, today, however, she needed to subtract.

A clerk from John's office knocked on the door and entered, putting various customer data on her desk. Kate acknowledged this with a nod of her head and the girl smiled and turned to leave.

Kate knew this particular girl. She was one of four she had employed about seven years ago under the Government Youth Training Scheme, for which the company received seventy five pounds a week for twelve month's work experience. The company passed this money on to the trainees, but as it gave them virtually nothing to live on, she paid their travelling expenses as well. They had all settled in remarkably well and in a matter of weeks appeared as though they'd held their posts for five years or so. At the end of the year they didn't want to leave and she didn't want them to go, so they had stayed.

Every company employee had fallen in behind her to secure contracts which enabled her to fund the increased wages bill.

She motioned for the girl to come and sit down, "Nothing serious," she assured her, "just give me details of how you have progressed in the company."

The unsuspecting girl went through her weekly work load and although Kate realised that she was trying to put herself in a good light, she knew she gave the correct information.

After about half an hour, Kate bent over the documents the girl had brought in and she correctly took it as a sign to leave. Kate turned to the profit margin on Alex's accounts and began jotting down the figures for the last three years. At the same time, half her mind was wondering that if that girl really was doing all she claimed, what were the other three doing?

This was crazy, because in the last seven years she'd purchased new computers and software, which at the press of a button took all the hard work out of typing up the company accounts and provided a host of other benefits.

The sales had only increased by a maximum of twenty-five per cent each year plus inflation, so there must be a massive overspend on staff hours, perhaps John Kitchen wasn't as efficient as he would have her believe. She kept coming back to the thought that the saga of the company deception should have been noticed well before it reached the stage it did.

Now it was the figures themselves that told some stories and that was what she had to concentrate on. Alex had fourteen companies and held fifty-one per cent of the shares. He was very much in control and had always ensured that she had all his business, be it a complete refurbishment or day to day maintenance. His requirements took precedence over other clients, because at one thousand pounds a week profit, it was paramount that no matter what notice he gave from time to time, everything was dropped in favour of him.

The entire workforce respected him and she had never, in all the years, received one complaint about the quality of the workmanship. Alex had shown his gratitude by way of insisting she add a rider to her invoices, which ensured they enjoyed added bonuses without even looking.

She knew she had to produce extra sales that gave fifteen hundred pounds a week profit - one thousand on Alex's accounts and five hundred for the bank loan. That meant finding seventy-eight thousand per year.

Well, she could find twenty thousand of that immediately. Her salary was thirty thousand a year. She had increased it gradually, the first time fifteen years ago, when she had discovered Annie. Then, she had added one hundred and forty pounds a week, so that she could give Annie a hundred. The next salary rise had only been three years ago on Paula's seventeenth birthday, when she had started giving her one hundred and fifty pounds a week. It may seem a great deal of money for a young girl but she had paid her own tuition fees out of that.

Well, thought Kate, it didn't matter any more because Annie was in a comfortable position, financially. She must be, her house was paid for when her husband died and as for Paula, she and Christian were sure that they wanted to strike out on their own, so it would be good housekeeping for them to have to live within their means.

Yes, she would reduce her salary immediately. It would be hard not to be able to buy anything that took her fancy, but that was a small price to pay if it went towards saving her company.

She had no mortgage, no hire purchase agreements and she drove a company car. Well, she only had another fifty-eight thousand to find. There would be extra sales, she would make sure of that herself, that would generate extra profit, but the rest would have to come off the payroll.

She pressed the intercom and Julia appeared immediately. "I think I need a drink."

Julia gasped, "Oh, Kate, I'm sorry, I was so busy after those two men left and I forgot all about you. I'll get you one now." She stopped and looked at Kate. "Does it remind you of something?" she said and they both burst out laughing.

The company had been in its seventh year and didn't have the organisation it had now. Kate did at least fifteen hundred miles per week and worked when she got there and worked when she got back, so it was easy to lose sight of what happened on a day to day basis.

It would have been the end of the financial year and once the final accounts were completed all the documents were put in big brown boxes and stored in the attic. Kate had told everyone where she would be and they had offered to help, but she had wanted the time to herself to sort through them all.

She had looked at her watch around ten-thirty and thought that her morning coffee would be welcome, but nobody had appeared. By noon her mouth was bone dry so she went to the top of the old flight of stairs and shouted down for someone to bring her a drink.

She could hear them, so she was quite confident they would hear her. Nothing happened. At two o'clock she was absolutely parched, so she made her way downstairs to a little office that was rarely used and had sent Julia a telegram saying, 'Does anyone mind if I have a cup of tea? Kate.' She left the door open and about half an hour later was delighted by the screams of laughter below her. The whole office must have bounded up those stairs. "We forgot about you!" they all said. Those were the good old days.

Julia came back with the tray. "Sit down," said Kate, "we're in big trouble at the moment."

"Well," Julia said, "I had an idea something was not right but I didn't realise things were so serious."

"We're going to have to make cut-backs and I'm sorry to have to tell you, but it's in head office."

Julia went white, "Me!" she gasped.

"No, not you," said Kate, "but do you think you can take over John Kitchen's secretary's work because that will be one wage gone?"

"I do his work already," Julia said in surprise,

"his secretary left over nine months ago."

"That's strange," said Kate, quietly, "he never told me. Can you get me the girl who does the payroll?"

"I think he does it," said Julia.

They both looked at each other. Kate didn't want to believe what she was thinking, because it would put a different light on everything. "What was his secretary's full name?" she asked Julia.

"Patricia Marshall," said Julia, "why?"

"Leave me, Julia, but get John to bring me the complete payroll, will you?"

Kate knew the minute he entered the office that her worst fears had been confirmed. She didn't have to look to see whether Patricia Marshall had been paid last month or all the previous months, she could see by the beads of sweat along John's top lip that she had.

Kate just looked at him, but he wouldn't meet her gaze. Eventually, she said, "I don't want to know if you did it, I already know that, I want to know how much, how long and why?"

"Coke," he answered bluntly.

"Cocaine! My god, you're on drugs?" She couldn't believe what she was hearing, "John, I never in my wildest dreams thought you were so stupid. How many more false names are on that payroll?" she asked, shocked.

"Only that one," John replied.

"I suppose you have a false bank account in that name, too."

"Yes," he admitted.

"That one hundred and sixty thousand pound sting, John, how much did they bribe you?"

"It was split five ways," he replied.

Kate reached for her calculator, "Thirty two thousand," she said.

"Well, they only gave me half of that, because they knew I couldn't do anything about it. Please don't get the police, Kate," he almost whimpered, "please, I'm over the top in debt."

Kate pressed the intercom and Julia came in. She looked at John and realisation hit her full in the face. "Does your husband still work around here?" Kate asked her.

"No," replied Julia, still staring at John, "but I can get him. He's on the fraud squad now."

"Then he may be just the person we need."

It was an hour before Julia's husband arrived. By that time, Kate had a long list of expenses that never existed and restaurant receipts from meetings that never took place. Once John started talking, it was extremely difficult to stop him.

She looked at him, "You are no hardened criminal," she said and John smiled at her. "Oh, don't smile at me, because the criminal I can cope with, you have at least a warning to be on your guard. No, the likes of you are much worse. You have almost destroyed over seventy households and if I were you, I couldn't live with that on my conscience. You have nothing to smile about."

There wouldn't need to be a lengthy investigation, John just 'spilled his guts' as the detective put it later. Kate was stunned. She gathered his personal belongings together in a carrier bag and handed them to him. The next time she wanted to see him was in court.

Court. That would be a problem too. John was as well known as she was, would it really do the company any good when the story hit the Press? Julia looked worse than she did and kept repeating, "Kate, I can't believe it and neither will everybody else."

"Do they know yet?" asked Kate.

"Well not from me, they don't, but one of the girls did come in while it was all going on in here and said it was a shame that John had all the pressure just because that company cheated us."

"Can you stay late tonight?" asked Kate.

"Of course," Julia replied, "what do you want?"

"Let all the staff go out of the building then get his expenses for the last six months and you and I will go through them. Don't let anyone know he's been arrested, whatever you do. I will call a staff meeting tomorrow to alleviate everyone's fears."

Julia looked at her watch, "They should all be gone in the next quarter of an hour. What do I say if anyone has decided to work late?"

"Oh, for God's sake, Julia, just think of something, but I need to know those figures tonight."

Kate hadn't meant to be so short with Julia and she just hoped she understood the pressure she was under, she didn't want to lose a friend right now.

Twenty six expense sheets shouldn't have taken long to analyse but it was difficult to decide what was authentic and what wasn't. There was a six week period when they were extremely low.

"Do you think he had a conscience then?" asked Julia.

"No," replied Kate, "he got a pay-off."

Petrol was the biggest surprise. Fifty pounds a week at forty miles a gallon added up to two thousand miles per week. He was rarely out of the office! Not only had he put in a false docket, he undoubtedly had to claim the VAT as well, which involved the company.

The hotel bills all needed matching up to his diary, but it was coming up to eight o'clock. "Julia, let's go home. We can do this tomorrow."

"Are you sure? I can stay if you like, Kate."

"No, let's leave it. I feel that relieved. I need to

drive home and get my thoughts together."

"Relieved!" exclaimed Julia, "I'd be hopping mad."

"Not if you've just realised that you've found the answer to saving your company, you wouldn't."

"Oh, Kate, what a way to find out. Can we really go on?"

"I've no doubt about it! Come on," she added, "let's go home, tomorrow's another day."

23

She hadn't really noticed the drive home, she was just glad to get there. She knew that was how accidents happened because it was difficult to remember the route she took, her mind had been so full of anger and relief.

There were fifteen messages on the answer-phone. She listened to Evert, Paula, Annie and her mum while she turned the heating to maximum, then she stopped as she heard John Kitchen's voice, "Kate, I know you don't want to know me, but I've called to say sorry."

"Go to hell!" Kate said aloud.

The last message was from Alex, who wanted

her to call him as soon as she could. She hadn't wanted to speak to anyone that night, but in the time she had known him she could count on the fingers of one hand the number of times he had phoned her at home.

Alex answered the phone immediately, he must have been waiting, "Kate, you've had quite a day," he said at once.

How did he know so quickly? She didn't have time to ask because he told her the answer himself, "John Kitchen phoned me. He told me everything. Well, he says he has, anyway."

"What did he tell you?" Kate asked.

Alex related the conversation with John. When he finished, she filled in the gaps, adding, "Tomorrow, I believe we will find out a lot more."

Alex sounded upset, "It was me who introduced you two," he said, "if you need any assistance, financial or otherwise, you only have to ask. In the meantime, I cannot advise you enough to keep it extremely low key, don't worry about him, because I can assure you he isn't going to breathe a word to anybody, but situations can be blown out of all proportion once word gets out. Are you going to be able to fund new business?" he asked.

"Yes," Kate replied, "just about."

She never mentioned the bank loan and neither did he.

Kate knew Alex would help her, but it was unfair, he had already told her he'd had enough and although she felt quite confident that the company would pull through, she wanted to put her own money at risk, not Alex's. She wouldn't risk his retirement.

Kate promised to keep in touch, saying she would call if she needed help and thankfully put the phone down. She knew good friends like Alex were hard to find. Annie was the same, but it was too late to think of calling her now, she'd do it first thing in the morning.

She selected a Roger Whittaker tape, it was just the sort of soothing music she needed at the moment. She particularly loved '*The Streets of London*' and '*The Last Farewell*' and she settled back and began to relax slightly as the gentle rhythms flowed over her.

She couldn't stop thinking about John. How could he put drugs into his body? How could anyone do that? She listened to '*A New World In The Morning*' and wondered what her world would be like in the morning - and what about John's?

How would he go on? These drug barons might have wealth beyond anyone's means, but they were surely the lowest form of life that had ever existed.

Her dad always said they should bring back hanging for murderers, but these people, the drug kings, were killers of thousands of people and yet when they got caught, what punishment did they get? Nothing compared to the misery suffered by their victims. Kate thanked God that Paula had never been involved in anything like that, another thing she had to thank Annie for.

She left the music playing and went to run a hot bath. She thought she might be able to really unwind in this for the next half an hour, which would enable her to sleep. By this time tomorrow, she knew her head was going to feel even worse than it did tonight.

She could hear '*The Leaving Of Liverpool*' in the background. How much different her life would have been if she had never left her home town. She sank deeper into the soothing water. Funny how everyone had songs that reminded them of people and places. She didn't know what song she would choose for today, she thought with a small smile.

She soaked for a while, then got out of the bath and rubbed herself briskly. She turned off the music and the lights, jumped into bed and tried to switch off her thoughts, she needed some sleep.

After an hour spent tossing and turning, Kate grabbed her dressing gown and went back into the living room. John was still kicking about in her head. She knew it was stupid, but she hoped he had really padded his expenses. Alright, the money he'd stolen was gone, but if he had stolen heavily, it was less she had to find immediately of the fifty-eight thousand she needed.

She also needed a new financial director, but for the next twelve months she would do the job herself, and as for paying an accountant two hundred and fifty pounds a week for a junior clerk, forget it.

There was a knock at the door. Kate's head swung towards the clock, one-fifteen in the morning. She peeped through the blind and saw Alex and his wife, Margaret. She opened the door, "Alex, what's the matter?"

"Kate, I didn't like the sound of you on the phone, so we decided to come over. Your light was on, so we knocked. We have been where you are now, it's shattering."

"I'm afraid I don't have anything to offer you," Kate said, apologetically.

"Not even tea or coffee?" asked Alex, making himself comfortable.

"Well, yes, of course, which do you prefer?"

"Oh, either," Alex replied.

When he had a mug of steaming coffee in his hand, Alex leaned forward, "Tell me everything, Kate, because from where I am sitting, you appear to be under considerable stress."

Kate had nothing to lose, normally she would have only told so much, because she depended so heavily on his business, but now he had sold it, it didn't matter.

When she had finished, she realised it was four o'clock and she still felt wide awake.

"Are you going to marry this Evert?" Alex asked.

"Maybe," said Kate.

"Go where your heart takes you, Kate, I did," Alex said, taking his wife's hand. "We have very few disagreements because before either of us makes a decision we both agree to what we should do first."

He leaned over and handed Kate a cheque. She looked at it - fifty thousand pounds!

"What's this?" she asked.

"It's for you, Kate, call it conscience money if you wish. I pressurised you into taking our Mr Kitchen in the first place. I can afford it, I got a good price for my business, but I'll give you a warning - you're going to have a fight on your hands to survive. The banks are very jumpy at the moment. Oh, not just with you, they're the same with everybody, which means many businesses are going under."

Kate looked at the cheque in her hand and then ripped it in half. Alex smiled and shook his head.

"What did I tell you?" he said, looking at Margaret, who smiled and nodded.

Kate looked at them, "Look, you've got it wrong, it isn't pride that stops me taking it and had you not told me that there will be many liquidations in the future, I may have done a deal with you to pay this back in five years or so. It will be bad enough if I lose my business and this," she said, gesturing around her home, "but to lose fifty thousand of yours, too. Thanks, Alex, but no thanks."

He held up both hands in a gesture of surrender, "Alright, but will you at least allow me to help by ringing my friends before we leave London? I can probably arrange some deals for you."

"Oh, Alex," said Kate, "when are you moving? I will miss you both, you two have been my closest friends even though we only meet occasionally."

"Come on," said Alex, "I need my bed. I've got a busy day tomorrow sorting our friend's sales out and she needs her sleep, too."

Kate broke down, she didn't mean to, but she couldn't help herself any longer. Alex pulled her to him, patting her gently on the back, "That's what you need, Kate, a hug. It may surprise you, but over the years I, too, have cried when I've been let down, but I have had my wife to fuss over me. You have nobody and everybody needs someone at some time. When you have your business back on track, I would seriously think about your Danish man again."

Kate nodded. Margaret spoke for the first time. "Kate, as an outsider looking in, you appear to have carried a hurt for twenty years that in the end turned out to be unnecessary. At one time, I used to be jealous of the relationship between you and Alex, but I quickly realised there was no need, because you never bothered with anyone. Sixteen years later, we find out why. Do you want my advice?" she asked, quietly.

Kate nodded again and looked at her gratefully. "Perhaps I do," she said.

"Be a woman for yourself, not a woman in a man's world. We still have a part to play, you know. Keeping the home together isn't such a bad job, after all. Are you alright now? Can I take this hunk of a man home with me now?"

"Be in touch tomorrow?" asked Kate.

"You can bank on it!" said Alex, walking through the door.

Kate suddenly felt sleepy, "Thank God for friends like that," she said aloud, before she finally drifted off.

24

Kate could hear a bell ringing and it took her a few seconds to realise it was the telephone, “Kate,” said Julia, “we wondered what had happened to you. Aren’t you well?”

“What time is it?” asked Kate, sleepily.

“It’s nine forty-five and it’s Friday!” replied Julia, with a laugh.

Kate jumped out of bed, of all the days to be late, “I’ll see you in about an hour,” she said, “and thanks for the call.”

Kate couldn’t believe she’d overslept, she’d never done that before, she had a clock in her head that woke her up at seven o'clock every morning.

Ten minutes later, after a quick shower, she was dressed and backing the car out of the garage with enough gusto to warrant a place in a car chase scene on the big screen. She joined the traffic into the city. This was the only bit of London she hated. In Liverpool, the same journey would take about ten minutes.

The modern motorway system - with the exception of the A74 in Scotland - was pure bliss, yet the capital was always clogged with traffic. It was getting so bad that long established city companies were moving their headquarters outside London, because of the business rates and lost man hours travelling.

She might do that herself, she thought, once all this mess was sorted out. With Paula in Denmark, there wasn't really anything to keep her in London any more. She even thought of going back to Liverpool, it was only two hours and forty-five minutes to London on the train and a couple of hours by plane to Karoup from Manchester.

That was impossible though, she realised, all the staff redundancy payments would be beyond her means. However, what she could do, was to find premises nearer her home and they could travel instead. There were plenty of vacant buildings now, some with a two year rent free period.

She remembered reading about a year ago, about a garage in the centre of London which had been sold for thirty thousand pounds. The property boom had had everybody scrambling to buy to make a quick kill, but now that was over and prices were tumbling as everybody appeared to want to be free of any commitment.

There was talk of the interest rates going up again. Well, she hoped not, she was paying 18% now on that hundred thousand pound loan and if the bank base rate was increased her repayments would rise accordingly.

She hoped Alex had rung his friends for her. Oh, she wasn't in any doubt that he would keep his word, but they were not of the same mind as him. They either sold up while the going was good or made massive cut-backs.

She was more than pleased to walk into her office, because her mind was all over the place and now she only had to concentrate on one thing, how much had John Kitchen misappropriated this last year? Once she had that figure, she had a basis on which to start.

"Sorry, Julia," she said, as she walked in, "I didn't get to bed until after four o'clock this morning. Alex and his wife came over."

"Well, I only rang because I was worried about you. I got in about seven-thirty this morning and thought you'd be here. When it got to nine o'clock I started to worry. But never mind, you're here now and the girls out of John's department want a meeting with you."

"What for?" asked Kate, "they don't know anything, do they?"

"Well, actually, yes, they do," said Julia, "you can't really expect them not to. Not if you go and clear someone's desk of personal belongings, stuff them into carrier bags and let them leave the building with a plain clothes' police officer whom they all know. It doesn't take much to put two and two together. I think you'd find it to your advantage to see them," she continued, "and without wanting to tell you how to run your business, you should tell them the truth, because they're not stupid. You never know what light they can shed on the situation."

"Yes, Julia, you're absolutely right, as usual, but before you get them in, tell me, how did I miss the fact that his secretary, Pat Marshall, left nine months ago? Didn't we have a leaving party for her?"

"No," answered Julia, "if you remember, she went into hospital for a hip operation, she'd been on the waiting list for a couple of years, so she grabbed the chance when it became available."

"Oh, that's right, it was more or less twenty-four hour's notice, but," added Kate, "I remember authorising that she got her wages no matter how long she was off. Don't tell me we've only found fifty pounds a week on his petrol expenses?"

"Stop panicking!" said Julia, "because Rob and I thought the same as you. The more he fiddled the less trouble we're in for this year. Anyway, ten weeks after the operation, Pat resigned and John simply carried on paying her wages into a false account. Alright, so it's not nine months as we first thought, but it will still be twenty-eight weeks.

"Rob says that it should be dealt with by the nearest police station and he's going to come and see you about it today. If you can show him all the paperwork he conspired with over the £116,000, his governor might let him take it on. There will have been a big fraud. Perhaps involving other companies as well, but he said to warn you not to expect a quick result, because these fraud cases can take up to two years!"

"Well, that would suit me fine," said Kate, "it would give us space before anyone found out. Also, our name would appear well down the list because the ones who would have suffered massive losses would be the ones who supplied the merchandise. Do you think his boss will let him take it on?" she asked.

"I don't know," said Julia, honestly, "Rob says they're snowed under."

"Can't you persuade him?"

"Well, it's not really up to him, because he'd do anything to help you, you know that."

"Yes," said Kate, "you were lucky with him, he's completely straight, isn't he?"

"Too straight for his own good sometimes, why do you think he's still a sergeant? But that's the way he is and it suits me, we don't have to look over our shoulders like some of them must do."

"Yes, there's been plenty in the newspapers about the few bad apples in the Metropolitan Police, but nothing about our London bobbies who do their bit for the tourist trade, plus the hundreds who keep us safe in our beds at night. Somehow they all seem to get tarred with the same brush. Look at this situation with John Kitchen, we've never had it before. I always thought I had no worries while he was controlling the expenses.

"Anyway," she finished, "let's get them in, otherwise we'll get nowhere near to solving our problems."

"Do you want to phone Evert or Paula first? They wanted you to ring them as soon as you got in."

Kate shook her head, "No, they can wait, let's concentrate on what we have to do. Go and get the girls in."

Kate arranged some chairs for them and decided

she would tell them the truth. She wouldn't leave anything out, not even the conspiracy against the company. The girls filed in and except for one of them who said 'good morning', they waited for her to address them.

It only took about ten minutes for Kate to fill in all the details and she ended by saying that up until yesterday, there would have been massive redundancies, but now, although there would still be some, the cut-backs would not be as stringent.

One of the girls handed her a sheaf of paper. "What's this?" she asked.

"I put all the expenses through the machine to check if they added up correctly and to extract the VAT. These are the last period restaurant bills from his expenses. I've noticed them for the last two years. It sounds a nice place, I'd love to go and see it, but it looks too expensive for me."

Kate looked at the receipts. It was apparent that on average, John had 'spent' four hundred pounds a week at the Coq D'Or Connection. "Did many orders match these expenses?" she asked.

"I don't know. It's taken me all morning to get those together."

Kate turned to one of the other girls, "Do you think you could man Julia's phone for the next few hours?"

The girl nodded.

"Why? Where am I going?" asked Julia.

"You and I are going to have an expensive lunch at this restaurant."

She turned to the girls, "You three, can you drop everything you're doing and try to establish what orders we enjoyed after this lavish entertaining?"

"Are we going now?" asked Julia.

"Yes," said Kate, "it's about time we found out how the other half lives."

They drove through London with Julia wondering whether she was dressed properly and wishing she had put her jewellery on. "It's alright," Kate assured her, "if we do stand out, we'll ask for a quiet table."

They found the restaurant without any difficulty, it had a bright red vanity blind with large gold writing. They parked and walked over, only to discover that the doors apparently did not open for anybody until twelve o'clock.

They waited for a quarter of an hour, but there was still no sign of life. They decided to have a coffee in the snack bar opposite.

"Yes, luv?" the big Cockney behind the counter asked.

Kate ordered. "Two coffees coming up," he said, "can I interest you two ladies in a sandwich? Five items for a pound."

"No, thanks," said Julia, "we're waiting for the

restaurant across the street to open."

"I'd have the sandwich if I were you, luv, it doesn't open until twelve o'clock tonight." He looked hard at them, "Bit long in the tooth to be going in there, aren't you?" he asked.

"Why?" asked Kate, puzzled, "is it a place for young people?"

The man laughed loudly, "No, luv, it's a strip joint!"

Kate looked at Julia and thought how silly she looked with her two bright red bunches. They certainly didn't match the crimson spots that had appeared on her cheeks, or her crimson ears.

"We do a nice toasted cheese with salad," the man offered.

"Alright," said Kate, "give us two of those, please," not bothering to ask Julia if she wanted one or not.

"Four hundred pounds a week to a strip joint!" said Julia, "I don't believe it, do you?" she asked Kate.

"Well, you don't know yet what clients he was entertaining and what orders he got, do you?"

"No, that's true," admitted Julia, "but I do know that I've been stood over him half my life and some stripper's had herself wrapped round him the night before."

They stopped in amazement as Rob walked in.

"What are you doing here?" asked Julia.

"More to the point," said Rob, "what are you doing here? I've just called in to the office and they told me where you'd gone."

"Well we couldn't get in."

"Good job, too!" he retorted, "they'd eat you two for breakfast in there."

Kate turned to him, "I was just saying to Julia, we'll turn up a client list and try to match up the orders for the night he entertained there."

"How much was he spending there?" asked Rob.

"About four hundred a week," said Julia.

"Well, dream on," said Rob, "he'd be lucky to get away with a hundred and fifty quid for a bottle of wine, plus the show and the chat with one of the girls, that would be his bill. If there had been two of them, he'd have doubled that, easily."

"Well, if that's all he wanted, why didn't he just go to the pub?" asked Julia.

"See what I have to put up with? If she knew the side of life I've seen, I'd never get any sleep. She'd be talking all day and night about it. I'll make my way in there in the next couple of nights and see what I can find out, I'll know a couple of them, they'll tell me what the scene is."

"Er, how do you know these people?" asked Julia, sharply.

"Look, don't judge a book by its' cover," he

answered, equally as sharp, "there are some good people in all these places, people who haven't been as lucky as you or me, because they don't know any different. Some of them have been left with kids to bring up on thirty pounds a week. I know one who paid for her kids' education to give them the start she'd never had. The owner's the one I've always been interested in, Julia, the girls are more to be pitied than anything.

"Come on," he said, patting her hand, "let's get you on your way to the real world, this twilight world is for someone else, not my wife."

Rob saw them to the car and Kate noticed he made sure they were away safely before he turned to get into his own car. She felt elated, twenty thousand a year in a strip joint, not bad going in two days. Yesterday she needed seventy-eight thousand to meet her commitments. She turned to Julia, who sat stony-faced. She hid a smile picturing Rob trying to defend himself by saying it was just a job.

"Julia, listen to me, I needed seventy-eight thousand yesterday for the company to survive. I intended to reduce my salary by twenty thousand, that's fifty eight thousand. If we haven't got those expenses of four hundred pounds there and fifty pounds petrol, that's another twenty-two thousand, five hundred, which brings it down to thirty-five thousand plus his salary and National Insurance, which is another sixteen thousand pounds. That leaves us with only nineteen thousand left to find."

Julia seemed to come back to life, "If you take a pay cut of twenty thousand, that will mean I'm on more than you," she said.

"It'll only be for about twelve months, then when it's over, I can always award myself a bonus if we do well."

"How much do we need to find a week?" Julia asked.

"About three hundred and sixty five," replied Kate.

"Leave it to me, you'll have it from today."

25

Back at the office they were met by the girl who'd been trying to find the clients John had entertained at the restaurant. "I can't find any," she said.

"It's alright," said Kate, smiling at her, "we've found the answer."

"Did he get results for us?" the girl asked, innocently.

"I don't know," laughed Kate, "but if I ever see him again, I'll most certainly ask him and let you know!"

The girl gathered her papers together and looked at Kate as though she had taken leave of her senses. Kate was still laughing as the girl turned for a final look before leaving the room.

She stopped laughing when she remembered she had to see the bank manager on Monday afternoon. She hoped he was like the last one. She realised that being new, he would want to make changes, but as far as she was concerned, there was a limit to how far he could go.

She suddenly thought of Annie. She'd be feeling isolated. Kate thought she'd call her and arrange to spend some time together that weekend.

"No, I don't think so," said Annie, when Kate rang her, "Paula phones every Sunday and I need to be here."

"Well, you don't need to be there tonight or tomorrow," Kate said, a little exasperated, "I'll pick you up - more for my sake than yours, Annie," she added.

"What do you mean?" Annie asked.

"I need a good friend and you are the one who comes to mind first," answered Kate, easily.

"Well, Kate, put like that, how can I refuse? What time do you need me for?"

God bless that woman, thought Kate. Annie was going to need her more than ever now and no matter what problems she faced in the future, she must never allow herself to forget that.

There was a wonderful restaurant on the North Circular Road. It was owned by an Italian family, but no matter what kind of food you ordered, it was always cooked to perfection. They could go there - or maybe they'd drive out to the French restaurant in Marlow, Buckinghamshire.

Annie preferred English cooking really, but it wouldn't harm her to taste what gourmet cooks had to offer from other countries once in a while. The first time she had tasted foreign fare had been in Denmark and she still mentioned it whenever you spoke to her. Yes, she'd ensure that she and Annie went out every weekend, she'd open her up to the world. Perhaps she could come to Liverpool with her the next time she went.

Kate thought she might as well call Evert and Paula. He was still in hospital but was hoping to be able to go home the next day. His main concern seemed to be when Kate was coming back. She told him as briefly as she could what had happened, but he didn't seem to understand English as well on the phone and at forty pence per minute it was too costly to keep explaining, so she kept the call as short as she could without appearing too abrupt. Paula wasn't in, so she left a quick message on the answerphone, before hanging up.

Then she rang her back and left another message, "Paula, I won't be contactable until Sunday evening, so don't try to phone me. I'll explain then. And don't tell your mum about this message."

Paula would wonder what on earth was going on, for although she and Annie had never felt the slightest pang of jealousy over Paula, at the moment Annie might be concerned if she phoned her a couple of times while she was staying with her that weekend, because she only got one phone call per week.

Julia broke into her thoughts, "I wish I could organise things like you," she said, wistfully.

"Give me your problem," said Kate, "you know I'm a genius."

"Well, you know I said I'd find the three hundred and sixty five pounds a week you need, I'll have it worked out for Monday."

"Alright, listen, it's been quite a week," said Kate, "so why don't we leave early today and make an early start on Monday?"

"What? All of us?" asked Julia.

"Why not?" replied Kate. "I want to do some shopping and then I'm picking Annie up, she's coming for the weekend."

"Oh, Kate, I am glad, I've never met her, but she sounds so nice on the phone. She always apologises for disturbing me, so does your mum. I bet Annie misses Paula. I was wondering whether you'd mind if Rob and I invited her over to our house. Our kids haven't got any grandparents, you know."

"Well, it's an idea, I'll ask her," said Kate, "but don't be disappointed if she says no, she tends to keep herself to herself."

Kate called at one of the largest supermarkets. Anything she thought Annie might like, she bought. She was going to wait on her hand and foot this weekend and every other one after this. Maybe it was pay-back time. If she couldn't have an adopted daughter, she'd have to make do with an adopted sister and instead of sitting alone in that house waiting for a weekly phone call, she'd probably meet different business contacts of Kate's which would enable them to attend the odd social event together.

She arrived at Annie's feeling much better. Doing something for someone else was a good way of forgetting about your own problems.

"Can you do without me?" asked Annie, when she opened the door.

Kate looked at her. She appeared to have no life in her. She was underweight and looked frail. "No, Annie, I can't do without you. I thought I could depend on you. I've had a terrible week and I thought that if I could tell you about it, you'd put me back on the right track."

"Oh, Kate, I'm so sorry, of course I'll come with you. Why didn't you phone me, I'd have come over straight away. After all, I've nothing else to do, have I?"

The minute Annie went to get ready Kate gave a sigh of relief. She'd always known she had a way with words, but now she was going to have to watch the way she phrased everything. She'd persuaded Annie to come this time, but Annie was no fool.

26

Once in the car Annie wanted to know everything that had happened and during the hour long drive across London, Kate related all the details.

"Are you going to survive it all?" asked Annie, concerned.

"With a lot of juggling, yes," Kate replied.

"Well, when we get inside with all the shopping you put your feet up and I'll make you a nice cup of tea, then we can talk some more."

"It's you who's putting her feet up," said Kate, with a smile, "I'm looking after you this weekend."

"I thought I was here to help you, Kate, that's what you said."

She looked across at Annie's earnest face. "Well, if you insist," she conceded, watching Annie relax again.

Once settled in her chair, Annie made some tea. It took her twice as long as it would Kate, but she realised the woman was happy pottering about.

"Kate," she said, as she brought in the tray, "you know that money you have given me for Paula each week, I've never touched it, you know. It's all been invested for her. If you need it to help you, it's in my name. You can have it all back. Paula would still have the house if anything happens to me and she doesn't know about the money, anyway."

"Annie, why didn't you use it?" asked Kate, stunned.

"I had my widow's pension and no mortgage, so I really didn't need it and when you started giving Paula an allowance I had money left over of my own, so it's there for you if you want it."

"Well, I don't," replied Kate, promptly, "that money is yours, not mine, you should have used it."

"Well, borrow it, then," suggested Annie.

"No," replied Kate, "I've already borrowed one hundred thousand and I'm not borrowing any more. Alex offered but I refused that as well," she added. "Anyway, you've found joy in building up a secret nest-egg for Paula, my joy has been building up a successful company and if my dream comes tumbling down, I don't intend to let yours fall with it. Now, that's an end to the matter," she finished.

"Well," said Annie, "I'll say no more about it, but if you send me another penny I'll send it straight back because Paula is in Denmark now and so I don't have to keep her, do I?"

"Alright," agreed Kate, "that's a deal." She was relieved Annie couldn't read minds, because she had been dreading telling her she had to stop her one hundred pounds a week. The way she was feeling at the moment, Annie would probably have thought she was cutting her ties with her.

"Kate! Are you listening to me?" Annie cut into her thoughts.

"Of course," she replied, "say that again."

"I said if I was you I'd stop Paula's money, too, it's the only way she's going to learn to stand on her own two feet. If she was going to university that would be different, but let Christian provide for her now. You need it more than she does."

"Well, to tell the truth, I'd thought that way myself, but she's going to have a shock when I tell her, isn't she?"

"I'll tell her on Sunday when she phones me. After all, it's my place to, I am her mother. I'll also tell her that she can have a loan at any time she needs one. Up to now," she added slowly, "Paula has had a pretty charmed lifestyle and I miss her so much, my world would be back to normal if she came home. But she couldn't find anyone better than that boy and you know what they say, when money goes out of the window, love flies out of the door, so maybe that will be the test which will put my mind at rest, one way or another."

"Have you ever thought about starting a little business yourself?" asked Kate.

"No, never. I've watched you over the years and I wouldn't have your worries for all the tea in China!"

"Annie, have you ever been drunk?" asked Kate, suddenly.

Annie looked at her in amazement, "No, you know I haven't. Why do you ask?"

"Because, Annie, there's a first time for everything and I'm going to open a couple of bottles of wine. We're going to drink them, talk a load of rubbish as the night wears on, then tomorrow we'll go out."

"Will I be alright?" asked Annie, alarmed.

"Well, let's hope you have a bad headache, then you'll know you've had a really good night."

* * * * *

It was Sunday night and Kate began to lay out her clothes for the next day. She needed to look her best, it was very important that she make a good impression on the new bank manager. It would be marvellous if she had the same dialogue with him as she had with the old one.

If this last week had been anything to go by, it wouldn't be long before she was back on track. She had expected to find Annie hard work, having to commiserate with her constantly over the loss of Paula. Instead, Annie had insisted she see to Kate's every need, starting with breakfast in bed on Saturday morning.

They had dismissed the idea of dining out and stayed at home, putting the world back to rights. Kate had thought, as she had driven Annie home earlier on, that she could quickly get used to spending her weekends like that and Annie herself seemed delighted with the thought. She had even offered to come over in the middle of the week to potter around the house for her. Kate had had to talk her out of that, because the local woman she'd employed for an hour a day for many years was excellent in keeping her home and laundry in order and she didn't want her feelings hurt.

The telephone broke into her thoughts. She turned the music down and picked up the receiver.

It was Paula. Kate braced herself for Paula's reaction to the news about her allowance being stopped, because she would have been told by Annie during her seven-thirty phone call.

"Kate," said Paula, "why didn't you want me to ring you until tonight?"

"Because I didn't know how your mum would react if you rang whilst she was here."

"Oh," said Paula, sounding relieved, "we thought it was because you were delaying about telling me you were stopping my allowance."

"Paula, I'm sorry," began Kate.

"Yes, you should be," interrupted Paula, "all the time you were over here you must have been worried to death and you never said a word. Wait till I tell my father. I hope he feels as guilty as I do. Kate, I've no money but I'll come there if you want me to."

"How are you going to manage, Paula?" asked Kate.

"Don't worry about me, my clothes will be good enough for the next five years and if we have to starve it will keep me in trim. Anyway," added Paula, "you only started giving me the allowance five years ago and that was the first time Mum and I had any money. She used to worry terribly when I wanted something extra for school."

Kate was glad Paula was taking it so well. She

continued the conversation for ten minutes or so, but was relieved to get off the phone. Sometime in the future Paula was in for a big shock and if Annie didn't want her to know now, then who was she not to respect her wishes?

Driving to the office the following morning, Kate felt good about everything. She wasn't really going to miss the money she was stopping from her salary and once she got over the meeting, she would phone Alex to see if he had been able to contact any potential customers.

Julia had the paying-in book ready for her with over £15,000 worth of cheques to pay in, that couldn't help but make a good impression. "How's Rob?" she asked, "has he been on the defensive all weekend?"

"No," answered Julia, "he was really annoyed about me being there. In fact, to save a massive row, I apologised. He was really uptight about it. At one stage I wondered whether he was involved with one of the women there, but then I thought how stupid that was, because when he's not working, he's at home with me every night."

"Oh, Julia," said Kate, carefully, "Rob would never dream of doing anything like that." She didn't voice her thought that there were twenty four hours in a day, not just eight at night, because she really believed that Rob wouldn't play around.

She knew, however, that nothing was guaranteed in a relationship.

Kate arrived at the bank ten minutes early for her meeting and was told to wait. Half an hour later she was still waiting. That was the first time it had ever happened. She had plenty of time to pay in her cheques, but it would be better to casually show him - if she ever got to see him, that is. She wished it was £150,000, but something was better than nothing at this point.

Eventually, she was escorted to a side room and not the office she knew to be the manager's. It was like something out of Dicken's time and she had plenty of time to look around because she was left there alone for ten minutes or so.

Brian Williams, the new bank manager suddenly appeared. "Nice to meet you," he said to Kate, holding out his hand, "I'm from head office and have now taken over the branch."

There was no warmth in his voice at all as he continued, "I wrote to you for two reasons, the first being I thought it best that we meet. Most importantly, however, it would appear on close examination of your account that it has not been conducted over the last six months as we would like it to be. You have a loan account of one hundred thousand pounds. Are you confident that you will be in a position to fulfil your agreement with us? That is, will you be able to meet your monthly repayments?"

"Yes," replied Kate, "I'm extremely confident. I've taken the necessary action to reduce my costs."

Brian picked up his pen. "Perhaps you will give me some indication as to how you have achieved this." Kate gave him a full account of the John Kitchen saga. "So you see," she finished, "with the four hundred pounds expense discrepancy stopped, plus his salary, your loan payment is already covered."

"You're not planning on replacing him?" he asked. "No," replied Kate, "I'll do the job myself."

"My understanding," he said at length, "is that you are the hub of the company. You have had long term contact with your clients. If you are going to take over the financial affairs, would the other side of the business not suffer as a result?"

"No," she replied, confidently, "I can assure you it will not."

"Hmm, debatable," Brian said, "debatable."

"Look," said Kate, slightly annoyed now, "I don't want to appear rude, but you have no problems concerning your hundred thousand. You may not be aware of this, but you have a debenture on my house and its current market value is two hundred thousand pounds, so your money is quite safe."

She tried to keep the sarcasm out of her voice

but found it very difficult. She decided she didn't like Brian Williams at all.

He looked at her now with disdain, "Yes, it is surprising how many of our customers with cash flow problems feel that they can sit back and relax once a property is signed over to us, but I would remind you that we only exercise our right over your property as a last resort, it would be an extreme measure to take and you," he said, emphasising the 'you', "might not be aware that we are not estate agents, there are costly procedures that must be put into place before we could expect to clear your account.

"Therefore," he continued, leaning back in his chair, "it is imperative that I have last year's accounts, not draft, final. Plus," he added, "an appraisal of your business by your auditors."

He concluded the meeting by standing up, extending his hand towards her saying, "Shall we meet in, say, four weeks from now? That should give you ample time to fulfil all my requirements."

Kate made her own way out of the bank and was relieved to feel the fresh air on her flushed face. Walking to the car, her annoyance turned to concern as she realised what he had said was quite true.

She knew her forté in business was ensuring her clients' premises were designed with the necessary impact that attracted the public to buy the merchandise displayed, rather than that of his competitor, who may offer similar wares.

She could do basic accounts but the manager wasn't far wrong in his observation that she couldn't really do both. Her dad would have summed it up by saying, "Jack of all trades, master of none."

She didn't relish the idea of eating humble pie to her accountants, but spending two hundred and fifty pounds a week for six weeks maximum was worth it to put everything in order. Mind you, she remembered, there would be an extra few pounds on timed phone calls, but what the hell!

Kate wasn't ready to go back to the office just yet, she needed to think about what she was going to do without anyone disturbing her. The optimism she had felt before the meeting with Brian Williams was now more than a little diminished, but everyone had days like this.

She slipped into one of the many cafés. Half an hour in here on her own and she'd know where to start when she got back to the office.

Settling back with a pot of coffee, she thought it was at times like this she regretted not having a partner. Oh, not a business partner, because that system rarely worked as one was always more dominant than the other. No, a husband or live-in lover - a soulmate, one who always knew when you were at a crossroads and who could wave a magic wand and put all your problems into perspective.

However, did she know couples like that? The nearest was Alex and his wife, but whether he ever took her advice was debatable, because in business he was very much his own man.

Well, every personal commitment would have to be put on hold for the next six weeks. She needed to throw herself into the business heart and soul now, which meant burning the midnight oil. It wouldn't be a problem, she had done it many times over the years.

Everyone would understand. She'd phone them when she got home. She was already beginning to feel the freedom and realised that after the last couple of months she needed her space back. She could justify herself if need be. She did feel slightly guilty about Annie, because she had enjoyed the weekend so much. Kate hoped she could persuade her that six weeks would fly by. Perhaps she could get Paula to call her twice a week, that would help.

She drained her last cup and left the café. She was glad she'd taken time, at least she'd sorted something out. She joined the people on the pavement and noticed the tourists window shopping. She felt a pang of envy, because she loved window shopping. However, her main priority now was to get back to her car and get back to the office.

27

As soon as Kate reached her office she settled herself behind her desk. She could see from Julia's expression as she passed through her office, that she expected Kate to volunteer her discussion with the bank manager, but if she was to get figured in time, it was imperative she got in touch with the auditors as soon as possible.

She'd be extremely surprised if they could drop everything to attend to her needs, but when a bank manager, especially a new one, committed you to certain requirements, it would be wise to comply.

The accountant seemed rather surprised to hear from her in such a short space of time after his visit. Kate told him she had thought it over and realised it would be better for his office to sort the figures out after all. The cost, she said, needed some discussion, because they would not now need an independent audit. The figures would be at their disposal at any time.

"Yes," replied the accountant, "well, no doubt we can come to some arrangement. Shall we meet sometime next week?"

Kate hoped he hadn't heard her gasp. She'd been hoping he would suggest a meeting tomorrow at the latest, because once he was aware that she needed him urgently, it wouldn't take him long to realise that unless she was contemplating a substantial purchase, she needed help to get at least a part of the accounts in order.

She crossed her fingers and told him a white lie. She said she could foresee herself not being available after tomorrow and she needed a discussion sooner than later, so she could concentrate on what she was doing next.

The accountant sighed and made a big show over trying to fit her in the next morning and she put on her friendliest voice as she wished him good afternoon before putting the phone down. Why did they always make her feel they were paying her instead of the other way round?

Kate hadn't done any conciliation for years, John Kitchen had seen to all that. He simply told her when she needed to make a few friendly phone calls to keep a balanced cash flow, but by the time the accountant arrived tomorrow morning she would ensure he didn't know how inexperienced she was because she intended to have the answers he would need.

She got up. Rather than have everyone running back and forth with paperwork, it would be more sensible if she worked from the accounts' office. She felt the girls were a little uneasy when they realised Kate wasn't simply making a visit for information, but they soon settled down again to their own work, once she had her head buried in the books.

After the first couple of hours, she felt she was beginning to get to grips with the figures and might just be able to show the company in the best possible light. She was so engrossed in her work that she began to talk out loud to herself, "Despite our loss on that big account, plus any misdemeanours, we appear comfortably off for this time of the month."

She suddenly realised the girls had all stopped work and were looking at her. "The cash flow seems better than I expected," she explained to them, slightly irritated by the lack of privacy. She had thought her open plan offices a good idea. Perhaps the accounts' department should be a little more private.

None of the girls indicated that they were pleased with the news, they simply sat there like zombies. She was aware of one of them reaching up for a box file, which she passed over to her, "When do you want me to pass these for payment?" she asked Kate.

"What are they?" Kate asked, taking the file.

"Outstanding invoices. The suppliers were screaming at John to put them through. I suppose he would have done eventually," she added quickly.

"How old are they?" asked Kate.

"Depends how loud they scream. The accountant's one we paid the other day was twelve months old, that's why they insisted on picking up the cheque when they were here."

Kate felt something akin to panic beginning to creep in, please God, let her tell me what I'm thinking isn't true. "Tell me," she ventured, "how come you're so far behind? Are you not aware that it is imperative that we invoice the customers the moment it is reasonably possible?"

The girl blushed deeply, "I have invoiced them," she said, indignantly, "we are up to date with the invoicing, because John wanted all the sales in the final figures."

"But you kept back the invoices that we owe to our suppliers," exclaimed Kate, "the one's that should also have gone into the final figures." She hoped the girl would not tell her she was correct.

"Well, what's different this year? We did it last year as well, but they got paid eventually."

"But surely you know that's wrong!" Kate shouted, "these accounts are useless, they are not accurate, we've even paid tax on profit we never had!"

The girl was close to tears, "I didn't make the decision what to put through," she said, "John did, he's my boss. I only do what he tells me."

"How much are these worth altogether?" asked Kate, wearily.

"About seventy thousand pounds," the girl replied, "but last year he only kept back about fifteen thousand."

Kate's head was buzzing and she could feel ringing in her ears. "Do you owe any labour expenses on the work we have done?"

"No," replied the girl, "that's up to date. It's only the suppliers' invoices he told me to keep back."

Kate stood up, "Someone get me the personnel file and bring it up to my office. I want it yesterday."

Julia looked up, startled, as Kate came hurtling through into the office. She followed her into her room and asked, "Kate, what on earth is the matter? You look just like you did when Evert phoned you for the first time."

Kate didn't stop to explain, instead she rapped, "When the girl brings in John Kitchen's address, get on the phone to Rob and ask him to meet me there. Tell him it is very important."

The girl arrived and Kate all but grabbed the file from her outstretched hand. She found the address and scribbled it down. It would take her an hour or more to get there and she hoped Rob would be there to meet her. Although she was only half the size of John Kitchen, she was going to kill him.

Why? Because that man had just lost her everything she had worked for twenty years to build. Well, if she was going to lose her house she was damn sure he was going to lose his, too. She wondered if it was possible to make him sign all his assets over to the company. Assets! That was a laugh, it had all been stolen from her anyway.

Kate's mind was in absolute turmoil. That would be the answer, even if it meant dropping the charges and if his house was mortgaged, he'd have to get a second one. There would be enough equity in it because every house price had risen in the last few years. Another way out was for him to get a short-term bank loan until the mortgage came through.

The more she thought about it, the better she liked it. What good would it do her if John got a prison sentence? If it even got that far, they'd probably try to blame everything on the fact his mother had given him a bottle instead of breast feeding him.

She was sorry now she had sent for Rob, because as far as she knew he was extremely honest and she couldn't see him being involved in any sort of deal. However, she had called him and she saw his car as soon as she turned into John's road.

"Hello, Kate. Julia said you looked very upset. What's happened? Why do I have to meet you here?"

Kate tried to tell him as sensibly as she could, but knew that her words were all tripping over each other.

"Kate," Rob said, shaking his head, "stop! Tell me why we're here!"

"I want you to be here when I get the truth out of him," Kate managed, "and I want my money back, whether it's against the law or not!" she added desperately.

"Well, it's not against the law if he offers to pay you back, in fact it would help his defence if all monies had been repaid, but if you were hoping to find him here, you're in for a big disappointment because he lives in a bedsit miles from here."

He took hold of her shoulders and she was glad he did because it stopped her from falling. "Look," he continued, "the best thing you can do is go back to the office, get together all the figures you can that he was involved with, let me have them and I will see him again. As a guide, Kate, he's got a one thousand pound a week cocaine habit, plus his club membership of one hundred and fifty pounds for a bottle of plonk.

"Come on, Kate, leave your car, get into mine. Let's find a pub, the next half an hour isn't going to alter anything, is it? You look as though you need a drink."

Kate realised why Julia loved this man. He was brilliant, totally in charge. He came back from the bar and gave her a brandy. "Talk to me, Kate, tell me all about it. It won't go any further, not even to Julia."

Two hours later she came to the end of the whole sorry story. She was fed up with iced tonic water and swirled the liquid round and round the glass. "So you see, unless I get my money back the business and my house have gone."

Rob nodded slowly, "And if he's the cause of Julia losing her job, I'll kill him! Kate, besides the house, couldn't you loan the business money then take it out in a couple of years?"

"I haven't got any money here," she said, miserably, "there is only seven thousand in my personal account plus about twenty-seven thousand left in Denmark."

Rob couldn't believe his ears, "Is that really all you're worth?" he asked, incredulously.

"I'm afraid so," said Kate, ruefully, "I ploughed everything back in over the years."

Rob rubbed his hands through his hair. "My God," he said, "look, Kate, I haven't told you this, but get that money out of your personal account as soon as the bank opens in the morning. Get cash, not a cheque, that's the best advice I can give you right now." He leaned over and kissed her. "Kate, I'm so sorry, don't worry about anyone else, worry about yourself for a change."

Rob escorted her back to her car. "Kate, forget what I said before, don't go back to work, go home, you look as though you need time on your own."

"Will you give me John's address, Rob?"

"No," he replied, with a grim smile, "I don't want you going anywhere near him."

"Please, Rob, I won't even go near the door."

"Then why do you want it?"

"I just want to see where he's living. I know

about his drug habit and even though he's destroyed me, I want to tell myself I can still win because no matter what, I'll never slip down the ladder as much as he has."

Rob looked at her hard for a minute, then took out a pocket book. He showed her the address on a page full of numbers and addresses. He couldn't tear it out, but it didn't matter, Kate knew she'd remember 2 Lilac Grove for the rest of her life.

28

John's address was not in the direction of the office nor her house, but she wanted to see it for herself. She looked at the speedometer in the car, thirty miles an hour on a dual carriageway, why wasn't she hurrying to get there?

She turned off at the next exit and stopped the car. What was the use of looking at someone's downfall? It was impossible to undo what John had done whether under pressure or because he was plain stupid. And what was she intending to do when she got there? Was she going to sit outside and gloat? Or would she knock on the door, shout at him, tell him he was a loser? If he really had a thousand pound a week cocaine habit, he already knew that. Anyway, at the moment he needed all the help he could get because otherwise he was going to end up dead.

Kate banged her fist on the steering wheel in frustration. She was not going to get involved in his rehabilitation, the National Health Service could have that pleasure. She started the car, turned round and headed for home.

Again, she couldn't get John out of her head. He seemed so intelligent. How on earth could he have got himself into the state he was so obviously in? The first she had ever heard of people taking drugs other than for medical reasons, had been the purple heart craze in the sixties. Twenty-five years on and she still didn't know what effect you were supposed to get from them.

She was glad she had met Evert when she did and travelled the world with him, because otherwise, she might have ended up trying them at college. Just the thought of it made her shudder.

Over the years, she'd listened to so many discussion programmes on the subject and as far as she was concerned, the fault lay with the Government. A policeman had made the most impact on her in one of these programmes. "We don't grow drugs here," he had said, "we have to import them. We have an advantage over other countries as we are an island, so why weren't stringent checks made on seaports and airports all those years ago? Alright," he had continued, "I know it's impossible to monitor the situation totally, but these days, drugs are in virtually every pub and club in the country. Why aren't the dealers found and convicted and thrown into jail for life?"

Kate thought he had the most commonsense attitude she had ever heard, but he'd been shouted down that the dealer's wife and children would suffer. He couldn't answer that and remained quiet for the rest of the discussion.

Kate shook her head and concentrated on other matters. She had decided to ring everyone tonight, but there was no way she could be bothered going through the details over and over again. She would call Alex though, she needed his business advice like never before.

Once inside, Kate closed the front door and got into her night clothes. She snuggled down into the settee. Once the water had heated up she was going to have a long soak in the bath, then she'd make her call.

Two hours later, she was still there. She had given up. What was the point, nobody was going to do anything. She was startled by a sudden banging on the door. She looked at the time, ten o'clock.

"Alex!" she said, as she opened the door, "I was just thinking of ringing you!"

"Yes? Well, you wouldn't have got through, because I'm not in! Julia's husband told me what happened today and she phoned me as well."

"What do I do, Alex?"

"Kate, the way it's going it's almost respectable to go into voluntary liquidation. You have your accountants coming tomorrow, Julia tells me, let them know everything, you'll feel a lot better, I promise you."

"You know I'll lose everything, don't you, Alex?"

"Maybe you will, maybe you won't, but at the moment you have a chance because until today you had no idea you were trading illegally. Once you made that discovery, you knew there was no way you could continue. Tomorrow you must be extremely correct in all that you do. It is very important."

"I have about seven thousand in my personal account at the bank. Could I get in trouble for taking that out?"

"Where did you get it from?" asked Alex.

"Well, from my salary," she replied.

"Yes, get it out then, it is your own money to do with as you please. You're going to need it, Kate, but all is not lost, get this business out of the way, then we'll get together and sort out a little business deal."

"But, Alex, you're retiring to Jersey."

"Yes, quite shortly actually and I'm looking forward to it. I'm going to miss this place, so I got to thinking that with you available, it wouldn't be a bad idea to have a look round for something that would interest us both, then I would have a perfect excuse to make the occasional visit."

"Thanks, Alex, but you're doing this for me, not for you."

"The offer is there, Kate," he said, "think about it." He stood up and passed her a card, "My number in Jersey is on that, don't be afraid to use it." He moved towards the door and kissed her cheek before saying goodbye.

Kate watched his car until it was out of sight. Well, whatever was going to happen, would happen, but she wondered just how many Alex's there would be when her situation became known tomorrow.

She went in and got into bed. When she next awoke, she was surprised to find she had slept right through. She spent more time than usual getting ready. If she was going out, she'd do it in style.

She didn't leave the house until well after nine o'clock. The accountants could wait. The first place she was going to was the bank. She filled in the withdrawal slip and joined the queue. The teller looked at the slip, then at her and pressed a key on the computer. "Just a moment please," she said, getting up.

Kate watched her go into a rear office and suddenly felt uneasy. She was waiting for a hand to clamp down on her shoulder. Eventually, the teller came back and said, "Would you go to the other window, please, someone will come and see you there."

The under-manager fiddled with the slip, "This withdrawal almost closes your account with us," he said.

"Yes, I realise that, but I do need that amount of cash today."

"Perhaps you'd better come through to my office," he suggested.

When she was shown through, all the details of her financial affairs were in front of him. He said, "You authorised a transfer of thirty thousand pounds to the Unibank in Denmark. Have you business dealings over there?"

"No," said Kate, "I loaned it to someone."

"You loaned thirty thousand to someone?" he said, trying to keep the shock out of his voice.

"Yes, until an insurance claim came through."

"Ah, I see! Once that is settled will you be

returning the money to your account with us?"

"Yes, of course," she replied.

"Well, let's hope they settle insurance claims quicker there than they do here. How do you want the money?"

"Oh, any way at all," Kate said, with considerable relief, "whatever is easiest for you."

"Wait here, I'll get this sorted out for you."

Kate looked around the room and wondered where the camera was. Keep calm, she told herself sternly, just for the next ten minutes, because that seven thousand is my only lifeline.

Eventually he returned and handed her an envelope, "Would you like to check it?"

"No, thank you, I'm sure it's all there. This is a bank after all." Kate felt elated and couldn't wait to get out into the fresh air. She didn't intend spending the money, but she did need to survive. She had about twenty-seven thousand left in Denmark and if her suppliers were short-changed, she'd have that available to enable her to settle their accounts privately.

Now, she headed for the office to start the process of liquidating her business.

29

Kate parked her car and walked the familiar short distance to her office building. She was surprised how calm she felt.

She imagined the accountants would be very annoyed to have been kept waiting, which, she supposed, was quite reasonable, but they would have an air of superiority on how they could turn the company around, but not before they had discussed their charges.

Julia pointed to her office, "They're in there," she whispered.

"Sorry to have kept you waiting, gentlemen,"

Kate said, as she walked into her office, "there was something rather urgent I had to do."

"Well," said the senior partner, looking pointedly at his watch, "perhaps we can hurry this through? We do have a limit on our time and it is our busiest period."

"Oh, this won't take long, I want to put the company into voluntary liquidation."

The two men looked at each other and then at her in amazement. Finally, the senior partner found his voice, "Why?"

"Because," she replied, "discrepancies have come to light that I cannot possibly hope to correct. I do not have the time to get new business so I could trade out of it. Also, if I did by some remote chance, I would not have enough capital to substantiate my payroll until the clients' invoices were settled."

"I see," the accountant replied, "and you want us to arrange this liquidation for you? How soon?"

"As soon as possible," Kate replied, "but before you do, I would like you to look at last year's accounts, when you charged me six thousand pounds for a full audit, but missed a discrepancy of fifteen thousand."

"I'm sure there must be some mistake," the accountant said, quite flustered.

"No, there is no mistake and had you done your

job properly, the company could easily have stood the loss. Now it has continued throughout the past year it has increased by another seventy thousand." She looked at them, enjoying their discomfort.

"Well, yes," the senior accountant finally spoke, "what you allege has yet to be substantiated and the Official Receiver during the investigation of the company will explore all the financial dealings with the utmost care and accuracy, so may I suggest we leave any further discussion of this matter to him."

Kate knew they'd find an explanation of the oversight from somewhere, but she had no intention of getting into an argument right now. "How soon can you arrange it?" she asked.

The accountant looked surprised. "Well, if we leave now, most probably later today. If not, then first thing in the morning."

"Does it happen that quickly?" asked Kate, in surprise.

"Oh, yes, once we are made aware of the situation, it is our duty as your accountants to put the wheels in motion immediately." They stood up and held out their hands. "We will be in touch once we have a time, but more likely, the Official Receiver will contact you directly."

Kate watched the two men leave her office, at

least she'd given them something to think about. They would no doubt come up with a mind boggling explanation for the oversight and she had no money to take the matter further anyway. Quite simply, unless she won the football pools there was no way to save the company now. Would she really want to?

Julia disturbed her thoughts with a big mug of steaming hot coffee. Even that had altered, she usually got a china cup! "What's with the mug?" she enquired.

"Thought you could do with a bigger one," said Julia, with a shrug. "Anyway, it keeps hotter in one of those. Can I stay?" she added.

Kate nodded, "Julia, we're going into voluntary liquidation, either today or tomorrow."

"Well, don't worry about me," said Julia brightly, "I'll soon get a job."

"Oh, that's good," said Kate, "because I *was* worried about you." She knew Julia wouldn't have caught the sarcasm, she was careful to keep it out of her voice. Kate had just lost everything and Julia thought she'd be worried about her! How long had she worked for her? More than seventeen years, you'd think she'd know Kate by now.

"Is there any chance of you starting up again?" asked Julia, "I would just take a month or so off, if there was."

"No, I'm sorry, there's no chance whatsoever."

They both sat there, absorbed in their own thoughts. The phone rang, making them both jump. "Yes," said Kate, "two o'clock will be fine, see you then." She replaced the receiver and looked at Julia.

"Was that the Receiver?" Julia asked.

"Yes, he's coming at two o'clock, so we'll know what's happening then."

"Kate, I can't believe it, you look so laid back. I'd be crying my eyes out or shouting, or something."

"Well, as my dad always used to say, 'you die if you worry, you die if you don't, so why worry?'. Anyway, after the last couple of months it's come as a relief really. I know I'm going to need a lot of support while these people wander through all the departments, but I'll just have to take one day at a time. Now, I'm going to get a sandwich, do you want me to bring you one back?"

"No," said Julia, "I'm not very hungry."

Kate walked onto Oxford Street and for the first time in years she took notice of the people. Every one of them would have a problem, some major, some minor, but a problem all the same. She looked at the blind beggar with his cap on the floor and guide dog sitting patiently beside him. She stopped to listen to the music he played on his accordion, then when she thought nobody was looking, threw five one pound coins in the cap.

The man stopped playing, smiled at her and said, "Thank you." Kate was startled, he hadn't said anything to the others who had dropped small change into his cap, could he possibly know the value of each coin by the sound?

She thought of Lis in Denmark, it made no difference to her if she travelled in brilliant sunshine or the dead of night, she could find her way equally as well.

These two people put everything into perspective and instead of feeling hard done by, Kate felt quite humble as she made her way back. She'd made sure she only had ten minutes to wait for the Receiver and she was still in the same frame of mind when Julia showed him through.

He told her his name and official title and then, in one of the kindest voices Kate had ever heard said, softly, "I had a company myself once and found myself in the same position you're in now. I want you to be aware that there is life after liquidation."

Kate nodded gratefully. The man continued, "Now, from what I'm led to believe, it's a cash crisis that prevents you from trading."

"Yes, that's exactly the problem."

"Well, don't worry, I will look at it over the next couple of days and see where we can go from here."

"I have a spare office," offered Kate, "or do you want to share mine?"

"There's no need for you to be here, all I need are the shareholder's names and addresses plus the two newspapers you would want the announcement to be in, should the worst come to the worst."

"Do I go now, then?" she asked.

"Yes, there really isn't any point in you staying here," the man said.

"Should I tell the staff?"

"It isn't necessary, but if you feel you must, then do so. Oh, one other thing, does your car belong to the company?"

Kate nodded.

"Ah, could you take out any personal belongings and leave the keys at reception, please."

"Can't I keep it until I find out what's happening?"

"Well, alright, you can always return it in the next couple of days, but if I were you, I'd clear your personal belongings from here. If we do have to liquidate, it would be extremely embarrassing to have to come back to clear your desk."

Kate called Julia, "Could you get me two black bin bags, please?" She turned back to the Receiver, who had already occupied her chair, and gave him the address of her brother who owned two per cent of the shares and the other details he had requested. By the time Julia brought the bags, she had some neat little piles of belongings ready on the floor.

Julia burst into tears. The Receiver looked suitably uncomfortable and bent his head over some papers on the desk. Kate managed to keep a stiff upper lip while she bagged her things and then she left the office without looking back.

Out on the street she hailed a black cab and directed him to the car park. He waited while she got her things from it and left the key at reception. "Where to, luv?" he asked and smiled when Kate gave him the address. Well, at least she'd made someone happy today, she thought, wryly. It would take about an hour and a half to get home and she didn't care how much it cost.

The house was spick and span. The smell of furniture polish hit her as soon as she opened the door. She wandered from room to room. Would she have to leave her home as quickly as her business premises once the bank was aware of the situation?

Where would she go? Annie? She'd welcome the company, but Kate needed her own space. Liverpool? It'd be like being a little girl again. Denmark? Was she really ready to settle in another country?

Her previous feeling of things being alright was beginning to recede. Everything was far from alright, but at least by the end of the week, she would have made a decision.

The house was silent and she liked it that way. She picked the phone up and made a call. "Annie? Can we cancel this weekend?" She realised she hadn't even said 'hello', so she quickly made some small talk and ensured that Annie was quite happy by the time the conversation was over.

She hadn't told Annie what had happened because she knew Annie would ring Paula and Paula would ring her and she really couldn't cope with that at the moment.

30

After her call to Annie, Kate put the answerphone on. She didn't want to speak to anyone else tonight.

Sitting down, she was soon lost in her thoughts and when she eventually stirred and looked at the clock, it was two-fifteen in the morning. All she'd had was coffee during the hours she had been home.

She was worrying about the Receiver. If he was really going to try and save the company, why had he wanted her to clear her desk and leave the car? It wasn't right. She owned the company and yet she was the only one who didn't know what was happening.

She made up her mind. Tomorrow morning she was getting a taxi into the office. She wanted to be there as things progressed. She went to bed.

In the morning, she awoke to the sound of the Hoover. She scrambled out of bed and hurried downstairs. The daily help, Edna, was surprised to see her, but she stopped work and put the kettle on. "There's some letters there for you," she said.

The first she opened said it all. She was requested to attend a creditors' meeting in twenty-eight day's time. So that was it, then. They didn't waste much time, did they? She didn't bother with the other mail.

"Tea's brewed," came a cheerful voice from the kitchen. "Not well, dear?" enquired Edna, as Kate came through.

"Sit down and have a cup of tea," said Kate, "I'm afraid today is your last day here, because I'll be here myself from now on. My company has gone into liquidation."

The old woman looked at her. "Well," she said, finally, "it might be my last day for getting paid, but you're going to need someone to pop in and see you're alright. What's happened to you, happened to my son. The phone never rang after that, he might as well have thrown it away."

Kate got up and went over to her phone.

Nobody had called and she turned it back over to normal calls.

Edna got up and put her coat on. "Can you manage without me for a couple of hours, then I'll be back." She didn't wait for an answer, but walked through the kitchen towards the front door. "You will be here, won't you, dear?" she asked.

Kate nodded and went to run her bath. She had to carry on as normal, she'd done enough sitting about last night. She'd just immersed herself in the luxurious hot water when the phone rang. She scrambled out, grabbed a towel and ran to answer it. At least she'd find out the state of play in the office.

"Kate," her mother said, "your brother's here, he wants to talk to you. Something about a letter he's had."

Kate had not thought about this. She didn't wait for him to go into detail, she simply apologised and assured him he would not end up with a massive debt, because she had it all covered with the money from the sale of her house.

She put the phone down and stood there, dripping. Should she ring the office? She decided against it, the Receiver would still be there, so it would be difficult to talk anyway.

Kate wandered back to the bathroom. She

couldn't be bothered getting into the bath again, so she dried herself and put on an old tracksuit. Now what should she do? What would happen if the house went? Where would she put all her stuff? She phoned Paula.

"Kate!" exclaimed Paula.

"Are you looking after your father?" asked Kate, with a sudden catch in her voice.

"Of course! What's wrong? Kate, don't cry, please tell me what's wrong. I'll go and get a plane home now."

"No need for that, I think it's just hearing your voice. Don't worry, I'll sort myself out."

"Kate, Evert wants to speak to you. Tell him everything," she urged.

At the end of the long conversation, Evert said, "Yes, I am also sad you have lost your business, but I am a little glad as well, because now I can look after you."

Kate promised to call back later, and replacing the receiver, once again counted her blessings. She'd had two offers, one from Alex to start a new business and one from Evert to be looked after. But what could she do? She had been independent since she was twenty-five years old. The thought of asking someone to buy her a new dress was unthinkable. Alright, she had the seven thousand here and she had money over there, but by the time she had paid her commitments, how much of that would be left?

Anyway, did she really want to live in Denmark? It would have been different twenty years ago, but now she was too set in the English way of life. Well, Evert wouldn't live over here, he thought the place was too dirty.

She heard the front door open - Edna was back with the biggest variety of home-made pies Kate had ever seen. "Put the kettle on, dear, these potato cakes need eating now. Just out of the oven, luv."

Kate paid this woman very little and had never really given her any attention over the years she had worked for her. But look who it was who was looking after her. Where were all her rich friends now? Nobody had called her. Right, it was about time she got her priorities in order.

She didn't really feel like eating, but to please Edna she made an effort. Once she started, she realised she was hungry after all and soon cleared the plate. The old lady was brilliant. She bustled about and made sure Kate was comfortable before she left.

The phone still hadn't rung and Kate was about to settle down to watch the mid-day news when there was a loud banging on the door. She sprang out of her chair and looked through the window to see a large Transit van.

"Come on, our Kate, open up, it's freezing out here."

Kate opened the door to find her dad and three brothers, "What on earth are you doing here?" she asked in amazement.

"We've come to take you home."

Kate sat on the stairs and wept.

"What are you crying for?" Billy, the eldest, asked. "You're no worse off than us. We've no money either and we enjoy ourselves, don't we? We have a good laugh and you will as well."

"Give us a brew, our Kate," said her dad, "and we'll start getting the lot in the van."

Kate stopped crying, "You can't do that, it's my home."

"Oh, yes we can," said her dad, sounding more serious than she'd ever heard him before. "When those bailiffs come they'll go through this house like a swarm of locusts. I've seen it happen. They sell it all and get you nowt for it. If it's all in Liverpool they won't be able to get their greedy little hands on it, will they? You have to move quick when they become involved, that's why we hired a van."

"I can't leave here," said Kate, in a daze, "this is unreal."

"Kate," said her dad, "what have you got to stay

for? There will only be letters demanding money and you can soon let them know where to send them on to, but they won't know where all the gear is. Anyway, it's my job to keep an eye on yer, and if everything works out we can soon bring all this stuff back again. So get the kettle on, lass, and make us a brew, me stomach thinks me throat's been cut!"

Turning to Kate's brothers, he ordered, "Right lads, start getting this lot loaded up."

He came and put his arm around Kate's shoulders, "Come on, love, because we won't be going home without you, even if we have to kidnap yer!"

Within four hours everything of Kate's was in the van, including her two other brothers, Dave and Robbie in the back. She felt like crying her eyes out, but instead, she laughed at them sat round a small table in the middle of the empty floor, playing cards.

Her dad insisted she sit up front in between himself and Billy. Travelling up the M1, all Kate could think of was that twenty years ago she had come here on a bus and now here she was going back in a Transit van with nothing. Somehow she felt an inner calm sitting next to her dad. He only had words, but they made her feel safe.

They were all shocked by a loud banging noise

coming from the rear of the van. Her dad got the van onto the hard shoulder as quickly as he could and they all ran to open the back. "Aren't we stopping for a brew?" asked Dave.

"Are you two crazy?" thundered her dad, "we thought you'd had an accident!"

"We will have an accident if we don't stop soon," quipped Robbie, "or should we just go in here?"

"You'll wait, like us," said the old man, "there's a service station up the road, we'll stop there. Now behave yourselves."

Considering one brother was thirty-eight and the other thirty-six, Kate found it highly amusing that neither answered their dad back. Call it respect or pure fear, but it just wasn't done.

They continued their journey and soon pulled into Newport Pagnall services. Dave and Robbie in the back made a run for the gent's and came out, laughing together. All Kate's brothers, although not rich, were in well paid jobs and owned their own houses. However, the thought of paying a pound for a pot of tea was beyond them.

Kate stood firm, "I am not having one of those paper or plastic cups!"

"Look," said Billy, "why sit here and pay five pounds for five cups of tea when we can buy it over there for two pounds and drink it in the van?" he pointed to the outside catering kiosk, "You'll have to learn to go careful, now you've gone broke."

The old man spoke up with quiet authority. "We are going inside and our Kate's paying like she's done for all of yer for years. This last couple of days she's taken a bit of a knock that's all and if any of yer try to take her pride away altogether, you'll have me to reckon with."

"No," said Kate, "Billy can pay for being so cheeky."

The tension was broken and they went inside. "Where's all your stuff going, Kate? You'll never fit all that in me ma's."

"Can you divide it up between you and take it? You can use whatever you take. If I go back to London or somewhere, I'll take it back, otherwise it'll belong to you."

Her brothers laughed, "We'll get a mint for all this along the Dock Road," said Dave, laughing. "Argh, only kidding, our Kate!" he said as Kate took a swipe at him.

"I'll take most of it," said Robbie, "and it won't be touched until you say you don't want it, then I'll buy it off you."

Kate looked at him. He was so like her father, not in appearance, but in the fact that he was as straight as a dye.

They got up, her brothers walking close to Kate, "Don't worry, you'll be alright, kiddo, we'll all look after you. Nobody's going to get at yer, we'll make sure of that."

The tension and stress of the last couple of days seemed to drain away and Kate thought that maybe Liverpool really was where she belonged. At times like this, she wondered why she'd stayed away so long.

31

It took a few minutes the following morning for Kate to realise where she was.

She had slept fairly well but the thought of returning to London was haunting her. She should be there now, the Receiver would want to see her and Annie would miss her terribly.

This time last year, she would never have allowed anybody to make a decision for her, it seemed funny she was doing it now.

She sat up and looked at her things stacked up in the corner - she could see some Royal Doulton figures and a Royal Copenhagen Christmas Plate. She smiled to herself. She had told herself when she bought it that it was because it was blue, but she must have had a deep rooted need somewhere.

She crept across the floor. She didn't want anyone bringing her a cup of tea just yet. She needed time to think. She looked through her things. There were a couple of oil paintings - one an original by L. S. Lowry, some silver, three Waterford decanters. She would get about ten thousand for the lot, she estimated. Add that to the seven she already had, the twenty-seven in Denmark and the sixty she should get from the sale of the house and she'd have one hundred and four thousand pounds.

She felt herself relax slightly. She had not gone without these last twenty years and not many could say they had that much left over after they went into liquidation.

If she had sold the house she would have had another hundred and forty thousand plus contacts and equipment in the company. Somebody a few years ago had put that at five hundred thousand, but now she would have to wait and see.

At least the Receivers were professional. If she only got twenty-five per cent of five hundred thousand that was one hundred and twenty-five thousand, added together with the one hundred and four and she would still be worth a quarter of a million. If she invested that wisely, she could easily live off the interest.

She needed a car. She rummaged through the pile of clothes on the floor and pulled on an old tracksuit. She had no idea of the time, but the sooner she got her life back on course, the better.

"Ah, decided to make an appearance, have yer?" said her father, good naturedly, "the kettle's been waiting for yer this past hour."

She looked at Robbie who was there already, "Fancy coming with me to buy a car?" she asked him.

He reached for the Liverpool Echo, "There are thousands of cars in here," he said, turning to the motoring section, "what kind do you want?"

"Oh, a cheap Mini, or something," she replied, "just something to get me from A to B."

"A Mini!" he exclaimed in disgust, "you don't want a Mini!"

"Well, after the trouble in London is over, I'm going to Denmark for a holiday and I don't know how long I'll be staying for."

"Forever," interrupted her father, "if Evert has his way."

"Anyway," Kate continued, "I'll be able to sell it quicker than a big car."

Robbie shrugged, "Well, you know better than me. If you want a Mini, I'll get you a good one."

They set off. By two o'clock that afternoon,

Kate was wondering if this had been such a good idea. They must have been through every district in Liverpool and although you paid more at a garage, at least you didn't have all this running about to do.

They rang the bell at yet another address and a little old lady took them to a lock-up garage. She opened the door to reveal a car covered with spotlessly white sheets. Once these had been taken off Kate saw that the red Mini, although seven years old, was in mint condition. It only had thirteen thousand miles on the clock and you could smell the polish.

Kate wondered if the old lady had a name for it and made sure she really wanted to sell it.

"Oh, yes," replied the old lady, "I haven't driven it now for over three years and it is taxed."

Each time Kate tried to talk about a price, the old lady sidestepped the question and spoke lovingly about the car, "I do so want it to go to someone who will take care of it," she said, flicking a speck of dust off the bonnet.

"Sure she's talking about the car and not a cat?" whispered her brother.

In the end they had to ask the old lady how much she wanted for the car, "Oh, five hundred pounds," she replied, "is that too much?"

"How about a thousand?" suggested Kate,

ignoring Robbie, who was looking at her as though she'd gone mad.

"Oh, no!" said the old lady, "give me six hundred and I'll be more than happy."

Kate paid the lady and took the risk of driving her new car to the nearest insurance broker. She was delighted with her purchase, it was a really nippy little car and such a bargain price!

Now she had some mobility again, perhaps she would stop wallowing in self-pity and get on with changing her lifestyle. Once this month was over, Kate decided to take herself off and relax, after all, she could afford it.

She could get to know Evert properly again. He would have been on the phone countless times and she would have a mass of return calls to make, but before she phoned him she'd catch up on all the news within the company.

She let herself in the house and sniffed. No matter what time it was, there was always a smell of home cooking. Since she had been in London she had kept to a relatively fat-free diet, but that was as impossible here as in Denmark.

"Did you get a car?" asked her dad. "Could you please ring Evert! He's been on the blower all day!"

"Did you remember to take all the numbers off him?" she asked.

"Of course, I'm not senile, yer know! Ring him

now, lass and stop him mithering us any more."

Evert picked the phone up after the first ring, "Kate," he said, "why are you there? Why are you not here now? I want to look after you and there is nothing to stop you. I love you, I think that you love me too, so we build a life together. Trust me. Everything will be alright, I promise you that.

"Paula and Christian have moved to an apartment together, the social, they sort everything out for me until my insurance gets settled . . ."

Evert would have been on the phone all night, so she had to cut into his flow, telling him she had other calls to make. She promised that within five weeks she would be there with him.

"Must cost you a fortune in phone calls," observed her dad. "Listen, Kate," he added, "don't you worry about anything. When that London lot have the manners to let you know when you've got to go and see them, I'll be coming with you."

Kate was worried. She had waited over two weeks for a phone call from the office but there had been nothing. She was disappointed, or, as her family would say, 'gobsmacked'.

She'd had a letter from the bank and the Receiver's bills for the services on her house, but nothing else. There seemed to be only Paula and Evert who believed she was still alive.

Her brother and sister-in-law had been brilliant.

They had taken her to the working men's clubs and the pubs and kept her amused with humourous conversation. She had missed the Liverpool sense of humour.

One chap in the club said he was sorry he couldn't talk business with her, but there had been sixty-one children in his class and by the time they'd called all the names out it was time to go out and play!

Now she cried with laughter and she was really beginning to wonder whether she should make her home up here again.

32

She and her dad had taken the 7.05 a.m. train from Liverpool to Euston. She looked at him sitting opposite her, he had been a tower of strength this last month - they all had.

She had tried to talk him out of coming to the meeting but he'd told her that even if he had to get there by himself, he was going!

Well, today was the day. This train arrived in London at 9.45 a.m. and they could get a taxi to the accountant's office and be there by 10.30 a.m.

Kate still couldn't believe that there had been no contact from her office, especially Julia - it wasn't as though she didn't have the phone number she could even contact Paula and Evert if she wanted to.

They had been absolutely superb, and so had Annie, bless her. She had begged Kate to take back the money she had paid for Paula over the years, explaining that as Paula didn't even know about the money, she wouldn't miss it. But no, what would be the use of throwing good money after bad? Kate had been grateful for the offer, but had refused.

That £100,000 from the bank had been a big enough problem. Borrowed money was no good, because you had to pay it back.

Her dad broke into her thoughts, "When this is all over, get yourself over to Denmark. But I want you to know, me and yer mam are there if you want us."

She leaned across to him, "I've always known that."

"Not for twenty years yer didn't, but we'll say no more about it, because you've got enough on yer plate today, I'll be interested to see what white rabbits they bring out of the hat for themselves."

"Oh, don't be so cynical! They are professional people."

"Look, love," said her dad, patiently, "nobody on God's earth is purely professional where money is concerned, money rules everything, you mark my words. These kind of people are only interested in getting as much off yer as they can. You might trust 'em," he added, "but it doesn't mean I've got to."

* * * * *

Kate was surprised there were only eight people there. The only one she knew was the Receiver. She was invited to sit at the top table, the other five sitting opposite and her dad on the sidelines.

The Receiver's senior partner explained the downfall of the company and added that the good news was that a buyer had been found. He was pleased to announce that once the purchase went through, except for the debenture to the bank, only £18,000 would be outstanding and that included the £12,000 Receiver's fee.

Kate felt sick to the pit of her stomach. Without the Receiver's fee, she had lost everything but £6,000. She saw no sign of her accountant on the way out - had she really expected him to be there? She was asked to go to another room to sign some papers. She took the pen the Receiver offered and signed automatically.

"Is it usual," she asked, "to be stitched up like this?"

The man shrugged, "You would never have had the time to sort it out, but if you don't agree with what has happened here today, you can always sue."

"You know that I have no money to take anyone to court," she stated.

"Come on, lass," her old man took her arm, "the sooner I get out of here, the better I'll be. They make me feel like I need a good bath."

"What are you implying?" the Receiver asked haughtily.

"That's for me to know and you to find out." The old man straightened himself to try to reach the same height, "but if you really want to know, why don't you sue me? Somehow I don't think yer will, an' yer can tell 'em that I said yer just a load of gangsters. Yer make Al Capone look respectable. I'll not say good day to yer because I don't wish you one. Come on, our Kate, let's find a pub. I need a brandy, even if yer don't."

Kate allowed herself to be led out onto the street. "I need to go to my bank first, I can't go smelling of drink, it just isn't done."

"Sod 'em!" said the old man. "You saw what happened in there and mark my words, the bank will be no better. When yer've got money everyone wants to know yer - they want some of it, see, but when ya're broke watch 'em go into the woodwork. If ya're very lucky, they won't even speak to yer and that's a bonus."

"Look, Dad, the bank can't do anything because I only owe them half of what the house is worth, so let's play by the rules and go there first."

"Well, I need a drink and you will as well, so

take notice of what I say to yer and come in here with me."

Kate gave in.

"Two double brandies," he said to the barman, "the best yer've got."

Kate thought he was going to need another one when she heard the barman tell him the price, but he just put his lips together and paid up.

"Could 'ave got ten doubles for that price in our club back home, don't know how you stuck living down here, anyway."

They eventually arrived at the bank. She looked at the clock, it was gone one o'clock. The manager was at lunch, but they were told to take a seat and the assistant manager would be pleased to see them shortly.

Kate wasn't bothered who saw her because it was only a formality - sell the house, pay the bank and whatever was owing to the company, then she could transfer the remainder.

The assistant manager was far more pleasant than his boss, he was almost apologetic. "I am not involved with this account, but looking through the papers we have already had an offer of £150,000 which we are about to accept."

"But it's worth much more than that!" Kate explained, jumping to her feet.

The assistant manager remained seated. He had

obviously seen it all before, but it still didn't stop him looking uncomfortable when he said, "The bank is only interested in recovering its debt, you have gone into liquidation, so there is no possibility that you can subscribe to the monthly payments as per your agreement with us."

She interrupted him.

"Are you saying I'll only have about £30,000 left?"

The assistant manager coughed, "As I told you, this is not one of my accounts, but I can foresee even that figure being greatly reduced after estate agent fees, land registry, solicitor's charges plus, of course, administration costs incurred by us. Ms Roberts," he added with concern, "can I get you a glass of water?"

Kate heard her dad answer for her and she was glad he had, because she felt ill.

"It's a money-making racket down here," said her dad in disgust, "and yer can get her nowt. The more I hear the more I keep thinking that the sooner we get on that train to Liverpool, the better I'll like it. So me daughter and me will bid you goodbye, but before we go, I want yer word that she doesn't owe yer anything else."

"Well," answered the assistant manager in some amazement, "the account should be cleared once the sale goes through and we have completion."

"Even I know that!" replied the old man. "In fact any fool would know it. Come on, our Kate, there's nothing to stay here for. Never trusted banks, now I know that I was right."

Once in the street, Kate told the old man she just wanted to go and see her house one last time.

"Ya'll do no such thing," the old man retorted, "I'm, taking yer home right now and it's a good job I'm here with yer, ya're no match for this load of sharks - and neither am I."

He hailed a cab and gave the driver instructions to take them to Euston Station. Instead of being her own woman, Kate felt like a little girl, especially when her dad held her hand and repeatedly patted it during the journey. She would never forget his support that day and was more than glad to follow him.

The train appeared to be waiting for them, because once they were on board it started to move back towards Liverpool.

"I need a drink and something to eat and you do as well!" declared the old man.

"Come on, Dad," it was Kate's turn to take his arm. "Let's go to the dining compartment."

Kate noticed all the other business people and thought that just a month ago, she would have been one of those. She wondered if any of them had the same problems she did right now. God help them! No home, no company, no job and very few assets. Tears sprang to her eyes and she turned her head away quickly and pretended to look at the scenery.

The old man interrupted her thoughts.

"Pick what you want, me lass," he said gently, handing her the menu, "don't dwell on the past, it's gone. I'll say this for yer, yer've done more than most people I know and who can say that around where we live?"

Kate put her hand over his. "Thanks, Dad, for coming with me."

"It's all right," the old man said gruffly, "that's me job to get yer there and back, safe."

Kate began to wonder who was getting who back, because once the drinks were served, he didn't know when to stop and his voice got louder as he emptied each glass.

"Banks!" he said, "never used 'em. Don't believe in 'em! They give yer an umbrella when it's sunshine and when it rains they take it off ya! Everybody knows that," he added.

Kate noticed the businessman opposite nodding his head in agreement. He was certainly listening to her dad, giving him the occasional smile.

Well, thought Kate, I hope he knows the word 'bloody', because when the old man drinks like this he usually puts the world to rights and 'bloody' peppers every sentence. 'Damn', 'blast' and 'bugger it' were usually reserved for when he cut his finger.

She pretended to listen intently to him because if she didn't he would talk even louder and the whole carriage would hear him then.

The Government was getting it at the moment. None of them were any good . . . "They only needed you for two things, fighting for 'em or voting for 'em. I've seen 'em send thousands upon thousands all over the world with guns in their 'ands and are we any better off? Are we hell! But they are. It's different if somebody comes here to take us over like Hitler tried, 'cause you 'ave to protect what is yours, but we fight everyone's battles. It costs a fortune and destroys families then when we've done all that, the one's we protected don't want to know us. They would be best spending on educating us properly."

"What do you mean, Dad?" Kate asked, trying to smooth him over.

"Now, there's a case," he went on, "when I was at school they told us that there was some bloke somewhere who led a load of rats out of town while he was playing his pipe and dancing."

"Yes," said Kate, "they told us that as well, but it was only a fable, a story."

"Well, there you are!" replied the old man. "That's me point! If you saw one rat you'd probably run a bloody mile, you wouldn't be bloody dancin'. So, instead of telling us stories, wouldn't it be better if they filled our heads with reading, writing an' arithmetic? But you see, our Kate, they don't want us to know too much. Look at you today . ."

"Shush, Dad," Kate said, hurriedly.

"Oh, never mind shush! You weren't educated enough to stand up to those people. They gave you all sorts of offers, I know, I read the papers, to start up a business, but they don't give you the education on how to keep it. Didn't happen to the Queen though, did it? The Royals were skint, anybody will tell you that and look at them today. I remember that Prince Phillip telling us to get our fingers out and start working. He's got a bloody cheek when the country's been giving thousands to his auntie Alice from Greece. Do yer know what she looks like?" he grumbled, "'cause I don't! Last time I saw her was on the telly when the Queen got married - over forty years ago!"

"Don't you like the Royal family?" asked Kate.

"Suppose they're all right, but there's too many of them to pay for, costs too much. What I don't like about 'em is that when everything goes right it's theirs, but once something goes wrong, it's ours. People like you and me end up paying through our noses for a wave on the telly now and again. I'll tell you, our Kate, there's only six sets of people you can trust."

"Who's that?" asked Kate, trying to keep him pacified.

"Police, Fire, Health, Army,Navy, Airforce - that's 'cause ordinary people are involved. The rest yer can forget about, they're only interested in making money out of yer."

The passenger opposite was laughing. He leaned over and took the old man's hand, "I should have got on the same train as you years ago," he said.

Getting the old man off the train at Lime Street was a problem, but the delighted passenger helped to get him to a taxi. Kate kept apologising.

"Don't worry, my dear," the man said, "that was one of the best train journeys I've had in a long time. Sorry, I couldn't help overhearing your problems. You'll bounce back, good luck to you."

Kate was glad to see the house. Her dad was still mumbling as he got out of the taxi.

"Had a good bevvy today, mate?" said the taxi driver. "Leave him to me, girl, I'll get him inside."

"Oh, I knew he'd take a drink today," said her mum, hurrying to meet them, "he's always the same when there's something on his mind. Let's get him up the stairs, then we can relax."

It was another half an hour before the old man was safely in bed. Her mum insisting that he was rolled over on his side in case he tried to be sick and ended up choking.

"Come on, now lass, I'll make yer a nice cup of tea. I'll bet yer've had a right day. Was it bad, Kate?"

"It most certainly wasn't one of the best times I've known, but it's my own fault. I shouldn't have been so trusting. I should have checked everything."

"Aye," said her mum, "drugs ruin everything. We never heard of 'em until the sixties. Well, he wouldn't like you being upset," she looked up to the ceiling, "he gets upset if anything happens to any of yer - yer know what he's like. Evert and Paula keep phoning to see if yer back, so yer'd better let them know what's happening."

"Do you think I should go over there?" asked Kate, sipping her tea.

"Well, lass, I would if I was you. Give yourself a rest from all this. Yer welcome to stay here as long as yer like, but really, yer place is over there. You should have been there years ago, if it wasn't for me yer wouldn't be in this trouble now."

Kate looked at her mum, whose lip was beginning to tremble. She hurried over and put her arms around her. "Don't be silly, Mum, I've had a brilliant life up to now, but maybe it is time to pick up the pieces."

"Aye," replied her mum quietly, "I think so."

33

Kate felt relieved now she knew how much she was worth and although it was nowhere near to what she was used to, at least she had a starting point.

Her mum brought her the usual cup of tea to wake up to, but apart from asking whether she was alright, didn't stop for her normal chat, seeming to sense that her daughter needed time to herself.

She'd had all the time in the world these last six months, but until that creditors' meeting yesterday she'd defied anyone to give an answer to what lay in the future. Well, today was 'make your mind up' time.

Although she'd never voiced her opinions, she thought she would have had at least £70,000 change off her house after the bank had exercised their debenture. That was disgusting, they had only been interested in getting their loan repaid, but there again, if she had lent someone £100,000, wouldn't she want it back again as quickly as possible?

The house prices were dropping so fast now, maybe it was just as well they had sold it quickly, at least she wasn't in debt to them. It cheered her to be able to count her blessings, at least she was better off than most people who went into liquidation, she could still hold her head up and didn't owe anybody anything.

She lay back on her pillows and wished for someone with a magic wand who could make up her mind for her. She had three options open to her at this time. She could take up Alex's offer and start another business - but was she really ready to get into the rat race again? The newspapers were always full of the deep recession that was looming closer every day. Even the Government had given warnings that it was going to get a lot worse before it got a little better.

She could get a job in Liverpool. But would she be happy working for someone else - it would be a first. However, according to the Echo, at least ten people were chasing every vacancy. She moved to the third option - going to live in Denmark. What would Evert be like to live with? It was one thing going for a holiday, but making a final commitment? This was the solution everyone expected her to take.

She'd heard the saying many times, 'Today is the first day of the rest of your life', but she personally had never even had time to think about what it actually meant, never mind experiencing it. She looked around the bedroom. Yes, it was very comfortable, but once you had left the nest there was no going back and she needed her own possessions around her.

She looked over at the clock, eight-fifteen. Well, it would be nine-fifteen in Denmark. She scrambled out of bed. Evert would be awake now, so she'd talk to him and tell him she wanted to bring all her furniture and if she couldn't, she was going to take a flat in Liverpool and look for a job.

Her mother looked alarmed when she came downstairs all dressed and ready to go. "What's the matter?" she asked anxiously.

"Nothing," replied Kate, "but if Evert agrees to my plan, I need to go into town and hire a container, then I need to sell my car, so I need to get an advertisement put in the paper for that. Where's Dad?" she finished.

"Still in bed. You'll be lucky if you see him for the next couple of days, he shouldn't be drinking like that at his age, he'll do himself harm one of these days, you mark my words."

"I know!" Kate laughed, "you should have heard him on that train and yet nobody seemed to mind."

"Oh, I admit he's never been bad with drink," said her mother, "but you always have to listen to him putting the world to rights. Everybody laughs at him but I don't. It's me that has to put up with him. When he does get up, all he'll do is moan about his bad head, I'm just waiting for it."

Kate smiled to herself. If she could fall into the same understanding with Evert as these two had, she would be quite happy to settle down. She got to her feet and dialled his number. He answered immediately, a lightness coming into his voice when he realised it was her. He listened carefully to what Kate told him.

"Well," he said, "you cannot bring your kitchen stuff because every apartment in Denmark has a fitted kitchen and the electrics are different anyway. The gas you get on the cooker is no good, because we don't have gas here and the bedrooms all have fitted wardrobes. Other than that you can bring what you like if it make you happy. You must get here soon, Kate, because I miss you."

Kate said goodbye and went out to her car. It

would be a shame to have to sell it, she loved it and would miss it. The travel agent was most accommodating and she felt relieved that she could leave the planning to him. She needed a container door to door and a return flight. She had decided to book an open return ticket, because it was always nice to know that you weren't stranded. Let's face it, she thought, it's not every day you emigrate!

Once she had made the arrangements, she nearly fell off her chair when he gave her a price in excess of £1,000. She must have looked fairly shaken because he asked her if she was alright. "Of course," she replied, "I just didn't expect it to cost so much. I'm on rather a limited budget and couldn't afford to do that very often. Is that charge a return on the container?"

"Oh no!" said the travel agent, "that's just one way. Why? Are you thinking of bringing it all back with you again?" he asked.

"Well," she replied, feeling stupid, "if things don't work out, I may have to."

He just looked at her. "Do you drive?" he asked eventually.

"Yes," Kate answered, "I have my own car."

He got up and went over to a display of North Sea Ferries' brochures and brought some over. "What is it?" she asked, as he handed her one.

"I don't want to pry into your business," said the travel agent carefully, "but it is very expensive to ship furniture about between Liverpool, Harwich and Denmark. However, there is another route which would be a fraction of the cost and you can still take all your belongings with you."

"Can you explain, please?" asked Kate.

"Of course," he said, sitting down again, "most of our clients choose this option if they don't want to fly. Anyway," he went on, "Liverpool to Hull is exactly one hundred and twenty-six miles, two hours at most. You take the overnight crossing at six-thirty and after a good night's sleep you will wake up in Rotterdam at eight o'clock the next morning."

"Holland?" said Kate, puzzled, "I'm going to Denmark."

"I know. Next, it takes about eight hours to get to Esberg, the same time it would take to get to Harwich and if I may make a suggestion," he went on, "get yourself the Baedekiss AA Scandinavian map and plan a route. Here, take the brochure with you and come back when you're ready. The ship is there every day and so am I."

She remained seated. Drive to Denmark? She'd never even considered that option. Two hours to Hull, another ten perhaps to Sunds. Whenever she had travelled abroad with her job, she had always had a Mercedes waiting for her at the airport. Be a bit different in a Mini. She mulled it over. She didn't need the furniture to go with her now and she could pack the car with as much clothes and ornaments as possible. She wondered whether she would have to unpack the car on the crossing and the travel agent laughed, "No," he said, "and that's an added bonus as you don't have to worry about any luggage except your overnight bag. Now, before you decide, go and get that map, it's important that you plan the route carefully, so you know exactly what you're doing."

She was home within the hour and her dad still hadn't made an appearance. Billy was there and so they spread the map out on the floor and poured over it. There was some easy chat between them on the best way to go and she was starting to find the prospect rather exciting. She thought carefully.

"I could go out of Liverpool on the M62, arrive in Hull two hours later and catch the overnight ferry," this was the only sticking point. The brochures made it look like a mini-cruise but having been to many summer camps in the sixties, she remembered that queuing up for chicken and chips had not been ideal and it had been impossible to sleep with so many people milling about.

"You could always book a cabin," Billy suggested.

"Good idea," she agreed and continued the route, "arrive in Rotterdam at eight o'clock. Take the E19, the E25, on to the E30 and straight through Germany, then the E37 to Bremen, the E22 to Hamburg, on to the E3 in Denmark and come off at Koldig, about an hour away from where I want to be!"

She knew it was easier said than done, but there would be no luggage to contend with and she could take her time and take an overnight stop on the way if she wanted to. She had made up her mind. Whoever had her furniture was welcome to keep it, providing that they agreed that if she returned within six months she could have it back.

There were some beautiful pieces but within six months she would have got over her homesickness and with the reasonable ferry prices, she could return to Liverpool anytime, but only to stay with her mum and dad. She had to give the long-term situation in Denmark her best shot, so she wouldn't buy any property over here.

Now she had decided, the sooner she booked the better. She knew her parents would never agree that she was in the way, but after bringing up the family, she felt sure they enjoyed their time together even more now. This last month must have been a strain for them and it just wasn't fair. She scrambled to her feet.

"Where are you going now, lass?" asked her mother.

"Denmark!" replied Kate.

"What? Now?"

Kate went and put her arm around her mother, "No, not now, but in a few days. I'll go and book now, but if Evert, Paula or Annie call, don't tell them what I'm doing, it will be a nice surprise for them when I turn up there."

"Oh yes, that will be lovely for them," said her mother, joining in the mystery of it all, "don't you worry, lass, my lips are sealed. Can I tell him?" she asked, pointing at the ceiling, "that's if he's up before you go!"

"You'll have to," replied Kate, "because although I'm nearly forty-six, he'll still have to tell me to be careful on the roads."

They both laughed quietly.

34

The travel agent made it all seem so easy, so two days and she would be ready to go. It was quite amazing what you could pack into a Mini and the belongings she had left behind would make a perfect excuse to enable her to come back often depending on what the journey there was like.

She didn't have many people to call and say her goodbyes to, because she hadn't really heard from anyone. "Fair weather friends," her dad had called them, "but if you won the pools tomorrow, you'd soon have them back on the doorstep."

She pretended she didn't care, but she knew deep down it really hurt. She'd known some of them for nearly twenty years. Annie was a different matter altogether. She was delighted that Kate had finally made up her mind to go over to Denmark, but what seemed to please her most was that she had been included in keeping the journey a secret.

There were a few wet eyes when Kate finally left Liverpool, but when she reminded them that she was only a few days away by sea and road and just a few hours by air, they settled down and waved like mad until she had disappeared.

She kept in the slow lane up to Leeds, but once the traffic thinned out she overtook when she needed to and took things easy. It was two hours to Hull and that included a stop for coffee. She filled up with petrol at the nearest point to the King George Dock, as it was bound to be cheaper on this side than on the continent and she intended to keep the journey as cheap as possible without missing anything out.

She joined the queue of cars waiting to board the ferry at the terminal and made use of the currency exchange facility. She had a selection of Dutch guilders, German marks and Danish kroner. So far so good, she thought, if the journey over to Holland went as well as the last couple of hours she would be kicking herself for not thinking of this before.

She walked casually back to her car, looking at the ferry brochures. Hull to Rotterdam, Hull to Zeebrugge. She thought of the fly-drive holidays she had taken which had normally involved a four hundred pound return flight ticket plus the cost of a hire car for ten to fifteen days.

The brochure told her she could go to Hull, Holland, Germany, Denmark, Sweden, Norway and even Poland and Russia one way and Belgium, France, Luxemburg, Italy, Spain and Portugal the other way, at a fraction of the cost. What's more, you could keep your own car. It would be ideal for the family to come and visit her every three months. With four people in the car, they would spend more on a good night out in Liverpool.

All the cars seemed to start moving at once and within a matter of minutes she was on the car deck of the *Norsun*. The travel agent had been right, all you needed was your hand luggage. This was great, because the stairs from the deck were a bit steep but manageable and even people thirty years older than herself had no problems.

She, like everybody else, found the reservation deck.

The surroundings were certainly plush, which surprised her, she'd expected something more like an up-market Birkenhead ferry, but this was actually a liner, she reminded herself.

She'd booked an economy cabin. She got the key and noticed that you could certainly travel very luxuriously if you wished, but her room was quite adequate. She showered and went to explore the facilities advertised in the brochure.

The duty-free shop was busy. She bought some Yves St Laurent perfume, whisky, cigarettes and some books. Once she had eaten, she would go back to her cabin and go to bed. She walked into the restaurant and selected a table in the far corner, asking the man nearest if he would keep an eye on her parcels. He looked foreign and agreed.

Kate was astonished when she saw the buffet, it was more than equal to that in any five-star hotel she had ever been in. She felt a certain amount of pride. Usually this country served good wholesome food, but paid little attention to detail, but this display could compete with any country she had visited. Imagine being a foreigner coming to Britain for the first time. The first impression was always a lasting one and there certainly wouldn't be anything to worry about here. It just proved what could be done with a little bit of effort.

She looked at her tray and decided that although she was being greedy, a half bottle of chilled wine wouldn't go amiss. Her purchases were safe and she nodded her thanks to their guardian. She tried not to eat too quickly, her beef was absolutely delicious. "Done to a turn," her father would have said.

She tried to squeeze another glass of wine out of her half bottle, but failed. She hadn't realised she had drunk it that quickly. The man who had minded her parcels offered her some of his. Kate protested initially, but the man insisted. She didn't object when he moved to join her, in fact she was quite enjoying herself. Despite her earlier thoughts, she didn't want to return to her cabin just yet and she studied her dinner guest.

He looked quite distinguished and was probably aged about sixty-five. He spoke very good English, and she was surprised when he said he was Dutch. He introduced himself as Johan Cluivert and they had plenty to talk about when he told her he came from Arnhem.

"My eldest brother was captured there during the war," Kate told him.

"Tell me all about it," said Johan, delighted, "the British were very good to us in the war."

"Well," replied Kate, "I don't really know much, except that he landed there in September 1944 and was captured. He managed to escape and was free until the SS picked him up in the middle of October. He told me he was very glad to see them because he had a bullet in his shoulder and shrapnel in his knee."

"What happened?" he asked, entranced.

"He always said that the ones who picked him up were good to him. He says the SS officers gave him food and he always maintains that there were good and bad."

"What happened to him after that? Did he tell you?"

"Only so much," Kate answered, "he never really mentions it now, but I know my mum told me a completely different story as to what actually happened. We used to get letters from him during the war, with 'censored' right across them, so I suppose she always believed those, but the truth is he was transferred the next day to Sargan, then from January to May 1945 he was marched in freezing weather across Germany. I don't think many survived and when you think that he was six feet tall and only weighed six and a half stone, you can see why."

"How did he survive?" asked Johan.

"Apparently there were only six left at the end of the journey and they were put in a camp, all extremely ill. One day, the Americans didn't wait to open the gates, they just drove straight through them and he was airlifted to the American hospital in England, where he arrived at four o'clock on the same day he was rescued. The following day he was passed over to the British. Do you want to know what happened to him when he was discharged fit, twelve months later?"

"Oh, yes!" he replied, "I am very interested."

Kate continued, "They returned him to his unit and they demoted him."

"What for?" asked Johan, shocked.

"I don't know," Kate replied, "but what a difference a few years make. He almost died for his country and nearly got the sack for his trouble. It's a crazy world, isn't it?"

Johan nodded his head, "Is he still alive?" he asked.

"Oh, yes," said Kate, "he's sixty odd now and as fit as a fiddle, except for the bullet lodged in his shoulder. He ended up a Major in the British Army and why I was so interested in Arnhem was that he represented his regiment at the opening of the graves there."

"Have you ever seen them?" he asked. Kate shook her head. "Then I insist you must. When we dock tomorrow morning, my wife and grandchildren meet me. You follow me to our house and I will take you to see them. I do not wish to offend you," he went on, "but I wish it was your *brother* I was going with. Now I think I will go to the bar. Will you join me? I assure you my intentions are strictly honourable," he added, with a smile.

Kate laughed, "I'd be delighted to," she said. It was two o'clock in the morning before she even looked at her watch. What an interesting night it had turned out to be. Regular passengers had joined them, Johan telling her he had got to know them over a number of years, because for him this was the cheapest and most relaxing way to travel to the north of England and Scotland.

They all promised to meet for breakfast and Kate hurried to her cabin thinking that breakfast would be in five hour's time.

Sleep hit her immediately - the lull of the sea saw to that. If she hadn't heard the knocking on her door, she would probably have slept her way back to Hull.

Johan was as good as his word. Evert and Paula didn't know she was going to Denmark, so they wouldn't worry if she didn't turn up on time. "You are not on the car deck?" she asked the man.

"No," he replied, "I'm a foot passenger. My wife comes to meet me and we will be waiting for you on the other side of the barrier. You will come to my house, you will be very welcome."

Kate was glad she had filled up with petrol. How much further was his house, she wondered. She felt like she had driven from Liverpool to London, but it was only seventy miles, she noticed as she glanced at the mileometer. She suddenly spotted the Arnhem sign and they reached his house soon after.

It was a beautiful house, with a thatched roof that seemed to envelope half of the outside. The whole family must live there, it was big enough. She was right. "My mother," he said, introducing her. He turned and spoke to his mother. Kate couldn't understand, but he must have put her in a good light because the old woman made an effort to get out of her chair and kiss her warmly on both cheeks.

"I like that I take you now to the war graves. I like that you see that we appreciate what people like your brother do."

"Yes," said Kate, "I would like that, too." She walked with Johan past the plaque that read, 'First Airborne Division'. The Dutch had kept their word. Except for the fact that they were man-made, the rows of white gravestones with the red flowers on each one could have been the eighth wonder of the world.

It was impossible to read every one, but there were children here and when he guided her to a far corner, the tears she had so far suppressed came and she felt her whole body shaking.

"Come," he said, "I think it is time we get out of here. You don't have to be concerned that you feel sorrow, it has the same effect on everybody."

They didn't walk back the way they had come, but went past rows and rows of graves of the British Armed Forces, whose sole aim had been to protect their sovereignty. She didn't read any more of the gravestones, the last one she had seen had said it all, 'here in Holland lies a little part of England . . .'

When they finally reached the exit they both stood for one minute's silence in respect. She didn't know what he was thinking but she was remembering Winston Churchill's words, "I have nothing to offer but blood, toil, tears and sweat." Well that was true enough. In two World Wars well over a million British people lost their lives and many more millions suffered. The Nazis had attempted to rule the world but had failed because of the many courageous, ordinary people like those brave young men who fell at Arnhem.

She shook her head. Twenty-two years after these stones had been laid the two countries had been joined in the Common Market. Her father said that Germany was being given the things they hadn't been able to take by force.

Johan had noticed her shaking her head, "Give me your thoughts," he said to Kate.

She didn't want to get into a discussion on Europe with him, so she said, "We have a saying in Britain that sums up my feelings."

"What is that?" he asked her.

"Ours is to do and die, ours is not to reason why," she said.

"We don't know that saying here," he said, "but perhaps we should. Come, we go back to my house now."

It was three days before they let her leave. She had a basket of home-made cooking and she had to make a promise that each time she came to Rotterdam, she was to make a detour and visit the family.

If Denmark was like this, she couldn't envisage any problem in settling there. The past four days had been better than any holiday she had taken in her life.

35

Was this Mini such a good idea, after all, wondered Kate. Oh, it was cheap to run and it really zipped along, but her back was aching.

It was going to put another two hours on her journey because she had to stop every so often to have a stretch and a walk around.

She had coffee at one of her stops in Holland and couldn't fail to be impressed by the way they even gave you a cup of coffee with a smile and friendly nod. Different countries had different ways - in Liverpool you would most probably have a cup of coffee slopped down in front of you, but if the waitress wasn't busy she would probably stop for a chat.

The Germans were a very different people. She had settled into one of the little cafés along the street and ordered herself a potato salad - the kind only the Germans could make - together with a Bratwürst sausage. It made a perfect meal. She looked at the people going about their daily business. She and her mum and dad's generation could never consider these people as friends and all because of one man.

And yet Paula would see them in a different light altogether, she would take them for who they were. Maybe a united Europe could bring people together, but Kate, like her father, would keep her reservations about that. Although Germany was a beautiful country, she shuddered at the thought of the country being the superpower and Great Britain just a satellite.

She finished her coffee and got back in her car. She hoped her dad wasn't right about them. He said they would always try to rule the world, because they were so arrogant in their outlook. They thought it was their right.

Kate shook her head, why was she even thinking like this? She should be looking forward to the friendly people of Denmark and her future with Evert. It would have been nice if the house in

Lemvej was still there, but Sunds was nice, also. She felt positive that she could fit into that way of life.

The minute she crossed over from Germany on to the Danish border she felt an urgency to get there. Evert would get the shock of his life and she felt safe in the knowledge that he would protect her, no matter what.

They say that life goes around in a full circle. Well, it certainly had for her.

It was nine o'clock before she arrived at the apartment. She could see the television on through the window and the back of Evert's head. She tapped to attract his attention and noticed that he turned himself around with some difficulty, but his expression turned to sheer delight when he saw her.

She seemed to wait forever at the door, but eventually he opened it, steadying himself on two walking sticks.

"Kate! Everybody be crazy with worry about you. It is best that you use that phone to say hello, but now you are here everything in the whole world will be alright, you can be sure of that."

"Where is Paula?" Kate asked.

"You phone her first, she and Christian have a flat together, the number is by the phone."

"Kate! Where are you?" screamed Paula.

"At your father's in Sunds," replied Kate.

Paula didn't waste a moment, "I'm coming there now!" she said before slamming down the phone.

By the time Kate had phoned Liverpool, Evert had managed to make some coffee. He touched her head each time he was close to her, "You are here to stay, Kate?" he asked.

"Yes," she replied.

He nodded, "Then the story closes with the correct ending. It take too many years for it to be so, but if I have you then my life be good, very good. Now, tell me, where have you been these last few days? Nobody knows anything. I think maybe you go back to London, but I hope it is here that you come. Paula, she not have the same worry about you as me. Maybe she knows more how you think than I do and that is not right. Kate, me and you get married together, as soon as we can, you think that as well?"

"Yes," replied Kate, with a smile, "yes, Evert, I thought you'd never ask!"

"Me not ask?" he laughed, "it was you who tell me all those years ago that we should and you be right."

Paula and Christian let themselves in.

"I knew you'd get here. I told them, but my father was very worried.

You should have phoned, Kate," admonished Paula.

"Your mother and me, we get married," cried Evert.

Paula burst into tears and Christian got hold of her. "Nothing for you to cry about," he said, wiping her tears away.

"I know," sniffed Paula, "I'm just so happy, that's all."

* * * * *

Kate lay in bed beside him, his big hand holding on to hers, both content in each other's company. Paula and Christian had gone home and tomorrow she and Evert would go and see their flat.

She went to sleep on the thought that they were two couples just starting out together. She felt comfortable about the whole situation.

She awoke to the smell of freshly brewed coffee. Every bone in her body seemed to ache; that journey had been horrendous, but she soon forgot her troubles as Evert came struggling through with a big beaker of black coffee - every step obviously an effort.

"Kate, you take this, then you feel better. Danish coffee is the best in the world."

She smiled at him, he would never change! No matter what you talked about, the Danes did it better.

She crawled out of bed, that was one claim he couldn't make, because the beds here were absolutely awful - it was like sleeping on a camp bed on the floor, the pillows being one little cushion.

She was going to have to get a proper sized bed from England - one with nice big, fluffy pillows and then she'd have a decent night's sleep.

She showered then went through to the kitchen. He had made an effort for her, with the bread board all in place with an arrangement of meat and salad. However, that was something she couldn't face in the morning and she was in too much of a hurry to see Paula's apartment. She knew the girl had good taste and she could already feel the pride in how she knew Paula would have organised herself on the limited income she and Christian would have now.

Kate had some difficulty getting Evert into the car. If she had felt twinges on the journey, then Evert was going to be in agony. He had problems putting one foot in front of the other. He never complained, only directed her to a small row of terraced houses off the main street in Lemvej.

"Oh, they've bought a house!" she exclaimed.

"No, not a house, just part of it at the side," said Evert. Paula appeared from nowhere at her father's side of the car, her face flushed with excitement that they had arrived at last.

It took Evert about ten minutes to get down the two flights of stairs to what looked like a basement. Kate had never seen anything like it in her life. There was a stone floor going right through it, a big pipe was running along the wall on which washing was drying and at the far side, there was a bed. There was no other furniture except for a clothes rack with freshly ironed laundry.

There was only one other room, which had a cooker, fridge and washing machine and a tap and bowl on top of the fridge.

Paula guided her father to one of the two picnic-type chairs and Kate went and sat opposite him in the other. She looked at the table with two candles on it and noticed that the only other items were a television, music centre and a coffee percolator.

All the lights were on because there was only one small window, through which you could see people's feet passing by.

"How long have you lived here?" asked Kate.

"Two weeks, we have been here two weeks."

"To make room for me?" asked Kate.

"No," replied Paula, "for me and Christian to be alone together."

"But you can't live here, it's a cellar."

"Oh yes we can," Paula's face was flushed. "We're very happy here."

Evert shrugged his shoulders when Kate looked at him and said nothing.

Kate couldn't wait to get out of the place. She couldn't stop imagining a big sewer rat running along that pipe. Once they were in the car, well out of earshot, she turned to Evert, who put up his hands in a helpless gesture.

"We have to get her out of there. I didn't know people lived in cellars in Denmark or England?"

"Yes," said Evert, "I think maybe that should not be allowed, but they only sleep there, because every day they be here with us, because I cook them food."

"You do?" exclaimed Kate.

"Yes, I got the kitchen lowered to fit my wheelchair, so I can cook all the meals for them and you."

"Can you cook?" asked Kate curiously.

"Sure I can," he replied, "I've been on my own all my life, so I have to do it. It was me who taught that bloody Helga how to cook. She could not make food when she came to my house."

"Don't let's talk about her," said Kate, "it's like a bad dream."

"I tell you now, because I not want that I tell you over the telephone."

"What's that? Has something else happened? Is it serious?" asked Kate anxiously.

"No, it is not serious, but maybe not so good. After I had my accident she came to visit me in the hospital to ask me to get you and Paula to go back to England."

"I know that," interrupted Kate.

"Yes, but she tell the police that me and her are in love and that I tell her to burn down the house because I know that I will not work anymore, then when the insurance pay out, me and her we build a new house together."

Kate looked alarmed.

"Do not be frightened, Kate. The police, they take no notice of her, but I think that maybe the insurance use it as an excuse to delay payment to me. That woman, she be completely crazy, but there is nothing I can do. I only get the Social Security payment to live on."

"Will you have to pay them back eventually?" asked Kate.

"I don't know," admitted Evert, "I never ask, but that is of no importance, the only thing that is important to me is that you and me be together."

"Don't worry about that," Kate said, "You're stuck with me for the rest of your life."

"I hope so, Kate, I hope so," Evert replied, struggling to put his arm around the back of her seat and pat her shoulder.

36

Kate settled into the Danish way of life. She and Paula usually went to the shops every day then made their way back home to watch television until Evert showed off his cooking skills - which tasted better than anything she could have prepared.

Initially, she had been dreading going into his bed - had it really been twenty years since she had felt the warmth of a man's body next to hers? But he had slowly and mystically aroused the passion she had experienced so many years ago. Long forgotten feelings came flooding back and overcame the fear that she soon realised had been completely unfounded.

Kate spoke to Annie every time Paula phoned her but she was always aware that it was only Paula that Annie was interested in.

The Liverpool lot were very different. They were never off the phone, her brothers always threatening to come over and take Denmark by storm to pay those Vikings back for raping Britain's women and beating up their men.

Evert always joined in by telling them they could try but he could give them a bottle of Old Danish and they could do nothing.

Money was short and Kate was always glad when the first of the month arrived, because that was when Evert's money went into the bank. She had her savings but that was for emergencies and money seemed to go a lot further in England, as there was fifty per cent tax on everything in Denmark.

The language was also a problem. She had tried but just couldn't get the sounds right in the back of her throat. Friends came round and if they didn't understand English it made her feel uncomfortable just staring into space, while everyone else chattered away.

Paula, on the other hand, was doing remarkably well. She seemed to understand the gist of everything that was said.

It was at one of the frequent house parties that Evert turned to her. "Kate, I tell my friends that you only be a visitor here and I think it would be better that we got married. You can choose dual nationality if you wish, but it allows you to stay here."

"I thought I could stay anyway," Kate replied, surprised, "we're in the Common Market now."

"It is still better that you are my wife and maybe the Social give me another half more."

Kate laughed, "Well, I've heard some reasons for getting married!"

"No!" said Evert seriously, "that is not the reason. I should do it twenty years ago, but we mess it up. Now I put it right and for the right reasons only."

"Yes," she said, "as usual, you make sense."

Evert turned and spoke to their waiting friends. A cheer went up and the bottles were raised, "*Skol! Skol! Skol!*" they shouted in delight.

The wedding was arranged quickly. Nobody from England came because they were only going to the Municipal Building with Paula, Christian, Lis, Pregan and Jenny and then on to a party at the Outland Club. But at last they had become Mr and Mrs Neilson. They hadn't bought another ring, Kate had insisted on the one she had worn ever since he had put it on her hand in Palermo - only now it was on the correct finger.

She looked at it. You were a long time getting there, she thought, with a rueful smile.

Life went on as normal and the months passed. She and Paula intended to spend a few days in Liverpool, then carry on to London to see Annie and do some Christmas shopping in Oxford Street.

Paula came off the phone, “You know Kate, every time I talk to Mum lately, it sounds like she's making an effort to speak to me.”

“Well,” replied Kate, “if you like, we can go to London first, then we can take the domestic flight up to Liverpool.”

“Yes,” said Paula, “I think I'll phone her and tell her, but do you think we could go a week early?”

“Why?” asked Kate. “You're not worried about her, are you?”

“As a matter of fact, I am,” admitted Paula, “she just doesn't sound her usual self to me, but maybe I'm being stupid.”

“Well, let's go tomorrow then,” suggested Kate, “put both of you in good spirits for Christmas, but don't tell her, let's make it a surprise.”

“Oh, yes!” cried Paula, getting excited at the prospect, “can you imagine her face when we turn up? It will be like old times.”

They went straight out, booked their flight and did a quick Christmas shop. Once back at home, still full of excitement about tomorrow's adventure, they displayed their purchases to Christian and

Evert. The men were pleased about their trip but gave them strict instructions to hurry back.

* * * * *

The taxi from Heathrow brought them to Annie's house and as soon as it stopped, Paula jumped out, rushing as usual to get to her mum.

Kate paid the driver and got their luggage. The taxi drove away and Paula was still waiting at the door. Kate joined her and they waited. The door was eventually opened by a little old woman weighing about five stone.

Paula looked from her to Kate and burst into tears. "Mum! What's happened to you?"

"Nothing," answered Annie. "Have you come home for good, Paula?"

"Come on," said Paula, "let's go inside and see what you've been doing to yourself. You don't look very well."

Annie turned and led the way down the hall. Once inside the living room it was immediately apparent that she had been sleeping on the sofa. In fact, the pillows and quilt were rumpled like she had just climbed out to answer the door.

Paula helped her lie down again, made her comfortable and sat beside her, holding her hand and stroking her hair.

"Have you seen a doctor, Mum?" she asked.

"Oh, yes," replied Annie, "someone comes in most days to have a look at me."

Kate spent the following week looking after both of them. Paula didn't leave Annie's side, telling her over and over that she would never ever leave her again. Kate never voiced her fears concerning Annie, but she was more than aware that she appeared to have lost the will to live. It was only when she and Annie were alone that her worst fears were con-firmed.

"Kate," said Annie, "I'm very tired. If anything happens to me promise you will mention me to Paula from time to time."

"Oh, don't be silly, Annie, nothing is going to happen to you," reassured Kate.

"The last few days, when I am quiet, I have seen my husband, he is waiting for me to join him. I'm not afraid, Kate, but I've been hanging on for Paula to come and now that I have seen her I'm happy, very happy."

Kate suggested to Paula that perhaps Christian should join them, but Paula said, "If I hadn't gone to live with Christian in Denmark, Mum would be full of life, so I don't want to see him again."

Once Paula was asleep, Kate overruled her. Paula would be comforted by having Christian and her grandad by her side.

One week later, Kate was glad she had made that decision as the four of them were by Annie's side as she went into her last sleep. Paula clung to her grandad and it became clear over the next couple of days that she wasn't going to let him out of her sight.

The funeral was a very small affair - only the four of them attended. Annie had never encouraged her neighbours and had no other relations. Kate looked at the casket waiting to take Annie on her final journey. "If anyone's going to the right place, it's you, Annie," she whispered softly. "Goodbye my friend."

Back at the house Paula was inconsolable. She hadn't bothered with Christian since his arrival and now he remarked to Kate that she seemed to be blaming him.

"Give her time, Christian," was all Kate could say.

As usual, it was the old man who took the situation in hand. He sat down beside Paula, took hold of her hand and said, "Now, you listen to me. I know it won't be long before I'm on me way, it's one one thing none of us can avoid, but when yer get to my age yer not afraid of dying, only of how yer die - and yer mum has gone the way I'd like to go. Yer either have a long sleep and don't know anything about it or there is someone else in another world up there. And, although I'm not religious I would like to think it's the last one, because when yer stop and think how we are born in the first place, that has to be some sort of miracle in itself.

"No doctor can make a human being, can they? So there has to be something else and if that's right, yer mam will be looking at yer right now, and do yer want her to see yer crying?"

Paula looked up at the old man, then got up, opened a drawer and handed the old man a gold chain.

"Grandad, take this. Mum really loved it because she knew it was the most valuable thing you ever had in your life yet you gave it to her for looking after me."

"Aye, that's right," agreed the old man, "I did. So now yer giving it back to me, are yer? Well, I'll tell yer, it's not hollow, it's solid gold. I didn't know how Annie was fixed for money so I 'ad it in me mind that if ever she needed money quick she could sell it, so now you won't mind if I pass it on to him," he said, handing the chain to Christian, "because he's the one who's going to see to yer from now on. Stop treating the lad like it's his fault, because it's not - and if yer need money then either of yer are very welcome to sell it, because I trust both of yer.

"And now, if none of yer minds, I feel the need to get back to me wife in Liverpool. I don't want her worrying about me. I'll find me own way," he added, "no need for any of yer to come with me. I got here so I can get back. It's only those moving stairs that bother me."

Paula hugged her grandad hard, then turning to Christian asked, "Will you travel with him?"

"Yes, of course," he answered. "Paula," he added, "I have to go back to Denmark, but I do not want that I leave you, so I stay, but how long do you think we will be here? I'm so sorry I have to ask the question at this time."

"Oh, Christian," cried Paula, "I've neglected you. Why don't you travel with grandad?"

She looked at Kate and asked, "Can you and I do what we have to here?"

Kate nodded, "Of course we can."

It was a relief for Kate to see her dad and Christian on their way in the taxi. With them out of the way, the house would be cleared in no time. The local vicar would know plenty of people who would love the furniture.

Paula would keep personal mementos and she herself needed something to remember Annie by. Then there was the solicitor to see. He would arrange the sale of the house. They could travel up to Liverpool and spend a few days there before flying home to Denmark. She gave a small smile, home to Denmark - yes, it was home now and she had to admit it, she did miss Evert like he missed her.

37

Paula went white. "Half a million pounds? Where on earth did she get that from?"

The solicitor leaned back in his chair, smiling broadly at her, "You are a very fortunate young lady, your mother invested wisely for you all these years, plus the fact that house prices in London at the moment are at an all-time high."

"Where did she get all the money to invest, Kate? Do you know? Did she ever tell you?"

Kate shook her head and looked at the floor.

Paula left a forwarding address and instructions to transfer her estate to the Unibank in Lemvej.

She got hold of Kate's arm to steady herself. "We have had one bar on the electric fire when it's been really cold and all the time she was saving everything for me. I don't believe it. I don't want to go shopping here, Kate, I want to go to Liverpool, can we go today?"

"If you want to. There's nothing now to keep us here."

They decided to go from Euston on the train. Paula was in another world. "What am I going to do with all that money, Kate?"

"Buy a house for you and Christian would be my first step, get yourselves out of that awful cellar."

"Yes, I suppose so," said Paula, "but what's he going to say? I suppose I should be excited but I'd rather have my mum."

Kate couldn't really get a word in during the three hour journey to Liverpool and even if she could have done, Paula wouldn't have heard, she was in a world of her own.

Once in Liverpool, they made straight for the house and knocked. "I'm coming!" called a familiar voice, then, "Oh, look who's here! Put the kettle on!"

The fresh smell in that house was always the same. The minute you stepped inside the front door, you felt you were home. Paula made straight for the old man to tell him the news.

"Bugger me! Half a million pounds!" he said incredulously.

"Wash your mouth out with soap!" shrieked his wife, "we'll have none of that talk, here!"

"Grandad? Feel like coming into Liverpool with me - just me and you?" asked Paula.

"I'll go anywhere with you, lass, yer knows that. Just give me time to smarten meself up and I'll be with yer. Now yer half a millionaire I'll have to watch I don't show yer up. I'll have to talk proper, like."

Kate and her mother watched as the pair linked arms and walked off down the street. "He looks as proud as punch, but I'm glad to see the back of him for a couple of hours, he gets under me feet sometimes and it'll give us a chance to have a nice cup of tea and a chat. I like that."

Kate enjoyed it as well, although she could lean on her dad and always depend on him giving her the right answer, it was her mum who had always shielded her. No matter if it was right or wrong she only had her family's interests at heart.

"Annie got that money off you, didn't she?"

"Well, yes," admitted Kate, "half of it, I suppose, but I really thought she was using it. I didn't know that she had invested every penny I had ever given her. She did tell me, a few months ago, that

I was welcome to what she had and that Paula didn't know about it. Just think, Mum, if I'd have taken her up on the offer, the company could have been saved, plus my house and Paula would still have got her inheritance. Isn't life strange?"

"Aye, lass, it is, but Paula will realise where it originally came from and see you all right. She knows that you've lost everything now."

Kate looked at her mother. "I feel awful talking about it. It's cold and calculating."

"Oh, don't worry, lass. There's only me and you here and I was just saying that she should give you half, but I won't be saying it to anybody else. My lips are sealed. Don't you think you could persuade Evert to live in England?" she went on, changing the subject, "because years ago he would have done, wouldn't he? And it would be good if you were nearer. The phone's all right, but it's better when we're like this, just me and you and the teapot. I could live like this for the rest of me days, I really could. Aye lass, I don't mind admitting I miss you."

Kate got up and put her arms around her mother. "Evert wouldn't come here, he doesn't complain, but he's in pain all the time and his main thing in life now is getting the insurance money and having the house rebuilt."

"I understand that, lass, but what about you? Is

that what you want?"

"Well," replied Kate, "I wouldn't like to be away from him for too long, but I miss England, I really do. My house in London, it was my own little bit of independence and sometimes I like my own company. You'd be surprised. It's nice to be on your own sometimes. I mentioned it to Paula on the way up here, whether she fancied buying something over here as well as in Denmark, properties are going up here as well as over there, but she didn't really give me an answer."

"Never mind, lass, when she's seen yer all right, yer'll be able to buy wherever yer want, but I wouldn't get a house here if yer going to live in Denmark. Why, if the two of yer fall out, which is bound to happen, it would be too easy for yer to move back over here. So long as there's no other woman involved and he doesn't hit yer, I believe it's a case of yer makes yer bed and yer lies on it."

Two hours talking to her mum was pure bliss for Kate and she could have sat there for twenty-two. There had never been a cross word between them and very few of love - there didn't need to be. They were interrupted by Paula and her grandad.

"Oh, get me a bowl of water," groaned the old man, taking off his shoes and socks, "she's walked the legs off me!"

"More fool you!" replied his wife, going to the

sink.

"Well," he shouted after her, "there's nobody better to do it for, is there, lass?" giving Paula a big wink.

Those two had hit it off from day one. Kate looked from one to the other, they were like two peas in a pod, despite the age difference.

Their time in Liverpool didn't seem long enough - it never did, Kate reminded herself. Paula felt the same way. "I could stay here for another week, couldn't you, Paula?"

"Well, yes, if Christian and my father were here, but tomorrow we go home."

"I know, but I hate leaving here," admitted Kate, "I always feel so guilty."

They sat until the early hours, talking, so it was quite a rush when they awoke to get to the airport on time. Kate had been surprised that her dad was unusually cheerful. He was normally quite subdued when she was going away. Maybe with Christmas so near he'd be glad of a bit of peace and quiet before the family turned up.

"I suppose you'll be house-hunting when you get home?" Kate asked, once their flight was underway.

"Yes," said Paula, "although maybe we'll leave it until the Spring."

"I'd have thought you'd want to get out of the cellar as quickly as possible," remarked Kate.

"It's not a cellar, it's a flat, and I happen to like it. So does Christian," Paula added.

"Well, you won't have to stay there much longer, anyway," finished Kate.

* * * * *

As they walked through the airport at Karoup, Kate was delighted to see Evert waiting for her. He was without his wheelchair and leaning on two sticks.

"Oh," exclaimed Kate, "you finally made it! Back on your own two feet at last."

"It is nearly a new year," replied Evert, "I do not intend to be in a wheelchair any more. But never mind about that, I am glad you are here, I have missed you so very much."

Kate looked at him fondly. England was nice, but she knew she belonged where Evert was. She said simply, "I missed you, too."

Paula and Christian were wrapped around each other. They had a language all their own.

* * * * *

Christmas and New Year passed quickly and everyone enjoyed the festivities, even Paula, although she missed her mother terribly.

Evert played the chef as usual and made a huge traditional Christmas dinner, which Kate enjoyed tremendously, but which just couldn't match the ones made by her mum.

Pregan, Jenny and Lis came over. They had invited Evert, Kate and Paula over to their house with Christian, but Evert wouldn't hear of it. "I never go to Lemvej. I only go to see my house get built, not to see a load of ashes."

Paula puzzled Kate. Every time they were in Herring she made a point of looking through all the estate agents' windows and pointing out different houses, but Paula always seemed in a hurry to go somewhere else. Oh, she looked occasionally, but never went as far as getting a brochure.

Kate decided to have a quiet word with Christian but soon realised that was a waste of time as well.

"It is her money to do what she likes with, but I think she leave it in England anyway. She doesn't need it here. I will make sure that she gets everything she needs."

"But can't you persuade her to buy a decent house?" persisted Kate.

"No, I will not tell her that, she must do what she like to do and I ask that you stop asking Paula to buy a house because it upsets her."

Kate decided never to mention houses again. If

they wanted to live in a cellar, that was up to them. They still came for their meals every day and Evert was in his element, making them different dishes to try - sometimes expensive ones.

"Does Paula ever give you any money towards this food?" Kate asked one day.

"No, I get no money off Paula. Why?" Evert asked.

"Well, here we are waiting for the end of each month for your money when she's got half a million pounds stashed away - and we buy all the food."

Kate was surprised by Evert's reaction.

"I tell you now, Kate, you never ever say that to her, never! You be sure of that. If I want to feed my daughter and her man, then I do it!"

Kate flushed, "Don't talk to me like that! And I'll tell you something, your daughter is completely selfish. Half a million and she never once suggests even taking us out for a meal."

Evert came and put his head on her shoulder. "Kate, what she does is her business, it should not concern me and you. We must not have angry words between us about it, so let the matter close."

38

Spring was turning into summer and Kate was feeling very uncomfortable. Nothing she could actually put her finger on, but Paula had altered so much since she had inherited that money and nobody seemed to notice except her.

They never went shopping together now, because Paula was always at the gym. She'd made a lot of new friends her own age and didn't appear to have time for Kate at all.

She also made sure she gave Evert a lift to his club most days, that's if she didn't want him to do a job for her in that cellar they called a flat.

Kate sat in the café in the centre of Herring and was glad that Annie wasn't there to see what a spoiled brat Paula had become.

Kate had always liked her own space, but during the past four or five months she seemed to be on her own all the time. She knew it wasn't just her imagination. Evert had altered as well. When he was home he was always deep in thought. Sometimes Kate felt she was getting the silent treatment, because as soon as Paula walked in, he came alive.

It was ridiculous, Kate thought to herself, she couldn't be jealous of her own daughter, could she? Well, jealous wasn't the word, but she had to admit she was beginning to resent Paula.

Everyone seemed to be under her spell. Pregan and Jenny described her as 'wonderful', Christian hung onto her every word - but there was something about her that Kate didn't like and the only words she could use to describe it was that she had become very deep and secretive.

What about the time when a couple of English women she had made friends with came over for a coffee? Kate remembered the occasion vividly. When Evert had come in, he said a terse hello and then went and sat in the kitchen, making everyone feel uncomfortable. The two women left quickly and Kate had tackled him about it, calling him ignorant. He simply shrugged and said, "The only one I want to talk to is you."

She was beginning to wish she'd never got married. Everyone said when you did you were taken for granted. Well, thought Kate, if things didn't alter soon on their own, she would do something about it.

Driving back to Sunds, Kate realised she was actually beginning to hate the place. She decided to give things another month. If nothing changed she would go back to Liverpool - at least she'd have friends there. Paula and Evert had become like strangers. She opened the door of the flat. The three of them were already home, which was unusual - it was usually quite late when Evert made an appearance.

"Kate, here you are, do you want our news? Christian and me are getting married and we're going to have a big wedding in Lemvej."

Kate turned to give them the biggest smile she could and said with not a hint of sarcasm, "I'm very happy for you."

"Oh, Kate! I know you are. Will you address all the invitations for me?"

"Of course, if you want me to. How soon are you getting married?" Kate asked.

"In about eight week's time, isn't that right, Christian? My father will give me away. We called in to Herring to look at wedding suits for him, didn't we?" Paula bubbled.

"Ya, ya! What she wants me to dress in I think make me look stupid," Evert grumbled.

"Where did you meet up?" asked Kate.

Paula and Evert looked at each other. "I saw him walking along the street," she said.

The evening was spent discussing the wedding. Paula even phoned her grandad especially, to tell him the news. Kate took the phone, she felt she needed to speak to her mum and dad, and wished they were with her now and not in eight week's time.

Her dad made her feel even more depressed. "You've got a lass in a million, there. I'll be as proud as punch to see her all dressed up, we all will."

Kate put the phone down. How could everybody be fooled by the spoiled brat? She didn't understand it, but in eight week's time Kate intended to put them in the picture - no matter whether they liked what she said or not.

Kate tossed and turned all night. She had heard Evert get up but pretended to be asleep and watched through the corner of the blind as he got into Paula's car and kissed the girl good morning. Kate showered, but didn't know whether the water running down her cheeks was the spray or her tears.

She dried and did her hair automatically, then

went in search of some coffee. She looked at the kitchen clock. It was eight-thirty. The gym didn't open until nine and who would be at the club at this hour? There was something wrong here and today she was going to find out what it was.

Kate tried to shake the thoughts out of her head, but she just couldn't get rid of the questions that flooded her mind. Paula and Evert couldn't be having an affair. Alright, the girl didn't know him as a father really, but she knew he was. He was still an attractive man. But why would she be getting married to Christian? And why, every time she came into the room, did her daughter and her husband stop whispering to each other? Why did they always laugh together but never when she was there?

Paula and Evert were like soul-mates and, whilst he was still attentive to her, Kate knew he was more withdrawn, as if he had something constantly on his mind.

She looked at the ashtray. Had she really smoked all those cigarettes this last hour? She decided to wait another fifteen minutes and then she would ring the club and the gym and get the pair of them back here. If she looked stupid at the end of all this, then so be it. Kate knew she couldn't go on like this for much longer.

"Paula who?" asked the man at the gym on the

phone, "I do not know anyone of that name. No, she is not here, nobody is, only me."

Kate dressed quickly and within fifteen minutes she was at the door of Evert's club. She banged hard to get an answer and the woman who lived above the club looked out and told her there was only someone there on Sunday mornings.

Kate drove back home, her head buzzing. She didn't even remember the road from Herring to Sunds. She hated liars and she was going back to Liverpool today.

She ran indoors and packed her case. She caught a taxi to Karoup Airport and was relieved she could get the next flight out to Copenhagen. She didn't care how long she had to wait there, just as long as she was miles away from Paula and Evert.

As things turned out, she caught a connection fairly quickly and was soon on her way to Manchester. The passenger next to her was very talkative, but eventually got the hint when Kate hadn't said a word for almost fifteen minutes. He probably thought she had a weak bladder as she dashed to and from the toilet, trying to hide her heartache. Once in Liverpool, however, it didn't matter and it was a very tearful Kate who banged on the door. The familiar sound of, "I'm coming!" made her break down completely.

Once inside Kate told them everything.

Her dad was very quiet, but her mum wouldn't shut up. "All yer've done for her, put her through school which she gave up, gave Annie an allowance for her every week for years, which she has benefited from now, given her everything she wanted - no wonder she looks the way she does, it was all yer hard work that's paid for it.

"How much did she give yer out of that half a million she got? You want to bank it and start getting a life for yerself and bugger them two, let 'em get on with it."

The old man spoke for the first time.

"Kate, there must be some explanation. If yer want my advice, yer've been too hasty. Why don't yer get on that phone and ask them both what's going on?"

The phone rang, making them all jump. Her mother got up, "I'll get that and if it's one of them I'll let them have a piece of my mind, no matter what trouble it causes."

After about ten minutes she came back into the kitchen. "It's Evert, he wants to speak to yer."

"Kate, I'm so sorry, *mine skat.* You must come back, there be nothing bad between me and you or Paula, you must believe that."

"Go to hell, both of you!" said Kate quietly and put the phone down."

* * * * *

During the weeks leading up to the wedding, Kate expected Evert to turn up on the doorstep, but he didn't. He had phoned several times a day, but it was too easy to pick up a phone, so she never spoke to him.

Paula had tried as well, but it was only her grandad that she spoke to, because there was no way Kate's mum was going to speak to her. Whoever upset Kate, upset her, she maintained.

Kate felt in limbo. There was only a week left to go before the wedding. Her dad and brothers were going, but she and her mother were staying in Liverpool.

The old man came and sat down beside her, "Look, lass, I know how yer feeling, but this needs sorting out. Come to the wedding with me, I'll get yer mam to come as well. Yer know sometimes things don't look as black as they're painted and I've said all along yer've been too hasty. Yer'll never get me to believe that either of them would do anything to hurt yer."

"They lied to me, Dad," said Kate, miserably.

"What lies did they tell you, lass? Because nothing yer've told me says they did. Think about what I've said to yer. Let's all go over and see yer daughter married and get everything cleared up once and for all. Me and yer mam will be with yer and if yer still unsettled come back with us."

"Well," said Kate, "my car is there plus I've got money in the Unibank, but I just don't know how I'll face them." The old man patted her hand, "That's better, let the three of us go into town and get ourselves rigged out, we want to look smarter than anybody else, don't we? By the way, I'll let 'em know that we're coming, don't bother yerself about that."

* * * * *

Kate's stomach had been churning all the way from Manchester Airport to Karoup. The food on the flight looked very tempting, but it was out of the question, so the old man ate Kate's as well.

Her mum, bless her, must have taken her hand a hundred times, "You all right, our Kate?"

"Yes," replied Kate each time, "I'm alright."

Once they arrived at the airport, Kate thought, this is where it all happens. She looked up to see Evert, Paula and Christian waiting for them. Evert couldn't wait and rushed forward to get hold of Kate in a bear hug. "Kate, my Kate, you don't understand, maybe the mistake is with me. I love you Kate, you must know that. I tell everybody, everybody in the whole world."

"Actions speak louder than words," Kate responded coolly, "and if you do love me, you have a funny way of showing it. But I'm here to see Paula and Christian get married, then I'm going back to Liverpool and you can find somebody else to love."

Paula came forward hesitantly, "Mum?"

"Aren't you forgetting something?" Kate looked at her daughter, "Annie was your mum, I'm your Aunt Kate. What was it Paula? Pay-back time for having you adopted?"

"Now, now," said the old man, "words will be said that will be regretted. We're here for a wedding, I haven't come all this way to row. Tell us where we're staying and let's make our way there."

Christian spoke for the first time. "Your sons and their wives are to be with my family in Lemvej and we think that you and your wife will like to be there also. I will drive you."

"Where am I staying?" asked Kate.

"You stay with me," replied Evert, "you are my wife and we have much to talk about. But that will be after the wedding tomorrow because Paula will be staying at the apartment, also. Christian will stay at home, then tomorrow, us three will drive through to Lemvej to see them get married together. Then after that, you and me can start a new life, you can be sure of that, no matter what you think today. Maybe I have to keep you prisoner to do it. Come on, Kate, everything will be all right. You'd better believe that to be true."

39

Kate waved her mum and dad off in Christian's car and went to get in the back of Paula's. Evert usually sat in the front but now he sat beside her, his arm around the back of her seat.

She only gave an occasional nod to what they were saying, the last thing she wanted was a tense atmosphere but she really couldn't help herself.

Paula got quietly out of the car and walked into the apartment. Evert helped Kate with the luggage.

"Kate," he said suddenly, stopping her, "you are the only person in the world for me, but you know that."

"Yes," she said, as pleasantly as she could, "but when I get in there do you mind if I have an hour's sleep? I can hardly keep my eyes open."

"Yes," he said, looking hard at her, "you want that I come with you?"

"No!" she replied, rather too sharply. "Look, I only want to sleep for an hour, then I'll be fine."

Kate awoke in the early hours of the morning with Evert beside her. She didn't know when she had fallen asleep, she had gone to bed to avoid being in the same room as Paula and Evert.

She looked at him now. She had loved him and Paula so much for all those years, but now? She was in such turmoil, she really didn't know how she felt any longer.

She crept out of bed and found Paula asleep on the couch, so she went into the kitchen and shut the door. A coffee would have been more than welcome but the percolator made such a noise and the longer they slept, the less time she had to face them.

Paula was the first to come through to the kitchen. She gave a start when she saw Kate sitting there, but she immediately came and put both arms around her shoulders.

"Kate, please don't stiffen up. You are one of the people I love most in the world."

"I love you, too," replied Kate carefully.

"You mean it?" Paula asked.

"Yes, I mean it."

Kate helped Paula get ready. Evert was waiting to take her to the car, but Kate thought Paula would need to help him, he'd never even see the wedding car through all those tears.

They got in the back and Kate climbed in next to the driver.

If ever there was a beautiful bride it was Paula. Evert leaned over during the fifty mile drive and said to Kate, "I never dream this day is possible. The two women that matter to me most look the best in the world. Today is a good day, Kate."

They arrived at the church and Kate thought there must be two weddings, there were so many people, but it appeared that the clapping and cheering was all for them.

Why all these people had been invited was beyond her. With the prices being what they were in Denmark, you wouldn't get much change out of five thousand pounds.

Evert seemed to know everybody, but even he looked a little surprised at the size of the congregation. After he had escorted Paula down the aisle to Christian he stepped back and took his place beside her. Kate noticed his hand was shaking as he took hers and gave it a comforting squeeze.

Once the service was over, Kate expected

everyone to start moving out of the church, but nobody moved. It must be what happens in Denmark, she thought and waited to see what would happen next.

She looked at Evert but he had his eyes on Paula. She looked around at her mum and dad behind them. They shrugged. Then she heard Christian say, "Shortly we will go for food, but first, my wife, Paula has something to do."

Despite herself, Kate whispered to Evert, "Is this what they do in church here?"

"I never see it before," he replied.

Paula came over to Kate and Evert, Christian just behind her. She handed Kate a big brown envelope and said, "Mum, Dad, this is for you."

"Open it," instructed Evert.

Kate did so and looked at what seemed to be legal papers written in Danish.

"I can't understand what it says," she said.

"No, you never understand," laughed Evert, "come now, we go for food."

They all piled out of the church and into the waiting cars. The road seemed familiar to Kate and she gasped as they turned up the drive that led to Evert's old house. At the top, instead of the pile of ashes she had expected to see, was the house - rebuilt in all its glory. She turned to Evert, "Who did this?" she whispered.

"We all did, for you. Only you and your mother not know."

"You mean my dad knew?" Kate asked in amazement.

"Yes, he knew before me. He and Paula planned it in Liverpool when you and she went to her mother's funeral. Paula came to me and told me her plan, but you weren't to know. Everybody joined in to make the best for you. But then when you went home to Liverpool and you not be at the apartment that night when I come home, I nearly go crazy."

"I'm going to kill my dad the minute I walk through that door and if I don't, Mum will."

Kate and Evert walked through the open front door hand in hand. Everybody was there to raise a glass of champagne.

Paula stepped forward, "Sorry, Kate," she said, "but it was the only way I could think of to repay you. You mean everything to me."

She handed Evert an envelope.

"What is it?" he asked.

Christian spoke, "Maybe you and me can work together because you will need me to steady your legs."

"Yes," said Evert, with a catch in his voice, "I like that." And he handed Kate a photograph of the new *Katie Paula* in the harbour.

[illegible]

She hugged Everett in embrace.

"What?" he asked.

[illegible]